SHIFTER

STOPE PACKS

REBECCA ZANETTI

ACKNOWLEDGMENTS

Like a wolf, every author needs a pack, and I want to thank mine. First, for being there for me with howls of encouragement, and second for nicely handling my very bad puns. Special thanks go out to:

Big Tone, my own grumpy sunshine hero. We celebrated the same anniversary two years in a row, and I'm pretty sure we know the right number now. Maybe. Either way, I'm so grateful to have you in my life, and I do appreciate a male who'd never bark away from a challenge;

To Gabe, who carries the spirit of the wolf and the heart of a champion onto the football field during college. I love watching you play and can't wait to see what you do next in life. I know you'll be the leader of every pack;

To Karlina, a truly talented film maker and art virtuoso at college, whose creativity and insight rival every possible vivid tale of a wolf shifter. I have no doubt your artistic footprint will be truly magical and can't wait to see where your path leads;

To Asha Hossain of Asha Hossain Designs for a cover that unveils the soul of a novel with one glance;

To Chelle Olson of Literally Addicted to Detail for edits as bright and illuminating as a full moon;

To narrator Stella Bloom, whose voice weaves through this shifter story with the elegance and mystery of a night prowling wolf;

To my agent, Caitlin Blasdell, whose wisdom and guidance have been the north star in my publishing journey;

To Anissa Beatty, whose steadfast support and organizational skills are as crucial as the keen senses of a wolf in the wild as my assistant and leader for Rebecca's Rebels (my FB street team);

To Rebels Kimberly Frost, Heather Frost, Madison Fairbanks, Joan Lai, and Gabi Brockelsby, whose keen senses are as important as an enforcer's duties for Beta reads;

To Writer Space for howling about my books to the masses;

To my constant support pack that always has my back and would never let me chase my tail: Gail and Jim English, Kathy and Herbie Zanetti, Debbie and Travis Smith, Stephanie and Don West, Jessica and Jonah Namson and Chelli and Jason Younker;

Finally, to you, the reader. Sorry about the puns. I just couldn't resist the call of the wild here.

CHAPTER 1

$\mathcal{P}$issing off an alpha male was definitely the wrong way to start her day. Perhaps Erik was just irritated. Nope, he was pissed. Yep, that was definitely a ticked expression. How could he look so sexy and angry at the same time?

Luna cleared her throat and tried to gather her stack of papers into some semblance of organization. "I apologize if I've insulted you. I mean your ego." She was fairly certain that all males, especially Alphas, had substantial egos.

Erik Volk sat back in his chair across the conference table, one dark blond eyebrow lifted. He'd cut his hair short—very short—making it look darker than his eyebrows. "My ego."

That voice. Seriously. Deep, growly, and thrumming with power. All Alpha.

It was shocking that the guy had let his brother become Alpha of their pack, instead of just ripping Seth's jugular right out. What kind of stranglehold did Erik have on his demons anyway?

She swallowed. "Yes." Trying to appear in control, she cast her gaze on the only other person in the opulent conference room, her current Alpha, Yago Yassi.

He sat at the head of the table, his expression showing... what was that? Shock, irritation, bemusement? Her stomach dropped. She truly needed to learn to read expressions better. Those online videos were *not* helping.

Yago cleared his throat and faced Erik. "I do apologize for any confusion." He glanced at the printouts. "Luna, I don't understand what you're trying to do here."

She had been extremely clear. "I'm trying to find the appropriate mate for our incoming Alpha," she said slowly. Again.

Yago shook his head. "You're the only descendant with even a drop of Alpha blood in your lineage. You're it."

This was not a game of tag, and the entire situation was probably a farce, anyway. "I understand that we haven't traced any Alpha blood to anybody else. However, there are definitely more suitable mates." She took a chance and looked at Erik again. "And then once you have children, they'll have Alpha blood, right?" If there were children, of course.

"Not Copper Pack Alpha blood," Yago said, his voice lowering to a growl. The current Alpha was several hundred years old, and his hand trembled slightly as he flattened it on the thick copper-edged table. "I know you don't see yourself as creating leaders for our people, but it's your role."

Actually, her role was as the lone—the one and only—scientist in any of the wolf packs. At least, as far as she knew. In fact, the pack's future might depend on her, and Yago knew that. He was just playing on faith and hope right now, and he should know better. Plus, she wasn't any good at keeping secrets. "I have other work to do," she said through gritted teeth. Her cheeks heated as she tried to face down the most powerful male she'd ever met. Well, until Erik Volk walked into the room.

"You can do both," Yago said.

She wanted to shake her head, but she lacked the nerve. She didn't have time to do both, and only somebody desperate would believe Erik Volk wanted to switch packs. He was Silver through and through, and most likely there to conquer the entire land. "I think we..."

"No," Yago said. "Enough of this." He stared directly at Erik. "I appreciate you coming into my territory and hope there are no hard feelings...well, about..."

Erik didn't move. "About you sending a kill squad of six males to murder my brother and slaughter his mate?"

A chill spiraled through Luna. "That really wasn't very nice."

Yago ignored her. "Your brother impregnated his human female before they mated. You know that's nearly impossible, and the offspring will probably be feral."

"That's an old wives' tale," Luna protested, her ears heating from the tension in the room.

Erik slowly nodded. "Yeah, and it's bullshit. You wanted to kill Seth because you thought I was going to take over the Slate Pack by mating Emily Nightsom, which would leave your pack in the cold when it came to alliances. You wanted to murder my brother and used an unborn baby as an excuse."

Yago leaned forward, his body taut. "And Seth killed all six of my soldiers. By himself?"

"You know Seth fought them alone," Erik murmured. "The bodies were brought back to you, and you could scent him. Well, what was left of the bodies."

Bile rose in Luna's throat. She didn't want any part of this kind of brutality. Erik seemed fine with it, and she'd never forgive him for so casually kidnapping her in September. She couldn't let him take over her life, and he would. She just knew it.

"So that's in the past?" Yago asked.

Erik tilted his head as if trying to decipher a puzzle.

Luna couldn't blame him. Yago wanting a different pack member as Alpha showed definite weakness. There should be viable contenders within the Copper Pack. "We do need a fresh start." She tried to assist her current Alpha.

Erik glanced at her. "I haven't decided if the insult is in the past or not, but if I do take over as Alpha, there will be no mercy for anybody who goes after my brother or his family. That's nonnegotiable."

"Unless we go to war," Yago countered. "Then your alliance must be clear."

Erik flicked his gaze toward Yago. Oh, there was no way Erik was here to help them. Why couldn't Yago see that? "We won't go to war."

Yago stood. "Good. I'm sorry the rest of the council wasn't here to meet with you today."

Erik stilled. "Council?"

Yago faltered. "Yes. As I've gotten older, we've formed a committee of sorts to lead. There were four other members, but your brother killed two of them."

"Having a council implies weakness. You have to know that." Erik's face showed no expression.

Yago swallowed. "I need to get to the copper mine. You two may work out the arrangements necessary for you to join our pack and your ensuing union." He glanced at his watch. "I have work to do." With that, he swept from the room, loudly shutting the door. The thick atmosphere of tension lessened just slightly.

"I have to admit," Erik rumbled, looking at the photographs Luna had provided, "I've never had a female try to get rid of me before."

That ego was probably earned. "I'm not trying to get rid of you," she said, throwing her hands up. "I'm just not the right person to be an Alpha's mate. I don't even know how to fight." She truly wasn't interested in learning combat.

"That's unfortunate because you should learn," he said.

It was nice of her to refrain from reminding him that he'd once kidnapped her. Jerk. "I don't want to learn. I like my lab, Erik. I like my job. I don't want to host society parties or go on hunts. It's just not me." Plus, she liked her freedom and didn't trust him. At all.

"I'm not saying I'm taking the job, but if I did, I wouldn't ask you to be anybody other than who you want to be." He sat back, his broad chest filling out his long-sleeve black T-shirt in a way that should be illegal.

She could admit to herself—and only to herself—that he was probably the most handsome male she'd ever met. Well, not exactly handsome, but rough and hard-edged. The strength in his face led to a beauty that could only be found in nature. He would make a fine Alpha, and the pack truly needed him.

Much more than he knew. She couldn't be the person to mate him. Wouldn't be forced to do so, damn it.

She slid two pictures across the table to him again. "Listen, I've done all my research, and one of these females will be the perfect mate for you."

He looked down at the photographs.

A surprising spurt of jealousy filtered through her, shocking her silent for a moment. What the heck was that? She had no claim on Erik Volk and frankly didn't want one. But she'd have to be dead not to recognize the power in every line of his body, in his very fit, muscular, and lithe form.

She cleared her throat and tried to keep from blushing again, knowing it was futile. She pointed to the first photograph that nicely showed Zelda Graytail, no doubt the fiercest female wolf in the entire pack. Stunningly beautiful with brownish copper eyes, Zelda had a wild mane of curly black hair, dusky brown skin, and finely cut muscles. She stood about six feet tall and had once taken down a grizzly bear—a real grizzly—all on her own.

"This is Zelda," Luna said. "She'll make you many fine sons, and she can train them if you're busy." It was nice to go with the positive aspects sometimes.

Erik looked up at her, a glimmer in his eyes. Was that

amusement? If so, she could work with that. "What about daughters?" he asked.

Luna blinked. "Well, yeah. She'll make you lots of daughters." She had figured he'd want sons. "Why? Do you *want* daughters?"

"Of course, I want daughters," he said. "Why wouldn't I?"

She shrugged. "It was my impression that most Alphas wanted males."

He studied her then in that way he had that made her feel like she was one of her specimens on a slide under the microscope in her lab. Well, her tiny basement that served as a lab.

"Females can be Alphas," he murmured.

Not in this pack. "If you say so," she said instead. "So, that's your first option." She then pointed to a lovely blonde in the second picture. "This is Francine Goodhouse. She plans the best parties and is the most organized person on the planet. She could take care of all your other duties, so all you have to do is work on protection and defense for the pack."

Francine also had a very kind heart and would probably be nurturing, which perhaps a male like Erik needed. He'd lost his mother a long time ago. Maybe he required a mate who was on the softer side.

"Can she cook?" Erik asked dryly.

"Of course," Luna said, brightening. "She's a wonderful cook. Her snickerdoodles at Christmastime are..." She paused. "Are you messing with me?"

"A little bit," Erik said, "though I do appreciate the time and effort you put into finding these females. Why these two? They seem to be complete opposites."

Luna lifted one shoulder. "I didn't know what you wanted."

"What if I want you?"

She sat back, blinking. Panic coated her throat. She was a logical female and didn't want this kind of attraction. Plus, she couldn't be what he wanted, even if she let herself ease into the whirlstorm he all but promised. "You really don't."

He cocked his head, and tension of a different sort spiraled through the room. "How do you know what I want?"

"You're an Alpha," she said slowly. "You want what they all want."

"And what's that?" he asked.

Why was he playing dumb? "To protect the pack, scare the other packs, make a bunch of money, and have multiple sons to carry on your lineage." Although, sometimes, that did create difficulties when the time to pass the torch arrived. Brothers fighting brothers could tear a pack apart.

"Huh," he murmured. "I wasn't aware those were my goals." He looked around the conference room before kicking back his chair and standing. "You want to get out of here?"

"Sure." She organized her papers into a file and stood. "I could show you around if you'd like. Then maybe we can track down Francine and Zelda, or you can see them at the welcoming party tonight."

He paused in reaching for her. "There's a welcoming party?"

"Yes." She rolled her eyes. Parties were her least favorite events—not that she enjoyed public events of any kind. "You need to meet everybody, the members need to meet you, and perhaps you can spend time with both of these females. Maybe a spark will fly." Sparks burned from her toes to the top of her head at being near him. What was wrong with her?

"Sounds like you have it all worked out. Who planned the party? Francine?" he asked.

"No." Luna kicked at an invisible pebble on the hardwood floor. "I had to plan the event, but Francine definitely executed the festivities. So, don't worry. It'll be perfect."

He grinned and reached for her arm to pull her around the table. "Sounds like you don't like party planning." His grip was firm and warm...and somehow gentle.

"I'm just not very good at it," she admitted, stepping in front of him and leading the way to the door, pushing out into a brisk, early winter day. November was chilly and rainy but hadn't seen snow yet. Headquarters was centered in the middle of their territory where the Alpha and his organization held office. The nearest road led a mile to the copper mine's entrance.

The Copper Pack was part of the Stope Packs Coalition, comprised of four wolf shifter packs, each with ties to mining. Copper had been in great demand for the last couple of decades, so their coffers should be full. However, their working force numbers were not.

"The mine is that way." She pointed.

"I figured," Erik said. "Mining copper isn't all that different from mining silver, so I can't envision a problem if they need help at the mine. I've worked in silver my entire life."

"Are you sorry you didn't become Alpha of the Silver Pack?" she asked quietly, curious. The breeze picked up, ruffling the maple trees around them and dropping scarlet and gold leaves in every direction.

"No. My brother is the rightful Alpha. I do miss working with him, but it's better to keep my distance unless he needs me. For now, it's time to create a good alliance between the two packs and maybe even intermingle a little bit."

Luna clapped a hand over her heart. "Don't say that out loud to anybody, especially Yago."

"I won't," Erik said. "I think it's silly that we keep these separations and fights. We created the coalition to protect against outsiders. Maybe it's time we adhered to that agreement instead of jockeying for position all the time."

She liked that about Erik. A lot. Of course, she needed a nice and mellow mate who wanted to putter in her lab or library with her and not a badass who'd no doubt killed more than once. That fire lived in Erik's blood.

He nodded toward one of several vehicles in the parking lot.

"I'll drive, and you can point out the entire territory for me. I'd like to get a feel for it before the event tonight."

"Sure," she said, not completely certain. It was one thing to sit in a conference room with his hard body for hours, but now he wanted her to relax in the cab of his truck? "No problem." She cleared her throat.

"Are you all right?" he asked, looking way down at her.

"Yes." Why couldn't she be tall like Zelda? How wonderful it would be to look eye to eye with folks. "Were you serious about wanting daughters?"

"Of course. I'd like lots of kids," he said.

"Were you honest about females becoming Alphas?"

He shrugged. "Why not?"

Why not was a very good question, except her people had never thought it a good idea. Yago certainly would not like this line of thought, but she couldn't exactly tell Erik, the possible soon-to-be Alpha of their entire clan, what to think or say.

He led her to his truck, opened the passenger-side door, and lifted her up. He frowned. "I don't have running boards on this. I guess I'll need to change that. There's no way you can climb in here yourself."

"I doubt I'll be in your truck much."

He leaned in, and the scent of wild forest and fresh rain came with him. "Are you sure about that?"

She was. She was absolutely sure. Wasn't she? For goodness' sake. Did she really have to remind her interested body that he'd kidnapped her?

He looked around. "It's pretty quiet in the area. I figured we'd see more people. How far is the school?"

"It's about five miles to the north," she said. "It's a small school."

He frowned. "How many members of the pack do you have?"

She had no idea whether she was supposed to share this information or not, but he needed all the facts to do his job. She couldn't share weaknesses, but if she showed him around, he'd see the truth. Erik Volk wasn't anywhere near stupid. "You know, we're like the other packs. We have about twelve hundred members." The lie nearly caught in her throat.

He slowly turned his head, staring her in the eyes. Man, his eyes were blue. Not as much blue as cerulean. "That's more than the Silver pack. Yet there's no activity around here."

"I heard something about a couple of big copper veins being hit, and everyone is working around the clock." That was the story Yago had insisted she tell, so she gave it her best shot. She sucked at lying.

"Why aren't there at least two guards on Yago?" Erik asked.

Probably a great question. "You'll have to talk to Yago about that. While he's several centuries old, he's tough, and I think he wants you to trust him. I'm sure he'll give you all the data about the pack—maybe after you've made a choice between the two females."

"I will," Erik said, his voice ominous. "Trust me." He leaned in, his gaze burning. "And it's three females, Luna. Right now, you're in the lead." His lips brushed hers before he leaned back and shut the door.

She gasped, her mouth burning.

CHAPTER 2

*E*rik turned from the door as the phone in his back pocket buzzed. He wanted nothing more than to dive back into his vehicle with the enticing wolf. Her scent had been with him for months. Juniper berries and female. Who the hell smelled like juniper berries? He pulled his phone free and walked around the front of the truck, already knowing who was calling. "Hey, Seth," he answered.

"How's it going?"

Erik's work as a spy had been rather boring so far. Well, except for sitting next to the flustered and too-adorable Luna. "I just met with Yago and am now going to tour the territory." The wind rustled leaves across his boots.

"Good. I want to know every weakness they have," Seth said tersely.

So far, the Copper Pack had revealed many more weaknesses than Erik had imagined, considering they let their Alpha meet with a possible enemy alone. "I don't know anything yet," Erik said. This could be a decent trap. Or at least an illusion. He wouldn't put it past Yago to give him a show. Made sense. Erik certainly hadn't promised to take over as the Alpha. As far as

Yago was concerned, this meeting constituted the first of several negotiations.

For Erik, this was a needed mission to secure his pack. The Silver Pack.

As adorable as she seemed, Luna might not have the full story about the Copper Pack. Why did Yago send a kill squad after Seth unless it was to take territory? Was he that afraid of the other packs combining to take him out?

"Do you know what Yago wants?" Seth asked. "None of this makes a lot of sense."

"No, but I'll find out. I'm going on a tour of the entire territory right now, and then I'll visit the mine. Tonight, they're throwing some sort of welcoming party."

Seth remained quiet for a moment. "A welcoming party?"

"Yeah." Erik ruffled a hand along his hair, wishing he hadn't cut it so short. It would grow soon enough.

"Do you think they'll try to kill you?" Seth asked.

"One can only hope," Erik murmured, his skin feeling too tight across his muscles. He needed a good fight—and soon. "If not, perhaps Yago truly wants an alliance between our packs."

Seth sighed. "It makes some sense, considering my cousin runs the Granite Pack, and we're pretty good friends with the leaders of the Slate Pack. It does leave Yago out in the cold."

"True. And his hands are trembling. He's older and more weakened than we thought."

"So, you could take him out?"

With little effort. "Easily." That had been Erik's initial intention, actually. He'd purposefully kept his gaze averted from the female in the truck. There had been an exasperated fondness between her and her current Alpha, and if Erik killed Yago, it'd hurt her. But his pack came first.

"Well," Seth said, "we could go to war."

Erik gave in and turned to look at the female in his vehicle's front seat, surprised to see her flipping through a book as she waited patiently for him. Damn, she was cute. "I know, but what then?"

"What do you mean, *what then?*" Seth asked.

"What do we do with everybody we don't put six feet under? We can't leave them unprotected." Especially Luna. He would never leave her unprotected. Even though the four mining packs had created the coalition for the good of all, they still hadn't worked or mixed. Ever. Combining packs would never succeed, and even if it somehow could, that wouldn't help Erik. Seth would always be the Alpha of the Silver Pack, which was as it should be.

But Erik couldn't stay too close these days—his blood demanded leadership. So, he'd stay alone, on the outskirts, and do what he could to help. "I don't have an answer to what Yago's up to right now, but give me a couple of days." His mind still reeled from meeting with Yago alone. Erik would never leave Seth's back unprotected like that. Even now, four good soldiers were rotating in a protection detail.

Seth's growl sounded tired. "We could hurt them bad enough they don't hit back and then kick them out of the coalition."

"That's an option," Erik agreed, his chest heating.

"Good. I didn't like the idea of you mating someone outside our pack."

Neither did Erik, and he thought he'd enjoy his new position of scouting weaknesses in other packs, both those in the coalition and the many outside of it. Surveying the Copper Pack was his first job.

Seth sighed. "You sure you're good traveling so much away from our people? So often?"

"What else am I going to do?" Erik said softly. "I can work as your Enforcer for short stints of time, but something in me wants to lead. This satisfies some of that craving."

"You need to lead," Seth finished for him. "I get it. I have

Alpha blood, too. Just don't let seduction go to your head. You're not meant to live with any pack other than your own."

"I don't think Luna wants to seduce me," Erik said dryly. He'd warmed to this new position instantly, knowing he could protect his pack from afar. It had been a while since he'd felt truly needed, and it surprised him how tempting the idea had become. "I'm going to seek weaknesses here and then go to this party. Did you know she has two other mating candidates for me?"

Seth chuffed. "Luna?"

"Yeah. She has two other females she thinks I should romance. One is a hardcore fighter, and the other is a homemaker."

Seth's deep chuckle came over the line. "That's hilarious. Isn't Luna the only one with any Alpha blood?"

"Yeah, and she doesn't think it matters. She believes they're better mates for me."

Seth laughed harder. "That had to be a bit of a blow to the famous Volk ego."

"You have no idea," Erik said, an unwilling grin tugging at his lips. "Right now, she's in the truck reading a book. I think she'd do it all day and not get irritated that I'm not inside going on her tour." That both amused and slightly irritated him.

Seth snorted. "You mean she's not undressing you with her eyes through the windshield?"

"Shut up," Erik retorted.

"You shut up," Seth said.

Erik shook his head. "How's Mia feeling?" His brother's mate was one of his favorite people on the planet.

"According to her, she has a bouncing watermelon in her belly. That kid is active."

"It's your kid," Erik replied. "Of course, he's active."

"Could be a girl," Seth said.

Erik warmed to the subject. "I'd love to have a niece."

Sudden tension spiraled over the line. "I'm going to ask you this once. Is my mate still in danger from the Copper Pack?"

Erik looked around the too-vacant area. "I give you my word that by the time I'm finished here, they won't ever consider crossing into our territory again." Although it appeared the lesson would be much easier to deliver than he'd initially planned—unless he was being lulled into a very false sense of security. He studied the female flipping through pages quickly. She must be a fast reader. She hadn't looked up to watch him once. Yeah, it might be insulting, yet his grin widened.

She looked adorable with her thick, dark hair piled on top of her head, dressed in a plain green sweater, jeans, and tennis shoes. No makeup covered her pretty face, as if she hadn't even thought of making an effort. Not that she needed to. Her eyes were a stunning mixture of blue and green, and her face was elfin and delicate beneath smooth, peaches-and-cream skin. She pursed her lips as she read, engrossed in the book.

"Erik?" Seth asked.

Erik wanted to tangle his fingers in Luna's silky hair and see her fighting mad again with her eyes spitting fire. The female hadn't been happy when he kidnapped her a couple of months ago, even though he'd been careful not to harm her. He'd just needed information to help Mia, which Luna had happily given with genuine concern in her eyes for her new pregnant friend. "Sorry, got lost in my head for a moment."

"Don't do that. You're in enemy territory. I'm still not entirely sure this isn't a trap," Seth snapped.

Erik looked around the vacant area where at least a few soldiers should be wandering around. "I don't smell betrayal on the breeze, but Yago has lived several centuries and probably knows a trick or two. Regardless, I had to come alone. You know that." He refused to show weakness by bringing backup with him.

"Every Alpha has an Enforcer," Seth retorted.

Erik placed a hand on the still-warm hood of his tall Ford truck. "Yago didn't have one in the meeting," he said slowly.

"Huh," Seth said. "There's no way he trusts you. Watch your back. I'm sure there are Enforcers nearby, even if you can't smell them. Be careful, brother."

Seth had no idea. For the first time, Erik wondered if he could kick this pack out of the coalition, where it would be fair game to enemies. Big time. This mission was to gather intel and see what kind of threat hung over his brother's head. Now, he wondered.

"Report in to me tonight." Seth ended the call.

Erik rolled his eyes, clocked the area around him again, and crossed to climb into his truck. The sweet and innocent smell of juniper berries shot heated desire right to his groin.

Luna hurriedly shoved her book into a small backpack at her feet. "Are you ready?"

He shut his door, his gaze taking in her flushed features. Delicate bone structure beneath smooth skin showed her fragility and tempted something dark inside him. The animal at his core, the one all wolf...and all Alpha. "What were you reading?"

She jolted, her eyes widening. In the dim light of the cab, striations of green sliced through the blue of her eyes. Fucking intriguing. "Um, why?"

Why? "Because I want to know." He tilted his head.

A light peach crawled across her skin. She reached into the bag and brought out a well-worn hardcover book. "It's Dr. Dolondson's treatise on natural treatments for animal ailments."

He blinked. "Oh." Yeah, he'd figured the novel was a steamy romance, which would've explained the blush. "Why are you embarrassed?"

She shoved the book back into place. "I don't know."

"Yes, you do." Could she be any more fascinating?

She sighed. "I'm thought of as eccentric and slightly, well, weird. Sure, our pack has healers, and I'm the current one, but I'm intrigued by science—even human disciplines."

"That doesn't seem weird."

Her eyes narrowed, and her gaze drew down. "Are you making fun of me?"

"No." He reached out and slid a wisp of hair off her cheek to tuck behind her ear. Even her ears were small. "What are you? About five feet tall?"

Her sigh held weight. "Yes. Damn it."

He grinned. "That bothers you."

"I'm a wolf shifter," she burst out. "I should be tall. Really tall. Like you."

"I'm only six-foot-five or six," he said. "Not ridiculously tall."

She crossed her arms and sat back in the seat. "School let out an hour ago, and I need to be home in case there are any injuries from the volleyball game, so let's get this tour started."

He ignited the engine, appreciating the smooth purr as his truck came to life. "I like your bossy side."

She swung her head so fast, more of her hair escaped the clip. "You do not!" Her frown darkened her eyes to a deep blue, making the green nearly disappear. "Stop ridiculing me."

All right. "That's it. We need to get a couple of things straight right now." He let a bit of the Alpha deepen his voice.

She gulped. "What?"

He captured her gaze and kept it. "I mean what I say to you. All of it. If I tease you, there will be no doubt that I'm messing with you, and you'll laugh. I won't ridicule you or make fun of the fact that you're a mad scientist. Okay?"

She shifted and then lifted one small shoulder. "I'm not exactly mad," she murmured.

Amusement lifted some of the constant weight off his shoulders. For a minute, anyway. "All right." He looked at the headquarters lodge with its many gazebos and public spaces leading in every direction. "Your headquarters is in the center of your territory, of course."

"Yes." She pointed down the pothole-riddled road. "The main area of town is that way, where we have the school, one store, and a movie theater. We also have a community garden that we've let go, and there's a community art center that just isn't used any longer."

Did she sound sad about that?

He eased the vehicle into drive and turned away from the lodge. "You mentioned a volleyball game."

"Yeah. The girls are playing a team from Puyallup. Let's go through town, and I'll show you the way to the copper mine."

He drove away from the lodge, and pine trees flanked both sides of the truck. "Actually, let's swing by the school and catch the match."

Her gasp filled the truck. "Seriously? Don't you want to see your possible new territory?"

He flicked a glance at her. "I do. All of it." His gaze swept her, and his chest heated. Apparently, the sense of possessiveness—a new feeling for him—reflected in his eyes.

The female paled and fumbled for her seat belt, looking away from him. "All right. I guess we'll catch the match."

CHAPTER 3

*L*ocated half a mile down the road from headquarters, the hand-carved pine school building showed signs of age with its many weathered and warping planks. The copper along the roof line and gutters had patinated to a rumpled green, and one of the many windows adorning the timeless structure had been boarded up near the corner.

Erik jumped out of the truck and crossed around to assist Luna to the ground.

She held onto his strong arms and then gained her balance, her lungs stuttering. "Thank you." Wincing, she looked down at the muddy parking area.

"Why isn't this place paved?" he asked, sounding merely curious.

She shrugged. "Not my monkey." Not that this made any sense. If he were in town to see their weaknesses, surveying the school didn't make sense. If he truly wanted to be their new Alpha, then the money and power lay in the copper mine. "Do you really want to watch a girls' volleyball game?"

"I do." He scouted the vehicles in the area. "These licenses are all from the other county for the opposing team."

She nodded. "Most people can walk to the school to watch the games, and the kids walk home or take the bus." Not that they had a bus, but Erik didn't need to know that.

"Still, shouldn't there be more vehicles from our county?"

"Come on." She grabbed his hand and pulled him toward the wide front entrance, surprised when he tangled their fingers. His palm was heated and firm around hers, and she realized too late the mistake she had made. Her breath quickened and heated. Just from being touched by him. She needed to introduce him to the proper mates soon before she tried to tackle his hard body to the ground. Not that she could. But the image amused her.

They walked up the wooden stairs inlaid with metal wolf paws. The accents had once been a bright, coppery color, but time had altered those to a metallic green, as well. Still, they were pretty cool-looking.

"How many students attend the school?" Erik pulled open the heavy, steel door.

What an odd question, unless he figured kids could fight. She sighed. "Listen, I can't deal with this any longer."

He paused, still holding her hand as he looked down at her. "What?"

She forced herself to meet his gaze and got lost in the myriad blue sparks. Or shards. Whichever word best described beauty and danger. The wolf within him lay right beneath his skin. "What you're doing here. I mean, *really* doing here."

One of his eyebrows rose. "Explain."

She swallowed, faced with a predator she didn't know. Sure, she could shift and hurt him, but probably not much. His broad chest blocked her view inside the building, and raw muscle showed in every line of his torso. Even his neck looked tough. "Are you here to hurt us or save us?"

He studied her for a moment in that still and somewhat

threatening way he had. The guy probably didn't even know it *was* threatening. "I'm not here to hurt you."

Did he answer her question? "Are you loyal to the Silver Pack or ours?"

"The Silver Pack." He waited patiently as if he had all day and shouldn't be counting the bars of gold in the mine safes. As Alpha, he'd have access to all funds. Wasn't that the draw?

She swallowed. "You have to be angry about the kill squad going after your brother and his mate."

"I am, and they're all dead. I don't hold you or anybody else accountable—except your Alpha."

That's what she'd figured. "You don't really want to be the Alpha."

"No."

At least he'd chosen honesty with her. She tried to dig into his head and find his true motives, but all she could see was his hard, cut face—angles and planes, starkly masculine. A light scruff covered his jaw, and she had the oddest urge to run her palm across those whiskers just to feel the burn.

His eyes darkened.

She gulped. "I won't let you hurt my people."

To his credit, he didn't laugh. Or even smile. "I understand. Now, answer my question. How many kids attend school in this run-down building, and why is it run-down? Copper is selling well these days."

"I think we have around three hundred children under the age of twenty." That sounded about accurate.

"That's a decent number," Erik said, pulling her inside the darkened hallway.

"The building needs some updating, but we've been busy with the mines." She pointed to the right. So, he didn't want to be Alpha and was just goofing off. No wonder he wanted to watch a game. At the thought, she finally relaxed. Nobody would push her to mate him if he didn't want to join their pack.

Why did that thought make her want to growl? She needed a vacation. "The gym is through here."

They walked past trophy cases on thin pine floors and around a corner, passing several classrooms to reach a double door that led to the gym. She opened it and walked inside with him on her heels.

While the floor was worn, it still squeaked plenty as the girls pounded the volleyball over the net. The bleachers for the other team held students, parents, and other visitors, all dressed in bright purple attire. The Purple Knights always supported their teams.

She gestured toward the pack's bleachers, where plenty of room remained. "Come on. We can sit up toward the top." She liked to rest her back against the wall.

"Sure." He looked around, his gaze probably missing nothing.

The copper and black uniforms the Copper Wolves wore were frayed in several areas, and none of them seemed to fit the players very well. All eyes in the place turned to stare at Erik as he made his way up the stairs to the top of the bleachers. His graceful movements somehow still held power. Several of the girls on the court even turned to look.

He glanced over at a group of elderly ladies who all appraised him from the front row by the other door. Dressed in copper and black colors, they'd bedazzled their hats. "I hadn't thought we'd catch this much attention," he said, looking down at Luna.

"Seriously?" She raised both eyebrows as they both sat.

"Fair enough. I just wanted to watch the game." He looked pointedly at the ref, who blew the whistle.

Luna glanced up at the scoreboard. The Wolves were behind by ten. Like usual.

"I figured there'd be more parents or other students from the

Copper Pack in the stands," Erik murmured, watching as the girls began volleying the ball back and forth.

"Everyone's still at work in the mine," she said. "When you hit a vein..." Was he still buying this? Hopefully.

He watched as the Wolf setter missed the ball. "Huh."

Luna winced. "Yeah, I know."

The match continued on with the Copper Wolves losing by twenty. Their shoulders slumped. The girls ranged from the ages of twelve to eighteen and trudged around the bleachers into their locker room without looking up at the stands.

The other side cheered wildly as the Knights jogged happily into the visitor locker room.

Erik looked down at her, his heated body warming her entire right side. "Where's the coach?"

She chewed on her lip. "At the mine, I think. They pretty much have to substitute themselves in, but they know what they're doing. Perhaps they'll play better in the next game." She could tell from the scoreboard that they'd already lost two of the five games. If they lost the next one, maybe everybody could go home.

"Huh," he said again. "Come on, let's go talk to them." He stood.

"No, I don't think—"

He grabbed her hand and pulled her up, holding tightly. "Wasn't really asking." Releasing her, he loped down the stairs and turned, heading to the locker room, where he knocked on the metal door.

Luna tried to catch her breath. "What are you doing?"

"Not exactly sure," he admitted, looking tall and broad against the door. He knocked again.

"What?" a female voice called out.

He opened the door an inch. "Are you all dressed? There's a male coming in."

There was quiet for a moment. "Of course, we're dressed. We have another stupid match to die on," came another voice.

Erik chuckled. "All right. Coming in." He pushed open the door and stalked inside the home locker room.

Luna winced. Several of the lockers were missing doors, and even the bench lining the center had cracked in two.

One of the girls looked up. "Hey, you're Erik Volk."

"Rumor has it," he said easily, leaning against one of the remaining lockers and crossing his arms.

"Are you the new Alpha?" Nikki, the setter, asked.

"We're negotiating that now," Erik said smoothly.

A couple of the girls straightened, and several blushed, all staring at him. Yeah, he was good-looking. Luna barely kept from rolling her eyes, but she understood their reaction.

"Why are you in here?" Nikki asked. Although the shortest, she seemed to be the leader of the group.

Erik looked around. "Sometimes, curiosity becomes too much for me. I had to ask, why'd you all throw the game like that?"

"Huh?" Nikki asked, flipping her blond hair with some spirit, although her brown eyes looked tired. Resigned.

He rolled his eyes. His very handsome, shockingly blue eyes. "Give me a break. I saw you blow three sets, and you"—he pointed at Ronnie—"could have spiked the ball down number two's throat three times, at least."

Ronnie stretched out her arm. At sixteen, the girl was a beauty with rich, dark brown skin with cool undertones, making her coppery brown eyes glow even more. Her curly hair had been pulled away from her stunning face. "Because we're wolves. That's the law. We can't let anybody know we're wolves, so..." She trailed off.

Erik frowned. "So, you lose? Every time?"

All the girls nodded sadly.

Erik looked down at Luna. "Did you know this?"

"Everybody knows," she said. "It's good that we keep a pulse on outside communities by using kids' sports for interaction, but we can't draw attention to ourselves."

He shoved away from the locker, appearing both incredulous and intimidating. "That doesn't mean you have to lose."

Ronnie snorted. "Right. You get in trouble with the Alpha and see how *you* feel."

He sniffed the air. "Who was vaping?"

The room went silent.

Luna looked around. They were all too young to vape, and why in the world would a wolf shifter mess with nicotine or pot?

Erik lowered his chin. "I'm not going to ask again." This time, his tone was all Alpha.

"I was," Ronnie said, glaring. "Just me."

Nikki sighed. "Me, too."

Erik yanked a discarded baseball cap off the top of a locker. "In here. All of them. Now."

One by one, half the girls tugged vaping pens from purses or lockers to drop into the hat, their gazes down as they retook their seats.

"I smell pot," Erik growled.

"It's legal in Washington state," Ronnie said slowly.

He waited until she met his gaze. "Not if you're under eighteen, and I assume not if you're a member of the pack."

"That's true," Luna whispered. "Where in the world did you girls get vaping pens, anyway?" They weren't allowed to leave the territory often.

A knock sounded on the door. "Time to match," the ref called.

Ronnie sighed. "What else are we supposed to do? Vaping calms us so we can lose our asses out there."

"Stand up," Erik said to the girl, only a slight hint of the

Alpha inside him coming through this time, although it was obvious in every line of his body.

She gulped and stood to just under six feet tall. Her body was lean and muscled, and she looked like an athlete.

"We'll deal with the vaping later." He extended one hand toward her, palm out. "For now, hit me as hard as you can."

The girl looked at Luna.

Luna shrugged. "Give it a shot."

"It's okay," Erik said. "Don't hold back. "

"Fine," Ronnie said, clearly exasperated. She pulled back and put all her weight into the strike. The smack echoed around the room, and a couple of girls gasped.

Erik didn't so much as flinch. He grinned. "Nice punch."

Ronnie blushed and shifted her weight. "Um, thanks?"

"Okay, good. Now," Erik said, his hand still in place, "punch me again, but at the very end, pull it. Still use your strength but show me your control."

Ronnie swallowed and looked at him for several heartbeats. "All right." She set her stance, took a deep breath, and concentrated, pulling back her arm and then punching, halting almost at the last minute but still connecting. The smack wasn't nearly as loud.

"Very good. Do it again."

She did it again.

"Even better. So, when you go out there for this next match, do that. Spike the ball where they can't get it. You don't have to hurt anybody. You don't have to show that you have extra strength. Pull your punches, but for the love of God, win."

The girls all looked at each other, excitement starting to fill their eyes.

"We can really win?" Nikki asked, her voice hushed.

"Sure. Next time you set, set it good." Erik gave her his full attention until she nodded. He pointed at Izzy Hollowgale, whose wild, red hair was up in a fierce bun. "How old are you?"

"Fifteen. I'm the youngest," she said. "But we don't have enough students for a full team, so anybody who wants to play does so on varsity. We don't have enough girls who want to lose all the time to fill more than one squad."

"I can't blame them," Erik said. "You're a hell of a server, aren't you?"

The girl blushed. "I can be."

"Let's see your talent out on that court today. Let's see you serve the ball in a way where nobody gets hurt. So, aim where they can't get it, and use half your strength—or maybe three-quarters."

"Are you serious?" she asked, hopping on one foot. She was nearly as tall as Ronnie, at least five-foot-ten, but she hadn't grown into her limbs quite yet.

"Yeah, I'm serious," Erik said. "What's the point of showing up for your team if you're not challenging yourself and them? But maybe only four or five times, and then you've got to let the Knights hit one back. All right?"

Excitement flushed the girls' faces as they all started to move.

"Is this okay?" Ronnie asked Luna.

Luna had no idea but was loving the feeling in the room. No more desolation. To think the girls vaped drugs just to deal with forcing themselves to lose. "Hey, he's looking to be the new Alpha." That wasn't true, but she couldn't diminish the hope on their young faces.

"I promise you, it's okay," Erik said, his voice lowering into a growl. "If anybody has a problem with you winning, they can talk to me about it. I'll make sure you're covered." He looked them over. "Hey, do you want to make it interesting?"

Ronnie frowned. "What does that mean?"

"How about you win this game by twenty-five to fourteen? Exactly. If you do, pizza and ice cream are on me tonight."

"We have that party tonight. The welcome party." Luna reminded him.

"Oh, yeah." He winced. "All right. As soon as it can be arranged. What do you say?"

The excited shrieks and cries hurt Luna's ears, but Erik didn't so much as grimace.

"All right, let's get out there and have some fun," he said.

"All right, Coach," Nikki said, hopping up and then running outside.

Luna waited until the girls had exited. "Are you sure you know what you're doing?" Her heart felt lighter, and her abdomen odd. Like butterflies winging through her stomach odd.

"I usually make it up as I go," he admitted. "But watching those girls have to lose badly, even just one time, was like a kick to the balls. No wonder nobody's here. It's a stupid law and a stupid rule."

"I agree," Luna said.

He sighed and looked down at his feet. "Does the football team have to follow the same rules?"

"They're allowed to win fifty percent of the time," she muttered. "It's not fair."

"No. It isn't."

For the first time, she wondered if Erik should become their Alpha. Well, if he decided not to kill all of them. When her pack went after Seth, and, more importantly, his pregnant mate, they'd declared war.

The Volks never lost a war.

CHAPTER 4

*E*rik walked outside the gym with teenage girls prancing all around him. He'd been given more high fives in the last few minutes than he had gotten his entire life. While he had no intention of staying in the territory, their exuberance was contagious.

Luna slung her arm around Nikki's waist. "That was amazing," she said.

"We did it," Ronnie said, hopping next to Erik. "We hit that score exactly."

"Yep," he agreed. "I'm buying pizza and ice cream for you all soon."

Izzy, the small server, giggled, turned to look across the parking lot, and stilled. "Oh, my mom's here." She waved hesitantly.

Erik followed her gaze to see a female about the same height as Izzy with similar features. She certainly didn't look old enough to be Izzy's mother. The female stared directly at him and straightened, leaning against what appeared to be a new, silver Chevy truck. The vehicle dwarfed her, even though she was tall.

"Um, I should probably go." Izzy faltered.

His ears prickled. "Is everything okay?" Erik asked.

"Yeah," Izzy said, holding the volleyball from the game under one arm. "She might've heard that we won."

"Oh," Erik said. "All right, girls, you get home safely, and don't forget the party whenever Luna can arrange one."

"We won't." Ronnie laughed. "Besides, we're coming to the party tonight. See you there, Coach."

With that, and in a cloud of giggles, most of the girls headed down the road. The Knights and their supporters had already left the area, leaving the parking lot calm and way too muddy.

Erik looked down at his boots. "Somebody should pave this place."

"No kidding," Luna muttered, casting a worried glance toward the silver truck. "Come on, Izzy. I'll walk you over."

"Oh, no, no, no. That's not necessary." Izzy started toward her mother.

Erik pivoted. "Really? I think it is." He walked toward the lone truck at the far end of the area, parked near a backdrop of pine trees with a couple of tamaracks thrown in. He reached the female, who paled the closer he got. "Hi," he said as calmly as he could, holding out a hand. "I'm Erik Volk."

"Oh, um, hi." She reached out to briefly shake hands. "I'm Haney Hollowgale. Izzy's mom."

"It's very nice to meet you," Erik said. "Izzy played a heck of a game."

This female had to have been a teenager when she'd given birth. There was no way she was even thirty years old.

"Oh, thank you." She reached for her daughter and pulled her into a sideways hug. "You guys won?" she asked, her voice trembling.

"I told them to," Erik said directly.

Haney instantly relaxed. "If you told them to win, they had to." The relief in her eyes was palpable. "That's good." She smiled at her daughter, finally appearing to relax. "Bet it felt amazing to finally win one, huh?"

"It really did," Izzy said with a sweet grin. "And honestly, Erik told us to, so it's okay, right?"

"Oh, definitely," Haney hurriedly assured her. "I'm sorry I missed the game. Your brother is sick, and I couldn't find a babysitter until just a few minutes ago."

"That's okay," Izzy said. "Nobody knew we were going to win." She chuckled.

A small smile lifted Haney's lips. "We have to get going. I need to pick up your siblings and get the truck back to your dad."

"Okay." Izzy turned and stared at Erik. "Thank you," she said softly.

It was like a blow to the heart. Erik forced a smile. "Anytime."

The girl rushed forward and hugged him hard, wrapping both small arms around his waist. She looked up. "I hope you become our Alpha." With that, she stepped back and rushed to jump into the truck's passenger side.

Haney faltered. "Um, it was nice to meet you. It was good to see you, Luna."

Luna smiled. "Thanks, Haney. Maybe we can get together next week."

Haney looked down at her feet and then back up. "Maybe. I'm really busy with all the kids, but I'll try." With one last look at Erik, she crossed around the truck and started the engine.

Erik watched them drive away. "Why is she so nervous?"

"I don't know," Luna murmured. "I don't see as much of her as I used to."

"How old was she when she had Izzy?"

Luna kicked a rock away from her foot, and it spun across the muddy ground. "I think around fifteen?"

"That's what I figured. Who's her husband?" Erik kept his voice level.

"Her husband's name is Butch Hollowgale. He's one of the supervisors at the mine. He's also on the council."

This council was already pissing him off. "I think I need to meet Butch," Erik said. Then he turned and lifted his head, smelling marijuana. "Interesting. I know that scent. Stay here."

Without waiting for an answer, he crossed the parking area toward the bigger pine trees and strolled through, following the scent. Branches crackled behind him, and a stick snapped. Luna definitely lacked subtlety and finesse. He heard her trip and finally just paused, turning to look. "What are you doing?"

"I'm following you. I'm curious," she admitted, pulling pine needles out of her hair.

He waited until she reached him. "Follow my trail before you hurt yourself." Dirt covered one of her knees. He frowned. "Did you fall?"

"Nah, not really. I kind of tripped into a tree," she admitted.

He figured he would've heard her fall. "All right. Do you smell that?"

She lifted her nose. "No, but honestly, I don't have a very good olfactory system. I can smell some things, but it's just not a skill."

How in the world had the female survived this long? "Stay behind me." He turned and strode through a makeshift trail until he reached a stand of blue spruce trees. "I know you're in there," he said calmly. "Come out." Then he waited.

Soon, a male walked out with a gun in his hand. "You have a problem?" he asked.

"My name's Volk. Who are you?"

The guy squinted. "I don't think that's any of your business."

"That's where you're wrong." Erik gestured toward the backpack over the guy's shoulders. "I can smell the pot and the nicotine. So, you're the source, huh?"

"You really are Erik Volk. I've heard rumors about you and have seen a picture or two. Are you looking to buy?" the guy asked.

Erik cocked his head. The dealer stood at about six feet tall and had shorter brown hair feathered over the side of his face. His nose took prominence beneath deep-set brown eyes. His lips were thin, his skin pale, and his ears wide. Truth be told, the guy was all nose and ears. He was also a shifter.

"Whose pack do you belong to?" Erik asked.

"I don't," the guy said. "I'm an independent."

"That's what I figured. So, here's the deal. You come into this territory again, and I'll take off your head." Erik tried not to sound bored, but this guy presented no challenge.

Luna gasped. "Now, wait a minute. Shouldn't we arrest him?"

"Do we have a police force?" Erik looked down at her.

She wiped a speck of dirt off her cheek. "Um, kind of? We have a couple of Enforcers."

"I'd rather just take off his head." Erik wasn't joking.

"I don't need to stay out of the territory." The guy kept his gun pointed at Erik. "You can call me Garth, and I'm your guy if you want to buy anything."

Perhaps the shifter had a death wish. "Not only do I not want to buy anything, I also want you to stop selling to teenage girls," Erik growled.

"And boys," Garth said cheerfully, apparently feeling pretty confident behind the gun.

"They're underage, and it's illegal. I know an FBI agent," Erik murmured. Truth be told, Mia was an *ex*-FBI agent, but she probably had resources. Not that he'd let things go that far.

"I understand, not that it matters. There's no way Erik Volk, one of the Volk brothers, is becoming the Alpha of the Copper Pack, so you can stop playing around with me. I'll leave for now, but we both know you're leaving, too."

So, word had gotten out. Interesting. Yet nobody believed he'd take over this pack—except possibly Yago Yassi. Also interesting. "I'm not going to tell you again. Keep out of this territory and stay away from these kids."

Garth studied him as if weighing the possibilities. Sure as shit, he looked like he might shoot. Erik dodged forward, swiped the gun out of Garth's hand, and slammed him against a tree. All five claws on his right hand extended, and he sank them deep into Garth's shoulder until he felt bark.

Garth cried out, convulsing. "What the hell, man?"

"Yeah. Alphas move fast," Erik said congenially.

Luna made a sound behind him. He looked over his shoulder to see her leaning over, holding her stomach and gagging, obviously trying not to vomit.

"What is wrong with you?" he asked.

"Violence." She coughed. "I can't handle such rage and destruction."

Part of life in a wolf pack. "I thought you were a scientist."

"Yeah, exactly. I'm a pacifist." She stood all the way up, her face pale.

"For goodness' sake. Turn around," he murmured. She nodded and swiveled.

Garth continued to shake while pinned to the tree. He tried to kick, but Erik was too close, so he lifted an arm.

"I'll break it if you hit me," Erik said conversationally, wondering if that sound would send Luna over the edge. He'd had no clue the female was that delicate. The urge to protect her dug deep inside, and heat boiled in his blood. For her.

Tears filled Garth's eyes, and a snot bubble popped from his nose. "Take your claws out of my shoulder." He took in a breath, and the air started to shimmer.

"You shift, and I'll cut off your head. I'll slice it right off," Erik said, meaning every word, leaning in with a growl.

Garth shuddered. "Fine."

"What have we agreed to here?" Erik asked softly.

"I'll stay out of the territory. I won't sell to the Copper Pack any longer," Garth gasped, paling as blood flowed from his shoulder.

"That's all I wanted to hear." Erik released him. "I'm not killing you because I'm not in the mood, and that's the only reason." Plus, Luna was behind him, apparently trying not to puke. "You come here again, and I won't think twice. You understand?"

Garth clasped a shaking hand to his wound. "So, you *are* taking over as Alpha?"

"It doesn't matter. You come into this territory again, I'll know it, and you won't live another day. Now, get out of here," Erik snarled.

Garth turned and headed west. Erik sheathed his claws and wiped the blood on his jeans before turning to reach Luna, who still faced the other way. With his clean hand, he touched her shoulder. She jumped almost a foot. "Are you okay?" he asked.

"I'm fine," she said again, her voice trembling. "I told you I wouldn't make a good Alpha's mate."

He clasped her to his side, warming her, and started walking back toward the muddy parking area. "I don't know why not. Nobody would ask you to fight as an Alpha's mate."

"Yeah, but don't you want someone who can fight?"

His gut ached for a second. "I've never really thought about it," he said. "I dated a wolf shifter once, but she died, and I wasn't strong enough to keep her alive."

"Did somebody kill her?" Luna tripped on an exposed branch.

Erik steadied her, wondering if he should just sling her over his shoulder so she'd survive walking out of the forest. "Yeah, someone killed her, but we caught him. Still, I've always thought it was my fault. I wasn't who I should have been with her. Didn't step up at all."

Luna turned and gifted him with a full smile. "You are definitely who you should be today. Those girls have never had so much fun on the volleyball court."

"Good." He had made sure to tell all the spectators—the few females there—that the win had been his decision and to spread the word. The bedazzled group had promised they would do just that. Even so, he wanted to make sure he made that fact clear at the party tonight.

When they reached his truck, he opened the door and lifted Luna inside, leaning in to check her color. She was still pale. "I should have warned you before I charged Garth. I'm sorry I didn't," he said honestly.

"No, you were doing your job. I just don't react to violence and blood very well." She exhaled. "Some wolf shifter, huh?"

Actually, she was pretty damn perfect. His gaze dropped to her mouth and then moved back up to her hazel-colored eyes. "Luna, what's really going on with this pack? Why are they trying to pull in an Alpha?"

Her gaze instantly slid away. "I don't know what you mean. We don't have a young, healthy one, and we need leadership."

"There are enough able-bodied males here who could mate you, but I haven't seen them, have I?" Since she had Alpha blood, the lineage would stay strong with whoever she mated.

She shrugged. "I'm sure I don't know what you're talking about."

He lifted her chin with one knuckle. "I will unearth what's going on, you know."

"I know," she whispered. "But I'm not going to be the one to tell you."

Cute and loyal. "Fair enough."

She stared at him. "I know you're not here to do what we want, but is there any chance you would consider becoming the Alpha of the Copper Pack? You did a wonderful job today with those girls."

He hadn't truly considered leaving the Silver Pack. Not for good. And yet... "I am tempted," he said.

"To be the Alpha?" She brightened.

"Not really." With that, he let the wolf inside him take over, leaned in, and kissed her.

CHAPTER 5

*H*eat flowed into her, lighting her entire body on fire. His firm lips easily overtook her, coaxing her to respond, compelling her to reach for his broad shoulders. She closed her eyes, opening her mouth to take more of him. Blood rushed through her head, pounding in her ears. Every nerve she had sparked from head to toe, spiraling a ravenous desire to her core.

Her wolf, the logical and reasonable animal deep down, started to howl. This was why it'd be too dangerous to mate him, even if he wanted her after knowing all the facts. How easy it could be to get lost in him. In his world, where violence and passion combined.

Her breasts tightened, and her thighs softened. Of their own accord, her nails scored his dark T-shirt, seeking flesh. His flesh.

Gripping her chin, he angled her face to the side, going deeper.

So deep.

She moaned, lost in the moment.

Finally, he lifted his head, his eyes an impossible and animalistic blue.

She blinked. Her body was on fire. "I'm not a passionate female," she whispered.

He burst out laughing, a dark flush highlighting the brutal angles of his face.

She uncurled her fingers, wincing at seeing that she'd pierced the cotton in several places. "Honestly."

His calloused thumb rubbed across her smarting bottom lip, shooting sparks right to her clit. "Whoever told you that was so fucking wrong it's comical. You're all passion, baby." With that, he released her, stepped back, and shut her door.

Baby? Passion? He had her all wrong. Except there was nothing in the entire world she wanted more right now than him. If he'd tried to take off her clothes, she would've helped.

His door opened, and then he was in the truck, overwhelming it with heat and the scent of the forest during a rainstorm.

She clasped her hands together. "I don't want you to get the wrong idea."

"Which would be?"

This was so complicated. "I know you're not staying, but if you somehow decide to stay, I'm not the right mate for an Alpha." How many times did she have to say that? "There are many reasons, but please just believe me." She couldn't give him the whole truth.

"I think you're still mad at me. I didn't hurt you when I kidnapped you a while back, and you know it. You even made a couple of friends." He grunted, which seemed to be a normal expression for him. "What time is this party tonight?"

She glanced at her watch. "We have an hour before the festivities start." He'd understand once he saw the other females, or at least viewed the pack. "For now, head away from the school, and I'll show you Main Street and the outlying areas. We have two main subdivisions, kind of, and then many cabins and homes scattered throughout the territory, which is flanked on both sides by the Cascades, as you know."

"I've hunted in the Cascades." He pulled out of the parking area and flashed her a grin. "I know. Probably broke a treaty or two."

She doubted anybody could stop him if he wanted to climb through the mountains.

He drove into the central part of town, and Luna tried to view the location from his eyes. The main store was in fairly good condition with wide glass windows and a copper roof, as was the movie theater next to it. Somebody had painted the theater a bright pink, contrasting oddly with its metal roof. Yet it held charm with the wide columns out front.

A little farther down, the door on the former art studio hung haphazardly with squirrels running around inside the vacant space. Beyond that, the community garden showed tons of weeds and sad neglect.

"We haven't done a lot in town lately." She felt lame.

"Why not?"

She coughed. "Like I said, everybody's busy working hard in the mine." Truth be told, she'd never been a good liar. Not that she was completely lying. Still, the look he gave her showed that he wasn't buying it.

"Keep going west." She tried to keep his attention off her, even though her mouth still tingled from that incredible kiss. "I'll show you the main subdivision. It's where the council and the Alpha live." The luxurious lots surrounded Mineral Lake, which was one of the most beautiful places she'd ever seen.

"All right." Erik drove quietly, his large hands capable on the steering wheel.

She slowly relaxed against the seat as the trees sped by outside. Clouds started to gather, and she smelled rain on the wind. Considering that it was late November, she should be scenting snow. She pointed ahead. "Through there."

"Interesting." He drove up to the gate, and it opened. "You all have a secured community?"

"Sure. Why not?" As wolf shifters, that likely did seem odd, but loyalty kept her tone level. "If you go this way, just follow the loop."

They drove by opulent, two and three-story homes situated around the small lake. They were high-end and well-kept, and this area of the territory definitely had asphalt.

"Pretty houses," Erik murmured. "Do you want to live here?"

"No," she scoffed. "I love my little cabin in the woods."

He drove out of the subdivision after she'd shown him each home. He had paused at seeing Butch Hollowgale's impressive Tudor-style house before moving on.

They drove for several miles, and she pointed to many dirt driveways leading off the main road. "There are different cabins scattered throughout the Cascade Mountains," she noted.

"You said there was another subdivision?"

"Yes. It's on the other side of the territory. You need to go back past headquarters."

He backtracked on the pothole-riddled road, his gaze seeming to miss nothing. They drove beyond the headquarters and into a more mountainous area, then to a grouping of ramshackle-looking trailers and wooden cabins.

"These definitely need repair. Who's in charge of that kind of thing?" Erik asked.

"I don't understand," she murmured.

"Who takes care of these places?"

What in the world was he talking about? "People take care of their own places. Many of these folks are retired, too old to work in the mine, and some younger folks are here, as well. Young families, I guess." She often brought extra food to this area if she had any.

His jaw tightened as he continued driving past the subdivision and into the woods, unerringly finding his way to her small cabin miles away, tucked against a rock alcove. "I remember this place."

"Yeah, you should. I hope it's not every day that you kidnap somebody."

He cut the engine. "I said I was sorry."

"No, you didn't."

He scrutinized her. "Huh. Maybe not, but we needed your help, and I thought you and Mia had formed a friendship."

"We did," she grudgingly admitted.

He didn't bask in the acknowledgment but instead focused on her again. "Do you need to grab anything for the party?"

She looked down at her jeans and sweater. Should she change? She hadn't even thought about it. Maybe she should dress up. "Yeah. Why don't we run inside?"

"Sounds good."

"Oh, I forgot. I was supposed to ask you if you wanted to stay in one of the houses in the Mineral subdivision or in one of the many empty cabins we have throughout the range."

He looked out into the darkening forest. "Definitely a cabin. I don't want to be anywhere near a mansion."

"All right. There are several just miles away from here you can choose from." She jumped out of the truck and hurried into her cabin with him on her heels. This place felt much smaller with him inside, and his wild scent filled the entire space. So much for her not being able to smell anything. He filled her whole head. "Can I get you anything? I have water." She chewed her lip. "And maybe some orange juice."

"How about a beer?"

Her eyes widened. "You know what? I do have beer." She'd held a poker game for a few friends a couple of weeks ago, and Maisie had brought beer. "It's in the fridge. Why don't you help yourself while I change? I should probably do something with my hair, as well."

"Your hair is beautiful as it is." He headed toward the fridge.

Her cabin was quaint in that she had a living room, a fairly large kitchen, and two bedrooms. The downstairs was comprised of her lab, where she conducted most of her work.

"I'll just be a minute." She hustled into her room and shut the door, taking several deep breaths. That had been some kiss. She hadn't known people could kiss like that. Maybe most couldn't. Perhaps that was all Erik Volk. Maybe he was the only male in the entire universe who could kiss like that.

That would make sense.

She hustled to her closet and winced, looking through her clothes. There wasn't much. Finally, she found a salmon-colored dress shoved in the very back. It looked nice enough. The A-line design fell to just above her knees, and the top was held up by straps, but it was a pretty color, and she liked it.

She hurriedly changed into the silky garment and then grabbed a gray cardigan to cover her shoulders since it would be a chilly night. She looked longingly at the tennis shoes she'd just kicked off and slipped on a pair of silvery gray kitten heels instead. She shouldn't trip too many times, but who knew? The more she was around Erik, the more off-balance she became. It wasn't fair.

Finally, she dashed into the bathroom and brushed her hair, clipping just the front part up on the top of her head before sliding some lip gloss across her mouth and swiping mascara on her lashes.

She glanced at her watch. They really had to go. So, she took a deep breath and moved into the next room, where Erik sat on her comfortable leather sofa, finishing his beer. He stilled. She looked down. Was there something wrong with her dress? "What?"

"You look gorgeous."

She blinked. Maybe there was something wrong with his eyes. "I look normal."

He stood. "Oh, no. You look gorgeous."

She knew better, but maybe the beer had gone to his head. "All right, we have to go." The tension spiraling in the room heated her breath, and she really needed to get outside.

"Are you sure about that?" he murmured, moving toward her.

She backed up, her butt hitting her bedroom doorframe. "Um."

Then he stood in front of her, washing heat along her entire front. "Why aren't you Alpha-mate material?"

She blinked. "Why does it matter?" Her breath came out odd. Kind of fluttery. Never had a male affected her like this. Perhaps there was more to the Alpha bloodline than she'd realized. "You're not really here to mate anybody, are you?"

"No." He leaned in, pressing his free hand against the wall and above her head. "But you can't deny we have an attraction. Why not explore that?" His eyes glittered, showing the wolf barely leashed inside him.

Tempting. Definitely tempting. But her brain ruled her body, not the other way around. Plus, there wasn't a doubt in her mind that Erik Volk had explored his passion with several females in his past. She'd hate to fall short. Oh, the need was there, but she didn't have his experience, and she also didn't want to be a mark in his no doubt impressively notched bedpost. "Casual isn't my thing. You mentioned you lost a past female. Was it casual with her?"

He changed then. Sharpened and withdrew at the same time without moving. "Yes. Too casual." Stepping back, he shot a hand through his hair and finished the beer in two swallows. "You're right. I'm sorry."

She liked that about him. For a big badass of an alpha male, he had no problem admitting fault and then actually apologizing. She hadn't realized that was an option with a male like him. "I like how you handled the girls' team earlier today. You did a good job." There. That should ease his ego and feelings.

A grin tugged at his lower lip. "Thanks for the support."

Was that sarcasm? No. Teasing her? Not really. Just amusement? Yeah. That was it. She smiled. "Sure. Now, let's get to this party."

CHAPTER 6

$\mathcal{E}$rik parked his truck and walked around the lodge to an area transformed into a welcoming November sight. Somebody had strung fairy lights from tree to tree and around all the gazebos while every light in the lodge glowed golden through the many windows.

Scarlet and yellow leaves created a carpet-like effect between the gazebos and the lodge, where a buffet table had been set up in the middle of a multitude of picnic tables. People milled about with glasses of champagne or beers in their hands while kids ran around chasing each other.

To the side, a band played a modern country song. Several volleyball girls ran up as Erik approached, all reaching for him.

"Come on, the bar's open," Ronnie said happily. "Then, as soon as you start the buffet, we can eat." The girl had changed into jeans and a sweatshirt with the school logo.

"Then we'd better get to it." Erik grinned.

Luna looked over to the side, where a group of females—the older ones still wearing their bedazzled hats—carefully placed centerpieces of colorful flowers on each table. "I'll be with you in a moment."

"All right." Erik let the girls lead him away. The festivities seemed peaceful. Even so, he scouted the forest for threats. The first one stepped in front of him just as he turned the corner toward a highly set-up and sophisticated-looking wooden bar against the side of the lodge.

"What do you think you're doing, winning a game like that?" a male around his age snapped.

Several of the girls stepped back.

"Why don't you go start the buffet line?" Erik suggested, positioning his body between them and this new male.

"We can't until Yago says it's okay," Nikki murmured, sidling closer to him.

Erik kept his expression calm. "It's all right. Find Yago and tell him we'll do whatever announcement or presentation he wants so you can eat. Go now."

The girls scampered off.

The male watched them go, his body vibrating.

"Who the hell are you?" Erik turned to face the asshole.

"I'm Butch Hollowgale." He stood at almost six foot eight and had long, brown hair and narrow-set brown eyes. Built like a lumberjack, Hollowgale appeared like he could take on a grown wolf without shifting. He'd worn a green-checked shirt, black jeans, and pointed cowboy boots for the festivities. "It's my understanding you told the girls to win today."

"I sure did," Erik said congenially. "You have to let them win once in a while."

"That wasn't your call." Hollowgale leaned in, his breath smelling like bourbon.

Heat flashed along Erik's arms. "Where's your daughter?"

"She's grounded," Hollowgale retorted. "She knows not to win."

Erik turned and looked around the area. "I don't see your wife, either."

"She'll be here soon enough. She had things to take care of. Not that it's any of your business."

"It might be," Erik returned evenly, facing him, energy flushing down his spine. It'd been a while since he'd had a good fight, and this jerk would give him one. It was too bad Izzy couldn't partake in the fun, and he wanted to make sure Haney was all right. "The win was my call. Why would you punish your kid for following orders?"

Butch leaned in. "You're not the Alpha here, so she had no right to disobey pack rules."

What a jerk. If the guy wanted a fight, he'd have to head into the forest and away from spectators so Erik could turn him into a bloody mess. "You have something to say to me? Say it."

Butch snorted. "I don't need to say anything. Anybody with half a fucking brain knows you're not here to become Alpha. You're pissed off we attacked your pack a couple of months ago and are looking for weaknesses."

Yeah, there was definitely some truth to that. "I take it you want the job," Erik drawled.

"I deserve it. You only left two members of the council standing—or Seth did, rather. We all know you're the little brother who never amounted to much."

"Haven't I?" Erik asked. "Interesting. I have a feeling you're trying to hurt my feelings."

Red flesh darkened Hollowgale's face. "Now that you've had your fun, it's time for you to leave our territory. Got me?"

Erik flashed his teeth. "Oh, I plan on getting you."

"You want to go?" Hollowgale asked, stepping forward.

"In a heartbeat." Erik smiled, letting the wolf inside him show.

"Excuse me," a dark voice said from behind him.

Erik didn't need to turn to know that Yago Yassi had stepped up.

"We're in the middle of something," Hollowgale snapped, looking away from Erik.

Silence reigned for a moment. "It'll have to wait," Yago said. "Erik, we need to introduce you to the pack."

Erik partially turned, carefully keeping the shock off his face. Nobody talked to an Alpha like that. Hollowgale should be on the ground and bleeding profusely for showing such disrespect.

Just how weak had Yago become?

"Who's your other council member still standing?" Erik asked, needing to know who else might be coming at him.

Yago waved over another male built like a brick shit house. This guy had blond hair and odd, copper-patinated eyes. A smaller-looking version of him trotted alongside him.

"This is Allen and Vernon Bushbalm," Yago said.

Vernon, the skinnier of the two, held out a hand. "Hi."

"Hi." Erik shook hands.

Allen stepped closer to Hollowgale and didn't extend a hand. "You're still here?"

"I take it you're on the council?" Erik asked Allen.

"I am. I'm also single and fully plan on mating Luna McElhanney, so you can leave our territory right now."

Something new rose in Erik. Something dark and primal. "I don't believe Luna is aware of that fact."

"She doesn't need to be," Allen said.

Vernon shifted his feet. His hair was cut short, and he had a similar eye color to his brother, but while his brother sported a beard, his cut jaw was clean-shaven. "Al, knock it off. Luna is a nice girl, and she can choose whoever she wants to mate."

"Actually, the pack is more important than one person's choice," Allen spat. "It's time for you to leave, Volk."

For the first time, Erik wanted to stay, if for no other reason than to protect Luna from this jackass. "As members of the council, do you run the copper mine?"

"Of course." Hollowgale's chest puffed out.

Hence the mansions on the lake. "Apparently, the mine is running right now. Why are you here?" Erik asked.

"We have it covered," Hollowgale snapped. "There are about five hundred people here for this ridiculous farce of a welcoming committee while everybody else is either busy or working in the mine. You're lucky we had that many people who wanted to bother coming to a damn picnic."

"Yeah, I feel real fortunate," Erik said. "Let me know when you want to finish what we started." With that, he turned his back on the male in a perfect insult. "Yago, you wanted to make some remarks?"

The Alpha looked from Erik to the other three males and then nodded. "Yeah, let's go this way."

Erik followed him toward the lodge's back porch, where a microphone had been set up, along with lights and beautiful flowers. His gaze instantly scanned the crowd and found Luna. She looked at him, her eyes wide and concerned.

What the hell was going on with this pack?

* * *

THEIR ALPHA'S message had been short and congenial while introducing Erik to the rest of the pack. The older ladies had instantly drawn Erik away to the buffet table, where everybody had begun lining up for the delicious-smelling food. Yago motioned Luna toward the lodge.

Sighing, she walked up the stairs and followed him inside. "That was a nice introduction."

"Does he suspect our weaknesses?" Yago asked without preamble.

She shook her head. "No. We told him we had to staff the mine tonight so many people couldn't make it to the party."

"Good." Yago sighed, the heavy wrinkles in his face appearing deeper than usual. "Has he agreed to mate you?"

"I haven't agreed to mate *him*," she said as gently as she could. "It's not going to happen."

"It has to happen. I don't care what you have to do. You need to draw him into the fold. It's either that or mate Allen Bushbalm, and he doesn't have the temperament to be an Alpha."

She shook her head. "I don't think you're understanding me. You're not going to tell me who to mate." She lifted her chin. "Plus, come on, Yago. You know Francine and Zelda are better choices—for obvious reasons."

"I'm not convinced of that." He sighed and looked down at his worn brown boots. "Luna, we have to draw Erik into this pack, at least for a while. Long enough for another leader to emerge, a good one. We're in trouble."

Her stomach churned. "I'm well aware of that. But we need to tell him the truth about the matings. He has a right to know." She was terrible with secrets and even worse with betrayals. Having Erik mate anybody in the pack without knowing the truth was just wrong.

"Sometimes, we have to do things we don't like for the good of the pack—even if only for a little while. We have several young leaders I see great potential in, but they're twelve, thirteen, and fourteen years old. It'll take a good fifty to a hundred years to prepare them."

She turned to see Haney Hollowgale arrive with her three younger kids, one boy and two little girls. "I'll talk to you later, Yago. I'll let you know how it goes." She turned and hustled outside into the brisk November evening and down the stairs. "Haney, you couldn't bring Izzy?"

Haney's eyes were puffy, and her nose was red. "No. Butch was adamant that she stay home, even though she'd been following the possible new Alpha's directive."

Luna leaned closer. "Are you okay?"

"I'm fine," Haney said, nodding at her young ones. "You guys can go get in line for food if you want." The kids giggled and ran off, all dressed in jeans and sweaters.

Luna leaned in. "Haney, if you ever need to talk, I'm here for you."

"I know. Thanks." Haney had dressed in a light blue sundress with a thick black cardigan. Her hair was up, and she looked pretty, even with her nose swollen from crying.

"Are you in danger? Is he dangerous to you?" Luna asked.

"Of course, not." Haney looked away. "You have enough to worry about, Luna. Have you found a cure for any of this?"

Luna looked around wildly. "No. Be quiet. Erik Volk is in the dark here."

"Don't you think that's something he should know?"

"Of course, I do," Luna whispered. "I'm trying to fix this. Honest."

Haney stiffened as she caught sight of her husband. He gestured her over. "I have to go." She hustled away, and Luna watched her leave, her heart hurting. She had to do something to help.

Sighing, she spotted Zelda Graytail near the bar, drinking from a bottle of beer. Luna crossed the leaf-covered ground, only tripping twice while trying to watch Erik interact with the pack, before reaching the beautiful female. "Zelda. Hi. How are you?"

Zelda looked down at least a foot, her copper eyes smiling. "I'm well. We trained some of the football team earlier in hand to hand. They did a great job."

"Excellent," Luna said. "I would like for you to meet Erik Volk. Yes, I'm matchmaking." She took her friend's arm and all but dragged her across the clearing to where Erik stood in the center of the volleyball team. She introduced them, her chest aching as she did.

"Hi," Zelda said, shaking Erik's hand. "We have training

coming up for some of the younger kids. What do you say you join in once we get it scheduled?"

"I'd love to," Erik said, smiling.

Luna's ears rang. This sucked, but it was also what she wanted. Zelda would be a good mate for an Alpha—so long as everyone finally leveled with Erik about the pack's problems, which might be too much for even a badass Alpha like him to fix.

She moved down to speak with more of her friends, trying not to watch as Erik and Zelda seemed to get along famously. Zelda had a fantastic laugh and used it often for the next half hour. Finally, Zelda wandered over to speak with a few of the elderly couples sitting at the tables.

Perhaps they hadn't hit it off. Was that wishful thinking? Luna needed to get a grip. The two had seemed to love each other's company.

She kicked at a rock and then found Francine Goodhouse fluttering around, picking up discarded paper plates. Her friend looked beautiful with her blond hair in a braid down her back, dressed in a hand-knitted gray dress that emphasized her narrow waist. "Francine, I'd like you to meet Erik Volk," she said, taking Francine's hand.

Francine looked across the distance. "You're crazy not to grab him for yourself. That body should be drawn."

Luna gulped. "I'm not an Alpha's mate." Even now, her feet throbbed in her kitten heels, while Francine wore three-inch stilettos and seemed relaxed and comfortable. "Come on." She escorted Francine to where Erik now sat, speaking with Yago. She introduced them.

Francine blushed beautifully.

"Have a seat." Yago gestured to the area next to Erik, narrowing his gaze at Luna. Francine pulled out a chair and sat. She smiled, instantly inquiring about Erik's family and his home life.

Luna listened for a few moments, marveling at how perfectly Francine put Erik at ease. She knew exactly what to say and effortlessly directed the conversation.

Feeling hollow, Luna turned, strode over to the volleyball players, and sat at a round table littered with discarded paper plates, soda cans, and a multitude of cake crumbs.

"Hey," Nikki said, nudging her. "What are you doing, introducing Volk to other females? Aren't you supposed to mate him?"

"No," Luna said glumly. "I'm really not." She hung out with the girls until the moon rose high in the sky while Erik and Yago visited with Francine. For hours.

Finally, Yago gave her a nod.

She swallowed and stood, heading to the edge of the gazebos where she'd set up a display earlier that morning. She cleared her throat. "Yago asked me to create a bit of a display that shows a commingling of powers." Drawing a lighter from her back pocket, she leaned down and ignited a flare, stepping away from the tree.

A lovely flame of silver wound around the trunk, followed by another one of copper, mixing until the entire tree glowed with the two colors.

Yago stood and moved closer to her. "That's beautiful. A symbol of how a Silver Alpha can mix with the Copper clan." He turned as Erik rose and walked nearer, the shadows from the flames dancing across his face.

He winked.

Luna's body lit up as much as the tree.

A sputter came from high above. She stepped back. Another sputter.

Yago moved away, gesturing for Erik to do the same. "Luna?"

She blinked. The concoction had been perfect, hadn't it? She stared up at the top. "Um. Everyone run."

The top exploded, sending flames in every direction. The girls screamed and ran toward the lodge.

Erik ducked his head and charged the hundred-year-old pine, pounding into it and pushing so hard the roots lifted right out of the earth. The tree landed with a loud thump, throwing flames, leaves, and dirt in every direction. "Water, now!" he yelled, jumping on the nearest burning branch. Yago ran and fetched a hose while more members of the pack beat out the flames. Luna winced as her toes burned but kept stomping.

Two gazebos went up, and everyone scrambled to extinguish the fires before they could spread to the lodge.

Soon, only ash and smoke filled the air.

Erik coughed and stepped back, soot covering his face and making his short hair stand on end.

Francine hustled forward from the lodge and touched his arm. "Let's get you out of that dirty shirt. You must have burns."

Yago turned and looked at Luna, exasperation clearly glowing in his eyes. "You said you had the concoction at a safe concentration." He nodded at Zelda. "You and Volk make sure the fire is out."

"You've got it," Zelda said, sauntering toward Erik, a smudge on her angled jaw. "Francine? He doesn't need his shirt for that. Feel free to take it."

CHAPTER 7

$\mathcal{T}$he cool night air was a balm for the burns down Erik's arms as he worked to separate burned branches from the trunk of the tree. Yago continued to douse the tree and both damaged gazebos with water as several pack members worked tirelessly around him.

Several times, Erik glanced at Luna, who squelched flames out near the lodge, her cute silver sandals now burned. Her toes had to be killing her. Every urge he had bellowed for him to move her away from the flames and stick her feet in a bucket of water. But since everybody else was helping, he didn't want to single her out. It was obvious that she felt bad enough.

A smile tugged at his lips, and he ducked his head to keep working. He'd never been so entertained in his life. While she might consider herself a boring scientist, he had learned that nothing was calm or placid around her. He liked that a lot.

"Hey, watch out. That's still smoldering," a kid to Erik's right pointed out.

Erik glanced down to see some flames on pine cones beneath several branches. "Thanks." He jumped in the middle and started snuffing flames.

"No problem." The kid kept moving, pulling branches away and tossing them toward the sodden, wet ground to the right. He'd stuck close to Erik for the last half hour or so and worked hard. He stood at about six-foot-five and had shaggy brown hair and nearly black eyes. His movements were smooth and graceful.

"I'm Erik," he said, breaking off another branch.

"No kidding." The kid smiled. "I'm Oakley Rockwood. I think you met my mom earlier at the picnic."

Erik had met so many people at the gathering that it was difficult to remember each one. "What about your dad?" he asked. "Is he working in the mine tonight?" It was odd that the entire pack hadn't shown up to meet who they thought would be their new Alpha. They didn't know he was only there to search for weaknesses.

"No." The kid ducked his head. "My dad died about five years ago."

"I'm sorry to hear that," Erik murmured. "How did it happen?"

The kid paused and then hurriedly leaned down to gather more branches into his arms, seemingly uncaring that a couple of them still smoldered. "It was an accident. You know, the mountains are treacherous."

Instinct ticked down Erik's back, but he didn't push.

The kid looked him over. "Do you want me to get you a shirt? Francine really didn't give you much choice in taking that off."

Erik chuckled. "No. Actually, the air feels good on the burns, but thanks. How old are you?"

"Seventeen."

The kid held some weight for being young. Muscled and fit. Good for him. "Are you still in school?"

"Yeah. I work in the mine part time, but I am trying to finish school."

"Why? Do you want to go to college somewhere?"

Oakley snorted. "We don't get to go to college, man."

"Yeah, the Silver Pack had the same problem, but that's changing now," Erik said, moving to pick up pieces of what used to be a gazebo.

The kid followed him. "What do you mean that's changing? The Silver Pack is letting kids go off to college?"

Erik nodded. "There's a plan in place. They need to attend in groups and return home afterward to contribute to the pack."

The kid whistled. "That's progressive and something new, right?"

Erik looked at him. "Would you like that here?"

Smoke filtered between them, and Oakley coughed. "I think that would be a great thing for a lot of the kids here, being able to go off to college and learn a skill that would be useful for the pack."

"But not you?"

Oakley shook his head. "I've got four younger sisters who need me." He shrugged and then leaned down to gather more of the gazebo's exploded lights. "Plus, I don't want to leave. I know a lot of people do, and I think that's great, but I like it here. I want to stay and maybe,"—he lifted a shoulder—"I'd like to be an Enforcer someday for an Alpha."

Ah, so *that's* why Oakley had stayed close. He was looking for a job in the future. Erik could respect that. "You'd probably make a good Enforcer."

"Yeah?" The kid's grin widened. "I think so. I mean, I know I'm young, but I can fight. And I know how to, well, *not* fight," he said glumly.

"Ah, you're on the football team?" Erik asked, rubbing at a burn on his elbow.

Oakley's grimace shifted the soot down his face. "Yeah. We're supposed to lose to a team out of Seattle this coming

Saturday. I don't mind blowing a game once in a while, but these guys are real assholes." He coughed. "I mean, jerks."

"No, if they're assholes, they're assholes," Erik said congenially. "Why don't you win?"

"We can only win fifty percent of our games."

Erik really hated that rule. It was stupid, and these kids shouldn't have to lose. "Why? I mean, even if you only win eighty percent, you don't make it to state, right? You don't hit the newspapers."

"Yeah. Maybe you could talk to Yago. I'd really love to beat these guys tomorrow. Last time they were here, they pissed on all the towels in our guest locker room. It was a crappy thing to do."

Erik frowned. "That is a crappy thing to do. I will talk to Yago because I'd love to see you guys beat these jerks. I mean, assholes."

"Great. Come to the game tomorrow, would you? Give us the nod." Oakley chuckled and then glanced up to see a bunch of the volleyball players working hard on the farthest gazebos. "Hmm, it looks like they need help. Good talking to you." With that, he jogged toward the girls. He was a kid after Erik's own heart.

Man, he barely remembered what it was like to be that young. Even though he was still under thirty, he sometimes felt a thousand years old.

"That was smoothly done," Zelda said from his right, handing him a glass of water.

"Oh, thanks." Erik tipped back the entire contents.

Her gaze appraised his bare chest, and she hummed. "Are you doing all right?"

"I am."

She looked down at the burns on her hands. "I can't believe Luna blew something else up."

"Something else?" Erik asked.

"Oh, yeah. She blows something up every few months or so. It's kind of cute." Zelda shrugged firm shoulders. "I like how she tried to matchmake us."

Erik shook his head. "She does seem to be determined. For some reason, she doesn't want to mate me."

"Well, she's not wrong," Zelda said. "You need somebody strong enough to defend and cover your back. If you become Alpha, it won't be an easy journey for you."

"Yeah, no kidding." Erik glanced over to where Allen Bushbalm and Butch Hallowgale smoked cigars near the lodge, apparently too important to help stomp out the flames. Even their Alpha was working to contain the mess.

Zelda followed his gaze. "We need to do something about those two guys, but I don't know what. Your brother did us a huge favor by taking out the other two members of the council, but don't tell anybody I said that," she whispered.

"It's been pretty bad, huh?" Erik asked.

She shook her head. "They're dicks."

Well, that pretty much summed it up.

She sighed and stood straighter, stretching her back. "So, there's probably a smoother way to say this, but it's all I've got."

He gave her his full attention. Under the moonlight, she really was beautiful with her darkened skin and glowing eyes. "What's that?"

"I'm not opposed to an arranged mating," she said quickly. "I think I'd be a good mate, and I would love to take charge of this pack in a way that's good for everybody. I like that you let the volleyball girls win. And the idea of allowing the kids to go off to college for a short time, well, I would've done it in a heartbeat. You could do some good here, Erik, and I could help you." It was a sweet offer, and it came from a good place. Even so, her gaze didn't quite meet his.

"What aren't you telling me?" he asked evenly.

She winced. "Pack business. You don't get to know pack business till you're in the pack."

That was a fair statement.

She cleared her throat. "I'd really like to have kids. Love to, actually." Her voice cracked at the end.

"I appreciate the offer," he said. A million years ago, he would've tried to lure her into the forest and had a great night to see if they were compatible. Of course, he'd been an asshole back then. Now, he didn't want to hurt her or anybody else. His gaze kept sliding to Luna and back.

Zelda smiled. "I see the draw, but you'd be spending your life putting out fires."

He was actually pretty good at putting out fires. The problem with Luna was that she didn't want to mate him. Well, one problem. The other was that he didn't want to be a member of this pack. He reminded himself once again that he was here on a mission—and not the one they all expected.

Zelda smiled. "Just think about it. If you want to meet up one of these nights and see if we're compatible, just let me know." With that, she sauntered off toward the final destroyed gazebo, her lithe body moving naturally in a way that would entice any male.

Erik glanced over and saw Luna glaring at her. She quickly masked it and looked back down at her work. Oh, but that glare had been there, hadn't it? Erik's phone buzzed, and he pulled it out of his back pocket, wincing as his burned fingers brushed the metal.

"Volk," he answered.

"Hey, it's Seth."

Erik glanced at the time on his phone. "Why are you calling so late?"

"I've decided I'm pissed off that the pack attacked us, and I want to take them out before they can try again. I'm thinking tomorrow night. How many soldiers do you think I'll need to destroy them?"

* * *

HER HANDS and feet stinging from burns, Luna bustled up the stairs of the lodge into the interior, wandering to the vast and spacious kitchen to search for more bottled water in the large stainless-steel refrigerator. She opened it, gratified to see a whole shelf on the bottom with nearly iced-over bottles. Excellent.

"I wondered where you got off to," a male voice said from behind her.

She jumped and nearly knocked her head on the freezer handle, turning to see Allen Bushbalm lounging against the kitchen doorframe, a lit cigar between his lips.

She shook her head. "Considering we're putting out a fire, do you think that's a good idea?"

"I think it's an excellent idea," he said, more than blocking the entire doorway.

No burns showed on his skin, and no soot marked his flannel.

"Are you even helping?" she asked.

"I'm supervising," he muttered, his eyes glittering.

Even from a distance, she could smell whiskey on him. For the first time, a sliver of awareness slithered down her spine. "Do you want to help me bring water out to everybody? I mean, those people who are actually working."

"I thought you and I could have a little talk instead."

She sighed, turning to pull water bottles out to place on the counter. There had to be a basket somewhere that she could use to carry them all out. "I don't see that we have anything to talk about." She turned suddenly, facing him. He had to be about ten years older than her, in his mid-thirties, and he'd been best friends with Butch Hollowgale for their entire lives.

"Do you think Butch is being mean to Haney?" she asked abruptly.

Allen blinked. "I don't know. What goes on in their marriage is their business."

"I don't think so." Luna crossed her arms. "Do you know something? Because if you do, you need to say something."

"I've never seen him hit her, but she's kind of a moron, so who knows?" He lifted one shoulder.

She wished she could fight. She would love to knock him into next week. "It's nice that you care so much, considering you want to be Alpha."

"I want to be Alpha to bring this pack back in line. We need to learn to fight because, you know as well as I do, the Ravencall Pack is coming back. They want our territory."

She threw up her arms. "Then why don't we tell the coalition? We're in the Stope Packs Coalition for a reason."

"If the other packs within the coalition knew how weak we are right now, they'd take advantage. In fact, that's exactly why Erik Volk is here," Allen spat. "You know that, right? You know he isn't here because he has some great love for you."

Allen's gaze swept her head to toe, and his lip curled.

"I have no illusions as to why Erik Volk is currently in our territory," she muttered. Of course, that didn't explain why he'd helped the girls' volleyball team or why he was currently working his ass off to protect the lodge from burning down— something Allen certainly could not claim to be accomplishing. "I haven't told him anything."

Allen puffed on his cigar, sending smoke spiraling around his big head. "It's good you finally learned to keep your mouth shut," he said. "And I'm not kidding. I am going to be Alpha of this pack, and you are going to mate me."

"You don't even like me, and I definitely don't like you," she said.

"That has nothing to do with it. You know why. It's that Alpha blood in you."

What a jerk. She needed to get out of this kitchen. "And you know it doesn't matter that there's Alpha blood in me," she snapped.

His eyes glittered even darker. "It has to matter with you more than with anybody else. You're our only chance. So, get on board. The second Volk is out of our territory, we're getting mated." He spat the cigar onto the floor, and ashes and little sparks flicked across the wood. Then he was across the kitchen and grabbing her.

"Hey," she protested before he lifted her onto the counter and yanked her close for a hard kiss.

She kicked his knees and punched his chest, but he shoved his tongue into her mouth, holding her still. She struggled wildly, panic echoing through her head as she tried to push him off.

A second later, he was pushed hard to the side and fell against a metal table.

Zelda put her body between them. "What do you think you're doing?" Her entire back vibrated with energy.

Allen straightened and punched out.

Zelda blocked the punch and kicked him square in the nuts. He fell back, leaning over, his eyes widening before an enraged *oof* burst from his mouth.

"Come on." Zelda grabbed Luna's hand and yanked her off the counter and around the table to where they could run through the lodge to the outside. "Are you okay?"

"I'm fine," Luna said, wiping off her mouth. "Thank you." It was quite pathetic that she'd needed Zelda's help and couldn't get away from the bully herself.

Zelda pushed her hair away from her face. "He's going to come after both of us now."

"I know. I'm sorry," Luna said, panting as her adrenaline flowed.

"It's not your fault," Zelda snapped, looking down and then softening. "We need to tell Yago."

Luna lifted both hands. "Why? Yago can't fight him any more than we can."

Vernon Bushbalm ran up, his hair covered in soot. "We got the gazebos all out." He narrowed his eyes at Luna. "Are you okay?" Then his attention diverted as his brother stormed out of the lodge, glared at Zelda, and then stalked away, still limping.

Zelda glared back.

Vernon moved closer. "What happened? Did my brother do something?" Anger coated his words, and he reached out to rub Luna's shoulder.

They'd been friends for a long time, since Vernon was closer to her age. "He's a jerk." She wiped off her mouth again.

Vernon's nostrils flared. "I'll talk to him. I promise." With that, he turned and followed his brother.

Zelda sighed. "Allen will kick the crap out of Vernon, like usual."

Frustration heated Luna's skin.

Zelda swallowed, looking toward where Erik worked alongside a couple of the high school kids near the edge of the forest. "He really is our only hope, isn't he?"

CHAPTER 8

*W*ith the flames extinguished and the area safe for the night, Erik climbed into his truck and drove away from the lodge headquarters before dialing his brother. He'd given him some terse answers earlier, but they needed to finish their discussion.

"Are you over your snit?" Erik asked when his brother answered.

"I'm not in a snit. And why are you calling me at two a.m.? I have a pregnant wife here who's asleep."

"We both know you weren't sleeping," Erik muttered.

Seth was quiet for a moment. "Fair enough. Anyway, I've decided I can't let the possible danger to Mia and the baby continue. If Yago sent out a kill squad of six, he'll send out another one."

"Not considering you took them out," Erik said easily. "You're allowing emotion over Mia and the baby to take over, and you need to stop and think. If we take out the entire Copper Pack, somebody else will just move in, and you know it'll be either the Ravencall Pack or the Ghostwind Pack. And we'd rather work with Yago."

The other two packs were notorious killers. If they got one foot in the door, they would gather strength and then come after the other three packs—without question. They wanted the money from the mines. "Yago's been an ally for centuries. He made a mistake, and I don't think it was him." Erik searched for the cluster of birch trees he was supposed to find on the way to the cabin they'd given him for his stay.

"What do you mean it wasn't him?" Seth asked.

Erik thought through the day, oddly reluctant to tell his brother everything, which was weird because he never kept secrets from Seth. "Yago's sicker and older than we thought. The pack has been run by a council for years. I don't know how long."

"What the hell's a council?"

"Exactly," Erik agreed. "The good news is that you took out two of the four council members after they attacked, but the other two are a couple of real dicks. One has high aspirations of becoming Alpha, and I'm surprised he hasn't already killed Yago."

If Erik decided to stay—which he was not going to do—he would ensure that Yago was always covered. It was shocking that nobody was guarding the current Alpha right now.

"How weak is the pack?" Seth asked.

"I've only seen half the pack members. Most work the mine around the clock." Erik turned left near a brilliantly golden-colored tamarack tree on a barely there dirt road. "So, I can't tell you. I assume the strongest members in the pack are working the mines—at least the strongest physically. But based on what I've seen, it wouldn't be much of a fight." It was sad but true.

Something creaked across the line as Seth must've sat. "So now would be a good time to attack."

"Affirmative," Erik said. "If that's the route you want to take, which is not the avenue I recommend." He'd try to stop his brother if battle plans were drawn, but gut instinct told him that

Seth would not destroy an allied pack. Well, unless they sent another kill squad after Mia. Then the Copper Pack would cease to exist in any form. "Give me a couple more days to identify all threats."

"All right. But then I also want a full battle plan," Seth grumbled. "How's it going with Luna? Is she still trying to pass you off to other females?"

"Oh, yeah. She introduced me to two. I like them both. Zelda's a great fighter, and Francine is a sweetheart."

"And yet…" Seth prodded.

Erik shook his head, turning left near a series of huckleberry bushes that were, unfortunately, now out of season. He could see a couple of the light purple berries at the bottom and made a mental note to pick them later. It was rare to find huckleberries this late. "There is no *and yet*," he retorted.

"Huh. I don't know, Erik. You might want to open your eyes to that one."

"Shut up," Erik said.

"You shut up," Seth retorted, bickering like they had since they were kids.

Erik pulled up to a nice-looking A-frame that fronted a narrow creek. "It looks like I'm home for the night. I'm going to check out the copper mine soon. I'll let you know what I see."

Seth chuckled. "Are you tempted to stay?"

Erik paused in jumping from the truck. "That was out of left field. Why did you ask me that?"

"Because I know you," Seth said. "It sounds like the Copper Pack needs help, and you've been somebody who runs into burning buildings to save people since you were two years old."

If only that were true. "Are you kidding me? You're the guy who saves people. I'm the one who gets people killed."

Seth groaned. "Ruby's death is not on your head."

"She was pregnant with my baby when she died," Erik retorted, knowing the guilt would never leave him. No matter the good he someday did in this world, if he did any good, that sin would always live in his soul.

"You didn't kill her."

"I didn't protect her either." They'd been good friends, and he'd cared about her. Maybe he would've grown to love her, and he should have. That was exactly the path he should've taken. But he'd been young and stupid, and, well, he deserved the pain. She should be alive.

"You have to let that go, brother," Seth said. "You're not going to get anywhere if you let that hold you down."

Erik jumped down and slammed his truck door. "I'm not letting it hold me down, but it's a lesson I'll never release." If he ever became involved with a female again, he would make sure, without a doubt, that she remained safe at all times. He fully understood his brother's nearly obsessive actions in keeping Mia protected.

"I don't blame you. Call me after you check out the mine." Seth ended the call.

Erik grabbed his bag and walked into the comfortable-looking cabin. It held a nice living room and kitchen, with what looked to be one bedroom off to the side near a bathroom. He tossed the bag on the older log-frame sofa.

Damn, he needed to run.

He ditched his jeans and boots and then returned outside, quickly shifting into his wolf form. He leaped off the porch and ran through the forest, letting the bright colors and sharper scents fill him before padding unerringly toward Luna's cabin. The female should be asleep.

She sat on her front deck, rocking slowly in a chair, her gaze on the forest and a cup of what smelled like huckleberry tea in her hands. Her eyes were sad, and her movements were slow. He didn't know what caused the melancholy and didn't like it. He padded closer until he came into her view.

She jolted and placed the cup on the railing. "Erik?"

He nodded and then gestured with his head toward the forest.

Her eyes lit up. "You want to go for a run with me?"

He nodded again, curious.

She seemed to think about it for several long moments. Finally, she stood and hustled back inside the cabin. So, the girl was shy. Good to know. "Turn around," she yelled.

Oh, for goodness' sake. He'd seen the female naked before. Even so, he turned around and faced the darkened forest between the pine trees. He felt her shift behind him as a wave of energy overcame him, then he turned to see her leap off the deck.

She was adorable in wolf form, smaller than he would've expected, even though she was petite as a human. Her coat was a lighter, thick, rich-looking brown, but her eyes remained the same: all blue and green mixed together in a color he'd never be able to describe.

He grinned and looked around. This was her territory, and she could lead.

Yipping, the cute little wolf dashed past him and onto a barely there trail.

His heart soaring and his blood pumping, he turned to chase after her.

The hunt was on.

* * *

WINTER'S chilling aroma rode the breeze as Luna ran on all fours through the forest, sensing rather than hearing the Alpha wolf behind her. Excitement rushed through her veins, and she kept her head down, sprinting fast along hidden trails and rocky ledges to the secret pond, surrounded nearly on all four sides by sharp rocks. It was her favorite place, and she didn't think twice about leading Erik here.

She skidded to a stop on the ledge, not surprised to see him padding leisurely toward her. In wolf form, he was every bit as powerful as she would've expected with his thick fur and sizzling blue eyes.

He came closer and peered over the edge. It was quite the distance, but the soothing water was well worth the plunge. Luna backed away, and he turned to look at her. Then, unable to help herself, she sprang forward, hitting his flank with both paws. He went over the edge silently and then made a snuffing noise before hitting the water.

Was that a laugh? It sounded like a laugh.

She looked down and grinned as much as she could in wolf form.

He rose to the surface and howled, the sound playful. She immediately dove into the air and fell, doing a belly flop on the water and sinking before rising to the top. He immediately planted one large paw on her head and shoved her under. She kicked back up, spraying him.

Who would've thought Erik Volk had a playful side, especially in wolf form?

She turned and swam toward the other side, knowing he would follow, and then catapulted up onto an outcropping. She couldn't count how many hours of her life she had spent on this very ledge, sunning herself in wolf form. Sometimes, in human form. Not many people knew about the hidden glen. As if Erik understood that fact, he sat before shaking his fur out wildly.

She yipped and batted away the water, even though she needed to do the same thing. He looked around curiously and then almost too quickly spotted her escape route. Smacking her on the shoulder with a paw, he turned and ran between two smaller birch trees and up the rocky slope.

She followed him instantly, trying to keep up, but when she finally reached the top, he sat waiting as if he'd been there all day. She rolled her eyes the best she could. He jerked his head and instantly turned, bounding into the forest.

Oh, yeah? She chased him now.

She did so, noting that he probably slowed his speed so she could keep up. They ran past headquarters and the ruined gazebos. In wolf form, the burned smell was sharper and more acidic, and she winced, happy when Erik kept bolting toward the school and across the football field. She often ran in the same place and didn't blame him. The natural grass felt good on her paws as her fur started to dry.

Then he turned and kept dashing. It took her a second to realize his aim, and when she figured it out, she tried to speed up. It was as if he knew she was coming, so he slowed down. She jumped in front of him and tried to force him in a different direction. He shook his head and bolted past her.

Damn it. She followed him, trying to catch up, but he didn't let her this time. Finally, they emerged into the copper mine's parking lot. He skidded to a stop, staring at the silent and closed building.

She gulped. Well, this was a disaster. The air shimmered and sparked, and she took a step back. Suddenly, he stood there in full male form—and what a male form it was. Sighing, she forced herself to shift back into a human. His gaze raked her nude body, and then he looked over his shoulder at the clearly shut-down mine.

"I thought we were working around the clock," he said.

She kicked a pebble, wishing she could shift back into her wolf form and be playful with Erik. "Yeah. Well, we shut down for a few hours. Everyone needs to sleep, Erik." The lie rolled easily off her tongue, but she couldn't meet his gaze.

He moved then, right at her, fast.

CHAPTER 9

One second, Erik stood across the parking lot. The next, he was in front of her, so close the heat from his body tingled on her skin. "Don't lie to me."

She lifted her head to meet his gaze, wanting to step back but forcing herself to remain in place. Why did he have to be so much taller than her? "I'm not lying."

His shoulders went back.

Crap.

"Luna." His voice turned all Alpha. Hard and rough.

Something inside her, all wolf, wanted to submit. She softened but held her place. "If I'm lying, then I have to do so." At least, that was the truth.

"I could get the full story from you."

Her legs trembled. Not from fear but from that voice. "Maybe." She gave in and stepped back, still meeting his gaze. "But you're not being honest either, are you? It's not like you truly plan to stay." Her mind flashed to how well he'd seemed to get along with Zelda, who could be an Alpha's match. Oh, Luna could learn the role and become all right with it, but she was also more of a risk for Erik and the pack, and she couldn't take that kind of chance. "So, who's really lying?"

"I haven't decided what I'm doing here." He seemed more than comfortable standing beneath the lone traffic light, bare-ass naked.

It was so difficult not to look lower. Cut muscles showed along his torso and down his arms, even to his abs, ridged enough that she could count them. But. Not. Lower.

Yeah, she wanted to peek.

But a female needed to have some pride. Or class. Whatever.

Not so for Erik. He'd definitely looked his fill at her nude and now-chilled body. His nostrils flared, and his wolf shifted just beneath his skin. "So, we're both liars, huh?" he asked softly.

"All packs have secrets." She tried not to shiver in the deserted area from the chilly wind. "I'm sure the Silver Pack has several, and I'd never ask you to divulge those. You can't know our weaknesses, our vulnerabilities, unless you're all-in."

"You have vulnerabilities, baby?"

More than he could ever know. "Yes." Desperation clawed through her, and she fought to keep her stance neutral when all she wanted to do was turn and run.

His gaze somehow warmed her even while stirring a warning deep inside her chest. "I'll happily take care of any threat to you. Right now. Give me a direction, and you'll feel safe by morning." A ring of truth, a deep vow, darkened his tone.

What would it be like to belong to a male like him? To be with a male like him? She'd enjoy making him hers, no question, but what then? "Not all threats can be banished." She attempted to keep the sadness from her voice but failed miserably. As his chin jerked, panic overtook her. She pivoted and shifted, landing on all four paws and running.

Hard and fast.

His shift blew the fur dry across her back as he pursued her.

Her heart raced as she zigzagged through the forest and then the town, knowing the territory much better than he possibly could. Even so, she could feel him breathing down her neck.

Turning for safety, she made it to the deck outside her cabin before he tackled her, rolling them both over and over on the pine needles. Then his jaw was on her maw. Enclosing it entirely.

She blinked and forced herself to shift back to human.

He released her immediately, backing away.

She scrambled to sit, crumpling dying leaves.

He shifted into a human form, standing tall and naked in the moonlight. "What the fuck was that?"

She forced herself to stand and wiped leaves off her legs. "I didn't want to talk any longer."

He prowled closer, right into her space, bringing with him the scent of male and dark moonlight tinged with pine. "So you ran?"

Yeah. Of course, she ran. How could she possibly stand up to a male like him? There was no question in her mind that he'd let her get this far, right to her home, before taking her down. Even then, he'd been gentle. A large wolf like him could've done serious damage, and all he'd done was roll her over and make her stop. She'd never be able to fight somebody like him. Suddenly, she was just tired. Exhausted from the subterfuge and the starkness of reality.

God, he was beautiful.

Her mind blanked, and her body took over. Just for a few minutes. That was all she wanted.

She leaned forward and placed her hand over his heart. He sucked in a breath, and she hummed as his heated flesh warmed her cold palm. "You're cut like a granite sculpture." Curious, she traced a path up to his clavicle and corded neck before sliding her hand down his arm, marveling at each hard ridge and powerful muscle.

She blinked, enchanted.

"Do you have any idea what you're doing?" His voice dropped to a low, nearly tortured growl.

"No." She caressed his arm to his flank, noting the burn marks across his ribs before moving around him to his broad back. "So much power." Using both hands, she planted them on his scapulae, feeling the energy pulsating in his muscles. "What is it like to hold so much strength?" He felt like a bomb that could detonate on demand.

Which she supposed he was—with full-force Alpha blood.

"Let me show you." He turned and lifted her easily against him, his mouth taking hers.

She instinctively grabbed his shoulders and raised her legs to tighten against his ribs for balance. Her eyelids fluttered shut, and she let him take over.

Completely.

He held her easily aloft in the darkened forest, his mouth destroying hers. Hot and wild, his lips glided over hers, one of his hands clamping on the back of her head to hold her in place as he plundered. Desire swamped her, landing hard in every nerve ending. She moaned into his mouth and returned the kiss, wanting to get closer to the fire.

And Erik Volk was all fire.

This was wrong, and for the first time, she didn't care. Didn't care that she was kissing a male who would be some-body else's mate. Maybe one of her friends'. He couldn't be hers, and it wasn't because she couldn't match him where it counted.

Right now, in his arms, she knew without a doubt that she could be his match. In this, anyway. She wanted to be his match. Her life might end up a lonely one, but she could have this. Have him for a short time. His body shifted against her, and he pressed her closer into him until her nipples zinged against his hard chest.

He moaned this time.

Then he released her mouth, letting her breathe. "We need to stop," he growled.

She blinked and ran her hands up into his hair, scraping her nails along his scalp. "Come inside."

He stilled. Head to toe, the Alpha turned into rock. "What are you saying?"

She found herself lost in his gaze, trying to decipher the color of his eyes. Not navy or turquoise. A combination of both that didn't have a name. "I'm saying, come in for the night," she breathed, her voice hoarse. "Just one night. Not asking or giving more than that." But she wanted this. Craved it. Just one night would be enough. It had to be.

Yet, he didn't move.

She spread her fingers, her palms filling with his heat. Even his ears were masculine. "I'm not seducing you."

"The fuck you aren't."

She pressed against him, her core meeting his groin above his obvious erection. Flashes of electricity sparked from her clit through her entire body. "I don't want to mate you, trick you, or ruin you for any other female. I just want one night." To feel what he could bring to her and maybe what she could give him. Erik Volk, heir to the Silver fortune, loyal to his brother, who he should've wanted to kill.

She knew all about him. But she also felt the loneliness, the desperate and raw desolation deep inside him as an Alpha without a pack. Tonight, she'd ease him. Tomorrow, she'd sacrifice any feelings she developed and find him a mate. Here, with her pack, where he could protect them all...and find himself. "Let's forget the world for a few hours. Just you and me. No lies, no pack politics, no future."

"Do the lies spell danger for the Silver Pack?"

She admired that. A lot. Here she was, offering her body, one he obviously wanted, and he thought about protecting his brother. His people. "No. You have my word. Any lies deal with our weaknesses, not yours." She blinked. "But are you going to hurt us?"

"I'd never hurt you." He tangled his fingers in her hair, shooting lightning straight to her clit.

Her mind blanked, and she forced herself to concentrate. "Not just me. My pack. Promise you won't hurt us." He could. There was no doubt in her mind that he could destroy her entire pack, and he might not need backup, although he certainly had it. "I have to know that."

He leaned in, his mouth above hers, his breath heating her lips. "So long as I don't find a threat to Seth or Mia, I won't let anybody hurt your pack."

As a promise, it was a good one. Better than he knew because there was no way the Copper Pack could be a threat to Seth or Mia again. "All right." She nipped his lower lip.

Then he was moving up her porch stairs and into her cabin, turning into her bedroom when she jerked her head that way, his mouth already back on hers. Somehow, he was even hotter against her. He settled her onto the bed, the muscles playing in his arms before he stood back. Just looking. At her, head to toe, his smile full of intent. "You're beautiful, Luna McElhanney. Don't ever forget it."

She felt beautiful. Right now, anyway.

He leaned over and ran his hands down her thighs, over her knees, and to her ankles, dropping to the thick rug as he caressed the arches of her feet. Every touch sent more flames through her, but as usual, her brain kicked in. She never would've thought he was a foot guy. Oh. He wasn't going to suck her toes, was—?

His lips found her. Right at her core. He sucked her clit into his heated mouth.

She arched off the bed, her hands scrambling for purchase and finding the comforter. The sound of the cotton shredding barely pierced her hazed mind. Her claws were out? "Wait, um —" She fell silent as he went at her.

A low growl, one of pure pleasure, rippled from his chest into his mouth and then deep inside her core. She felt him. Then she had no choice but to close her eyes and just feel. Pleasure shouldn't be this dark. His wide shoulders forced her legs farther apart, and he hummed, licking her and forcing her up way too fast. Faster than should be possible.

She bit her lip and rode his mouth, shrieking when the orgasm consumed her, ripping through her entire body. Gasping, she came down, her ears ringing and her toes curling.

He stood, a powerful male with a handsome smile. "You're a screamer, baby."

Screamer? Not her. No way.

She blinked. Wow. There was a lot to Volk. Head to toe, all muscle, all male. And that ego was well earned. She reached for him, and then he was on her, pressing her into the mattress. "I don't usually scream," she gasped.

He kissed her, going deep before releasing her mouth. "You sure about this?"

"Yes." She scratched her way down his back to his firm butt, leaving her marks. For a short time, he'd wear them. Pleasure filled her at the thought. "Are *you* sure?"

"Yeah." He shifted his hips and paused. "I didn't bring a condom."

She blinked. "They only work half the time with shifters, anyway. Plus, we're safe. I promise."

"Ah. A female who knows her cycle." He nipped her nose. "I bet you have a chart."

She didn't, but it didn't matter. Forgetting reality, she leaned up and kissed him. "You have a sweetness to you."

He prodded at her entrance, slowly filling her. "Don't you think of telling anybody that."

She chuckled, widening her legs and trying to relax. Even so, pain tinged the pleasure from his girth. She winced.

He kissed her again, nipping at her lip and sending more wetness spilling from her. She gasped and tangled her fingers in his short hair, holding on as he took her over again. He kissed along her jawline and to her ear, down to her clavicle, and then her breast. Once entirely inside her, he took his time with each breast, licking and nipping until she was a bundle of nerves beneath him, trying to get him to move. He pulsed, full and heated inside her. His control remained impressive.

She pulled his hair. "Erik, move."

He leaned back, his body holding her in place, his eyes a glittering blue. "I'm in charge here, little Luna."

She clutched him with her internal muscles, truly enjoying the growl that spilled from him. "Prove it."

He pulled out and pushed back in, bringing her so much pleasure it might just be enough for forever. Then he did it again, setting up a hard-pounding rhythm that had the bed squeaking across the floor.

She gasped and held on, delighting in the electricity burning through her body. He powered harder and faster, his gaze never leaving hers, the intensity there so raw it should've given her pause. But it was too late. Way too late. The orgasm swept over her in a rush of heat and wild flames, and then she was climbing again.

Somehow.

The next orgasm had her shuddering beneath him and digging her nails into his back.

Yet he didn't stop. Didn't even slow.

The final orgasm had her yelling his name and holding on for her life.

Turned out she truly was a screamer.

CHAPTER 10

*E*rik leaned over to search Luna's fridge for something to eat. The female really needed to stock up. Old lettuce and several sad-looking oranges filled the bottom shelf, while coffee drinks lined the top.

His phone buzzed from the back pocket of his jeans, and he lifted it out to press to his ear. Earlier this morning, he'd run back to his place to grab clothing and his truck before returning to snuggle with Luna for a couple of hours during the misty and chilly dawn hours, awakening her once again for another round of sex.

"Volk," he answered.

"Hi, it's Yago. We need to have a meeting at headquarters. Can you be here in about fifteen minutes?" Stress lifted the Alpha's consonants.

What the hell was going on now? "Give me more info." Erik shut the fridge door.

"The council has called a meeting, and it's important. We have humans coming into the territory in a few hours for the football game, and we'd like to get things settled before that." Definite stress.

"Are you in danger?" Erik stiffened.

Yago chuckled, but the sound seemed forced. "Of course, not. The council is here, which means my two Enforcers are at my back."

A rustle sounded behind Erik, and he turned to see a tousled Luna emerge from the bedroom. God, she was adorable. Her thick mass of brunette hair curled wildly around her shoulders, and those multi-colored eyes were still sleepy. She'd thrown on a T-shirt, and her feet were bare. Even they were cute and small.

"Yes, I can be there," he answered into the phone, his gaze on the female.

Just then, her phone dinged from the other room.

"I'll see you then," Erik cut off.

Luna turned to enter her bedroom and then came out, yawning wildly. "I'm supposed to be at headquarters."

"Ditto. Why don't you get ready, and I'll drive you?"

She paused, looking at him for a moment, whisker burn across her delicate chin. "Maybe we should arrive separately."

So, she was still going that route, was she? "No, I'll drive."

She shrugged and returned to the bedroom, emerging exactly fifteen minutes later, wearing dark jeans and a pretty white sweater with her hair in a ponytail. The scent of lavender soap lingered on her skin, no doubt banishing his scent so nobody would know they'd spent the night together. He didn't like that. She'd brushed lip gloss across her mouth, but other than that, she was free of makeup and looking young and vulnerable.

He'd never been good at the morning-after talk, but he had to admit to himself that he'd never given it much effort. He used to be kind of a jerk, which was a fact he'd never forget.

So, he moved toward her and gently rubbed his knuckles along her jaw. "I was too rough with you last night."

She rolled her eyes, still looking sleepy. "You were not. Don't be silly. Now." She looked him up and down. "Your jeans and shirt are perfect. Do you know why Yago has called a meeting?" She wrung her hands.

Going on instinct, he pulled her against him and hugged her, holding on tightly. "Everything's going to be okay, Luna." He had no idea how he could make that promise, but he would keep it for her.

She hugged him back quickly and then stepped away, a pretty peach blush highlighting her high cheekbones. "Last night was last night, and it was fantastic. The best ever. But we need to move on to our plans." A hint of sadness wafted around her.

"What makes you think you're not my plan?" What was he doing asking that question? Even though he'd spent his youth as a cad, he never made promises he couldn't keep.

She looked down, once again not meeting his gaze. "You have to trust me on that."

"I'm done with the secrets," he murmured, a sense of possessiveness filling him. Heating him.

She nodded. "I don't blame you, but we need to go."

He'd let her off the hook until after the meeting. She'd need some time if she was as off-balance as he felt right now. But he wasn't bluffing. The secrets were done. They could figure out where to go from here. "All right. Is there any chance we can grab food on the way? I'm starving."

She frowned. "Isn't there a yogurt cup in the back of the fridge?"

He shook his head. "We're definitely finding something to eat."

"The restaurant went out of business a couple of years ago." She rubbed a mark from the fire near her ear. "I forgot to show you that part of the area on the other side of the high school. None of the businesses are open, except for the lone gas station."

"Why the financial problems?"

Her sigh was so heavy it moved her chest.

Oh. Another fucking secret. Irritation ticked through him. While he understood her loyalty to her Alpha, enough was enough. Grasping her hand, he pulled her out of the cabin and down to his truck. "After this meeting, are you comfortable checking on Haney and Izzy Hollowgale? I hate that Izzy was grounded because I let them win that game. I promised I'd take the heat." Not in a million years had Erik expected her asshole father to ground her.

"Yeah, I was planning to head out there today anyway."

Once Luna was safely ensconced in the truck and they were on their way toward headquarters, his phone buzzed again. "Volk," he answered with more than a little exasperation, his phone to his ear.

"Hey, it's Seth. You get those weaknesses yet?"

Erik glanced sideways at the female peering intently at the trees outside. "I'm working on it."

"Good. I spoke with Jackson, and we're working out some sort of agreement where his pack and ours can take over the copper mine and split the profits."

Erik turned onto the main dirt road. "That seems like a violation of the treaty."

Luna looked at him and he shook his head. She frowned but turned her attention to the world outside the truck.

Seth cleared his throat. "The Copper Pack violated the treaty when they sent a kill squad into my territory. You know that as well as I do," he said. "You're there for one reason and it's to find vulnerabilities. They shouldn't have invited you, which shows not only weakness but also stupidity. I don't want to be aligned with a self-destructive pack. It's bad for all of us."

Erik's gut churned. "I can't really discuss this right now, but I promise I'll call you back in an hour or two. I'm currently going to meet with Yago."

"Good," Seth murmured. "You can bring Luna into our pack. Or whatever female you decide you want if you decide to mate."

"Gee, Seth. I appreciate it." Sometimes, his brother needed a good punch to the head. It had been too long since Erik had delivered one. Yeah, he understood Seth's need to protect Mia, especially since she was pregnant, but the guy needed to get his brain back in the game. "Like I said, we'll discuss it later."

"I'm drawing up battle plans. Jackson wants to take the lead, but I won't let him. My pack wants revenge for the insult and deserves to draw blood."

The longer Erik gave Seth to think about the kill squad, the worse things would become for the Copper Pack. At this point, Erik might actually have to step up as Alpha just to keep the Coppers alive and functioning. "Don't you have a pregnant mate to worry about?"

"That's exactly what I'm doing," Seth growled.

Erik rolled his shoulders back. "I swear to all that's holy, if I ever knock up my mate, I won't be such a complete jackass. You need to start thinking and stop feeling your decisions."

"Are you countering an order?" Seth's voice turned all Alpha.

Erik's Alpha rose fast and hard inside him, and he took a moment to keep his voice calm. "I'm discussing this as your brother and the one person in the world who isn't afraid to tell you to pull your head out of your ass. Besides Mia, that is."

Tension spiraled across the line so quickly it was a shock the thing didn't just burn up. "If I give the order, and right now I'm fairly sure I will, you'll act as my Enforcer. Period."

Erik had neither the time nor the patience to deal with this right now. "Tell Jackson to cool his jets. For now, just hold tight. Later." He clicked off.

Jackson Tryne was the Granite Pack's Alpha and also Seth's distant cousin. They'd been at odds for years until Seth fully took his position as Alpha of the Silver Pack. That they were planning to unite against the Coppers would be a disaster.

"What was that about?" Luna asked.

"Family matters," he replied tersely.

She clasped her hands in her lap. "Like I said, I'm not the only one with secrets."

He couldn't disagree.

"I wasn't trying to eavesdrop, but it sounds like your brother wants to attack my pack. Can you stop him?"

Erik looked down at the pretty brunette. "Probably. Definitely, if I mate somebody from the pack." It was the first time he'd truly considered the possibility. Sure, they could pull many of the members into the Silver Pack, but merging two full packs with some Alpha blood never went well.

Luna brightened. "Then you should meet with Francine today."

Insulting. He snorted. "You really want to get rid of me."

"I don't," she said quietly. "But the pack comes first. You know that."

He had to figure out where this insecurity came from because she'd been anything but that the night before. The female had been all passion and wildness with no inhibitions.

Fuck, he hated secrets.

They reached headquarters, and he stretched out onto the now-muddy ground before stalking around to open her door and lift her out of his truck. The burned remains of the gazebos and the tree had been hauled to the side, but the smell of smoldering wood still filled the air.

She looked over at the mess. "Honestly, I had that concoction just right." Her sigh was heavy and cute.

"Come on," he said. "Let's go see what Yago wants."

She preceded him across the ground and up into the lodge, where he followed, and then she turned right to enter the sprawling conference room. Yago sat at the head of the table with Butch Hollowgale, Allen Bushbalm, and Vernon Bushbalm next to him.

Luna smiled. "Vernon. What are you doing here? Are you taking over for one of the former council members?"

His brother snorted. "No, he's just a placeholder for today. We'll find somebody who can handle it."

"Actually, an expert in accounting would be a perfect member to serve on the council. Our investments need serious work." Vernon turned red to the tips of his ears. "It's good to see you, Luna. Sorry about last night."

"Oh, that was my fault. I screwed up the concoction," she said.

Vernon shook his head and winked. "There's no way you made a mistake. Francine and I talked about it, and we're sure something else went wrong. Sometimes, the weather can mess with things."

His brother shoved him in the arm and pushed him over. "Stop flirting with my female."

Luna's head jerked so hard it was a shock she didn't pull a neck muscle. "I am so far from being your female it's not even funny."

Erik let his teeth show. Her taste still filled his head, and the wolf at his core tried to jump its chains and leap for Bushbalm. The male had no idea how close he was to getting decapitated.

Yago sighed. "Erik, Luna, please have a seat. We need to discuss the future of the pack."

Erik pulled a chair out for Luna at the opposite end of the table from Yago. She faltered and tried to slide to the side, but he gently placed her in it. Then he sat next to her. Close.

"You should be in this chair," she muttered.

"I like you there," he said. He could intercept anybody before they got to her because he could kick her chair out and push her to the wall if necessary. Not that he expected an attack, but his job was to always look for one. "So." He turned to face Yago. "I don't really want to deal with the council. I'm fine dealing Alpha to Alpha."

Hollowgale scoffed. "That's too bad because we manage things by council here. We're about to take a vote on who will be the next Alpha, and I'll give you a hint. It isn't going to be you."

Erik studied the male. "We never did have our little meeting out in the forest. Maybe we should do that now." He had no intention of adhering to a vote by any council. That's not how things were done. Could he actually kill this guy? It might be the best thing for the pack, but he didn't want to start any relationship he might've just created with Luna with him killing somebody the next day.

"That's unnecessary," Yago said. "Everyone just needs to take a breath."

Luna sighed. "Listen. We invited Mr. Volk into the territory for a reason. I think we—"

A loud explosion rocked the entire territory.

CHAPTER 11

*L*una jolted and then turned toward Yago. "I didn't blow anything else up, I swear."

Another explosion knocked the glass pitcher off the table. Erik instantly jumped up and lunged through the door, running outside with the rest of the members behind him. He halted on the deck. "Smoke that way. Isn't that the school?" Then he lifted his nose into the wild breeze. "You smell that?"

Yago nodded, his chin hardening. "Yeah."

"Do you recognize their scent?" Erik asked.

Yago frowned. "Yeah. It's the Ravencall Pack. Many of them."

Erik looked over his shoulder at Luna. "Do you have any sort of hospital or doctor's office set up?"

Gulping, she shook her head.

He shrugged out of his shirt. "All right. Use that old, abandoned restaurant you mentioned and create a triage center. Find assistance because we're under attack."

Without waiting for her answer, he leaped into the air, shredding his remaining clothes as he flew, landing hard on all four paws in full wolf form. Then he was off and running. Yago,

Allen, and Butch followed suit, catching up to him as they ran full bore toward the smoke rising into the sky.

Vernon grasped Luna's arm. "Come on. I'll help you with the hospital."

She rapidly thought through their numbers. "How many members are in the Ravencall Pack?"

Vernon scratched his head. "I think they have maybe about three hundred these days. My guess would be one hundred and fifty fighters."

She calculated the odds quickly. "Okay, so if they have one-fifty possible fighters, they would've sent maybe...what? Seventy-five, tops? No way any pack would leave themselves unprotected, especially a wild, feral outsider pack like the Ravencalls."

"That sounds about right."

She shook her head, panic seizing her lungs. "Vernon, we have to fight. Let's worry about the hospital after."

His hand shook when he wiped off his chin. "You're right, especially if they're at the school. I'll tell you what, you go set up the hospital, and I'll fight. Stay safe, Luna." With that, he turned and stumbled down the stairs before dropping to all fours and shifting into a light brown wolf.

She wanted to create a trauma center more than anything, but at the moment, they needed bodies. So, she sprang into the air and tried to shift like Erik had. Instead, she landed on her hands and knees before her body completed the action. Leaving her clothes behind, she ran behind Vernon. She wasn't a physical fighter, but she didn't have a choice if they were outnumbered.

Reaching the school, she watched all the football players leap out of their uniforms and shift into wolf form as a fight ensued near the nearest goalpost. The day was misty and cold, and it was easy to tell the Ravencall Pack from hers. Not only did she know everybody, the Ravencall Pack members were mainly a lighter gray and bigger than many of her friends.

She saw Zelda leap onto the back of a Ravencall wolf and sink her teeth into its neck, just as Erik took on three by himself. Luna jumped into the melee and tried to block a couple of the smaller football players, keeping them from danger.

They were too young to be fighting grown soldiers, but they vaulted in without a thought. Her pack was hugely outnumbered, so she went for a smaller female with claws and teeth.

Smoke spiraled from the part of the schoolhouse that was still on fire, clouding the misty day with soot and smoke. They had bombed the schoolhouse? She couldn't believe it. There was no doubt the Ravencall Pack was the enemy they'd been fearing.

Three wolves went for Erik, and he shockingly ripped one's head off with just a swipe of his claws. Luna knocked out the wolf right after the bitch slashed her claws down Luna's face, and then she bounded over to cover Yago as best she could. He was fighting alone. Where were his Enforcers?

Her pack was outnumbered, at least one hundred fighters to fifty right now, so the Ravencalls had sent more than she would've thought prudent.

Then, enemy wolves threw several of the teenage Copper wolves all the way across the field and turned to take on more of the kids. Yipping, she tried to dive between them. A full-grown male wolf came at her. Suddenly, Erik vaulted out of nowhere, knocking the attacker to the side and digging his claws into the wolf's chest before ripping down.

Footsteps sounded, and all the Copper wolves from the mine rocketed into the fray. Finally. Thank goodness.

Blood filled the air, as well as cries of pain and growls of anger. Erik was a wolf possessed, showing no mercy in taking down all the attacking wolves within his reach.

Several football players lay unmoving on the field, and Luna started to help them as another wolf tackled her from behind.

Vernon was instantly there, clawing and fighting. Between the two of them, they dispatched the younger male attacker to hell.

Her face hurt, and her flanks ached from claw and bite marks as she turned to assist the wounded. Several additional older pack members lay unmoving on the other side of the field, and she tried to get to them.

Yago stumbled and fell, and two enemy wolves jumped on him. Luna and Vernon instantly ran that way, smashing head-first into the enemies and knocking them off their Alpha. He struggled to his feet and swiped out with a massive paw, stabbing through the face of one of the wolves.

Pain flared along Luna's hip, and she yelped, twirling and trying to dislodge the wolf biting her. A young wolf instantly pummeled her attacker, and she turned as Oakley viciously bit the wolf's neck until he stopped moving.

Oakley was too young to be fighting.

She turned to see Erik dispatching two more members of the attacking force. With the increased numbers from the mine, the Copper Pack slowly pushed back the enemy until those still able to move ran away and out of the territory.

Erik started to follow and then stopped, turning around. He shifted into his human form, bleeding and gasping, his eyes furious. "We need to put out the fire in the schoolhouse," he said, his voice a low growl as he took in the scene of downed wolves. "Pile our dead over to the side, and let's get everyone we can to the hospital to see what we can do. I want to know how many we lost."

Despair clouded Luna's mind as she shifted into human form, looking at the downed bodies. Who had they lost?

* * *

WITH ONE BANDAGE on her hip and another over the claw marks on her face, Luna hustled around the makeshift hospital that had once been a restaurant. They utilized the worn tables as gurneys, and she tried to categorize the most crucial injuries by using different areas in the diner.

Her medicine cache wasn't impressive, but she'd done her best over the recent years to stockpile different herbs and minerals she knew could help. She treated several internal wounds, having at least four patients return from their human forms to wolf, where it was easier to heal.

Erik dropped in several times to check on her status before returning to the battlefield and ensuring a second wave wasn't coming. For the moment, everybody worked together. There wasn't anything she could do about the people they'd lost in the battle, but she was determined to ensure that nobody else died.

She finished with two heart wounds and moved to where Oakley Rockwood lay on a table, holding a football jersey to his neck.

"You were very brave out there today, Oakley. In fact, you might've saved my life. Thank you." She gently pried his hand away. "You need stitches, but you'll be okay." She reached for a suture kit and quickly went to work.

The kid remained silent, looking up at the ceiling. Gashes and wounds showed down the side of his body, and after she took care of his neck, she spread salve on several areas. She couldn't do anything to repair the multitude of bruises on his battered flesh, though. He'd fought hard the entire time.

At the moment, she was more concerned about his heart than his body. "Oakley?"

He still didn't look at her.

She sighed and placed a hand on his shoulder. "I know we lost Jarod Randallberry." Her voice choked on the young kid's name. He'd been a bright boy with shining green eyes and a hilarious way of telling jokes. Both of his parents had been lost five years ago, and he'd lived with his aunt, who was still unconscious on another table across the restaurant.

"He shouldn't have been out there," Oakley said tersely. "He was only fifteen years old. What was he doing in battle?"

"Same thing you were," she said gently. "He was protecting his pack. I'm so sorry."

Oakley just stared at the ceiling. "I don't want to talk about it. Are my mom and sisters okay?"

"They are. They're at the lodge, where we put everyone who's uninjured. At least, for now. Erik is shoring up the grounds."

"Why?" Oakley asked. "It's not like we can prevent another attack. We don't have the numbers. Yago should have taken care of this a long time ago."

Luna couldn't fault him, and she also couldn't help him. "Stay here and let the salve take effect. I'll check on you in a few moments." She pulled a blanket up closer to his chin. "You might be going into shock, and I need you to stay warm."

Her heart aching, she turned to Vernon, who was working on the patient next to her. "Would you call his mom? I think she needs to be here."

"Sure." Vernon secured a bandage over an elderly male's jawline. "I'll do that right now."

"Thank you, Vernon," she said. "You've been a great help."

He shook his head, his eyes sad. "I can't believe this. We weren't even remotely ready. If Volk hadn't been here..." His voice trailed off.

Yeah. If Erik hadn't been there, they'd all be dead. She'd never seen anybody fight like that. He was brutal and merciless and had somehow kept them from being taken over. Yago had done his best, and even Butch and Allen had fought wildly, but it had definitely been Erik who had scared the enemy enough that they retreated.

She wanted to throw up, but she had work to do. She continued through the restaurant until she noted Erik in the doorway. Blood still flowed from a wound in his neck, and claw marks scored his torso, but he had drawn on jeans and thick boots. Blood already seeped through the material over one thigh and his knee.

"You probably need stitches." She moved toward him.

"I'm fine. Just wait until you've helped everybody else. What's the count?"

She sighed, her head down. This hurt so much. "We lost four elderly, three males and a female, and one teenager."

It was shocking that they hadn't lost more pack members. Even so, each death hurt her personally.

"How old?"

"Fifteen." Jarod should be playing football and planning fun with his friends, not dead on a football field from a pack that never should've had the guts to attack them.

Erik's growl came from deep within his chest. "How old for the older people?"

"They were all over three hundred. Too old to fight," she said. "Way too old to fight."

Fury and a wounded desolation flickered through his eyes. "I need to make sure the fire's out in the schoolhouse. I can't believe they attacked with a bomb first." He shook his head. "Fucking weak."

Anger rode his tone, and she realized she truly didn't know him. Oh, she knew he could fight, but she hadn't imagined the brutality living inside him. He'd make a good Alpha and a horrific enemy. God, she hoped he wasn't their enemy. He'd defended them today, but was that out of instinct? If Seth ordered Erik to destroy the Copper Pack, he probably wouldn't even need help. Even so, he had saved them all today.

"Let me at least patch you up," she said.

He leaned down and looked at her, every line in his body hard and angry. "Later. Where's Yago?"

She couldn't breathe. Right now, her body felt sensitized— probably because he'd claimed every inch the night before. She cleared her throat. "I gave him thirty stitches, and he went to survey the damage. He's with Butch and Allen. I don't know where they are."

"All right. When this is all over, we are meeting again in the conference room. I want the full truth."

With that, Erik gave her a hard look, turned on his heel, and stomped out the door.

CHAPTER 12

*E*rik finished rolling up the ancient fire hose as several football players somberly stacked burned wood and scalded copper over to the side of the demolished wing of the schoolhouse. They all wore thick gloves, and nobody seemed to be talking much. He knew what it felt like to lose a friend and didn't know how to help.

A battered Jeep pulled up alongside the still-standing part of the school, and Francine Goodhouse stretched out, her hands full of platters. Two of the boys ran over and helped her carry them to a still-standing but definitely damaged picnic table, where the kids had no doubt eaten lunch during school.

"I brought sandwiches and some water," she called out, returning to her Jeep for another pile of goodies.

The kids descended on the food, maybe not eagerly, but with well-earned hunger. They'd been fighting or working all day.

She walked over to Erik and handed him a paper bag. "I brought you a clean shirt and some bandages." In the still-smoky day, she was lovely with her blond hair in a ponytail and her intelligent eyes looking sad. "Thank you for what you did today."

"It was no problem." He pulled out a double-extra-large gray shirt and tugged it over his head. "Thank you. I don't need a bandage."

She looked pointedly at the blood on his thigh, obvious through his jeans. "I think you need more than one bandage."

"I'll get it taken care of later." Many of his wounds had already healed, but he might need help with the slash in his leg.

She looked over to where the kids were eating. "I can't believe we lost Jarod. He was such a sweet boy."

The mere mention of the kid's name slammed hard into Erik's chest. Everything had happened so quickly, he hadn't had time to tell the kids to vacate the area, yet he could admit that the pack had needed them. "Francine, what's going on here? We're missing half the pack."

She looked down at her feet. "I think that's something you should discuss with our Alpha."

Oh, it was definitely something he was going to discuss. "Speaking of whom, where the hell is he?"

Francine looked around. "I don't know. I haven't seen Yago or his Enforcers."

"They should be here helping put out the fire."

She chewed on her lip. "Maybe they're securing the perimeter the best they can. There's probably another attack coming, right?"

"More than likely," Erik muttered. "We're definitely weakened, and while we hurt them, we didn't kill enough of them. I need to know more about the Ravencall Pack."

Francine fluttered her hand in the air. "I'm not the person to talk to about defense. You need to speak with Yago or Zelda. She should be an Enforcer, but Yago didn't think she'd be up to the job."

"She's an excellent fighter," Erik countered. "I think she'd make an excellent Enforcer."

"Me, too." Francine ducked her head, and a light pink filtered across her cheekbones. "Though I'm not sure she's the right mate for you. Don't you want somebody...I don't know, calming? A peaceful oasis to get away from the pressures of, you know, all this fighting?" She looked toward the still-smoldering wood.

Luna's face instantly flashed into his mind. "I don't know that calm is my thing."

Francine twirled her hair with one finger, creating a curl. "I'm just saying think about it. I have no problem with an arranged mating because, from what I can tell throughout history, those last. We have shared common interests, and we definitely need a new Alpha. I would do an excellent job as your mate. I'm very organized."

Her grin was cute. She was sweet, and Erik liked her, but he didn't feel the need to reach for her and pin her down like he did with Luna.

"I think we can be friends," he said, trying to soften the rejection with a smile.

She lifted a shoulder, looking like a young surfer from California. "That's not a no, so do give it some thought, though I understand if you want a powerful fighter like Zelda."

He figured he could be friends with Zelda as well. Plus, it wasn't like he was taking this Alpha gig. His alliance had to be to the Silver Pack, though what then? Who would protect all these young wolves? He watched as the football team returned to work, just as two carloads holding more teenagers—including the volleyball girls—showed up to pitch in.

Francine followed his gaze. "They've been helping at the hospital and trying to secure the southern part of our territory. I don't know how, but they scattered in wolf form to make sure no other enemies were close. Besides the Ravencall Pack, I've heard that the Ghostwind Pack is also gunning for us."

Erik shook his head. Just great. Both packs were notoriously dangerous and had been trying to encroach upon the mining areas for years. They were one of the reasons the four mining Stope packs had created their coalition for protection.

"Why haven't any of you reached out to the other packs in our coalition?" He tried to keep command out of his voice, wanting her to continue talking.

"Again, that's out of my purview," Francine said quietly. "I'm not in the know when it comes to that kind of thing, though I could be. I'd be a great sounding board." She looked him up and down. "And I find you quite handsome."

He grinned. "That's very sweet of you. I find you beautiful, as well."

"I didn't say beautiful," she retorted.

The more he got to know the people from this pack, the more he liked them. All of them.

Nikki approached and handed him a bottle of water from the picnic table. The young volleyball player had lost the hop in her step. "Have you seen Oakley?" Her eyes filled with tears.

"Yeah, he's recovering at the restaurant hospital," Erik said. "I don't think he's doing so great."

She looked down.

"Are you friends?"

She shrugged. "Yeah. We've been on a couple of dates, and we talk a lot."

"Why don't you go see him?" Erik gently prodded. "He could probably really use a friend."

Her eyes lit. "Are you sure?"

"Yeah. Take my truck." He reached into his back pocket and tossed her the keys.

She looked at the ring in her hand, up at him, and then back at the keys. "You're letting me drive your truck?"

Erik eyed Francine, who just smiled. "Do you have a disastrous driving record I need to know about?"

Nikki shifted her feet. "No, it's just, I mean, it's your truck."

"Ah, well, I appreciate that you see the importance of that," he said. "But yeah, you can drive my truck to go see Oakley. Okay? Stay out of the woods."

"All right." She gave one hop and ran toward his truck as if afraid he'd change his mind.

He shook his head. Had he ever been that young? He didn't think so.

Francine sighed. "So, I guess it's Zelda, is it?"

"I didn't say that," Erik said, wondering again how Luna was doing.

Francine blinked, and then her jaw dropped. "Oh, Erik, you're not still considering Luna, are you?"

Of course, he was. He'd spent half the night memorizing the female's body. "I don't mind that she's a bit eccentric and blows things up once in a while."

"A lot." Francine leaned forward. "You don't understand. She blows things up a lot, but that's not why."

"Why, then?" Erik asked.

Francine looked away, obviously flustered. "You need to talk to somebody else about that, but Luna, she's not the right choice." She patted his arm. "Please, just keep me in mind. All right? I really would like to strengthen our pack, and I think we'd make a good alliance."

With that, she sauntered away in dark jeans and a light pink sweater to fuss over the kids and make sure they were all eating enough of the sandwiches.

Erik looked up at the cloudy sky and then back down at the partly cleaned-up area. He was so finished with these secrets.

* * *

AFTER DARKNESS FELL, just as Luna finished organizing the remaining bandages, Francine walked into the makeshift restaurant-turned-trauma center.

"How are things going?" her old friend asked.

"I think all right. I had to stitch more people up than I would've expected, and I didn't lose anybody here in the hospital." Thank goodness. She hurt so badly from the deaths on the battlefield that the thought of someone dying under her care made her hands shake.

"Good." Francine reached for a mop and automatically started cleaning the floor.

They only had five patients left on the makeshift beds, all sleeping peacefully. Luna looked over at the darkened area, making sure everyone was still breathing.

"Why don't you go get some rest? I'll cover for the night. I don't have anything else to do," Francine said.

"You don't have to do that." Luna was so tired her eyes ached.

Francine looked up from her mop. "You worked really hard today, Luna, and you're half-asleep on your feet. Let me help. Okay?"

Luna nodded, guilt spiraling through her at her jealousy toward the female earlier.

"I took the kids food and Erik a clean shirt. I also offered him, well, me." Francine grinned, and a dimple winked in her right cheek.

Luna snorted, feeling both despair and humor. "That was quite the offer. Did he take you up on it?"

"Not really," Francine said, returning to her work.

"Maybe he wants a good fighter like Zelda," Luna murmured.

"Who wouldn't? It's weird to be competing with my best friend," Francine mused. "Although, if you ask me, that alpha male only has eyes for you."

Butterflies winged through Luna's stomach. "That's unfortunate because I'm not the right choice, and we both know it."

Francine rubbed her chin. "We don't really know much right

now, do we?" She shook her head. "I don't know, Luna. We've been friends our entire lives. What do you feel for the guy?"

"Too much," Luna muttered. "I feel too much." With that, she grabbed her handbag off the counter that had once served toast and bagels and now held bandages and disinfectant. "I might go take a nap, but I'll try to be back before dawn so you get a break."

Francine waved her off. "Don't be silly. Take the whole night. Get some sleep. We can regroup later. I'm sure we'll have the funeral ceremonies tomorrow night."

The mere idea made Luna want to throw up. "All right. Thanks, Francine. I owe you."

"Nope, we're even, girlfriend. We all worked hard today. We do need to get Erik Volk into the fold no matter what it takes, though. You understand that, right?" For the first time, Francine's gaze held an intensity that matched her tone.

"I understand," Luna said, wearily opening the door and walking out into the too-chilly night.

November had roared in, with December coming with definite snow. She caught her breath and walked along the hard sidewalk to reach her older Volkswagen Bug. While she tried to follow many human laws, she still hadn't found time to obtain a driver's license. Most shifters had fake ones, anyway. She might think about getting one. In addition, maybe she should put her snow tires on earlier this year.

"Hey, there, I've been looking for you." Allen Bushbalm pushed away from the building, his customary cigar in his mouth and his swagger more evident than ever. He wore pressed jeans and a black shirt. No burn marks, wounds, or soot showed on him. He'd obviously showered.

"I take it they're finished cleaning up the mess?" she asked, setting her stance.

"I have absolutely no idea what they've been doing. I've been scanning the perimeter of the property, looking for any vulnerabilities and threats. No threats, plenty of vulnerabilities."

She relaxed, her body so tired it just couldn't stay alert any longer. "That sounds about right. We definitely need an Alpha in place."

"That would be me," Allen said. "Combined with you, we could lead this pack."

She looked way up at his face. He was a good decade older than her, and they'd never been friends. They didn't really even know each other, and what she did know, she didn't like. "You fought well today," she said. Although nowhere near as brutally as Erik had. The Ravencall Pack would have overtaken her people if Erik hadn't been there.

"You fought well, too," Allen said. "I was surprised that you physically engaged the enemy. You don't really know what you're doing."

"I'm well aware of that fact," she said. "But there wasn't a choice."

She'd been pretty lucky that both Oakley and Erik had come to her defense, but she had caused some damage to the enemy, and she took comfort from that. If only she could have somehow been in the right place to protect Jarod. "Have you talked to Jarod's family?" she asked.

"No, that's not my job," Allen muttered.

She shook her head and then winced as pain echoed through her temples. Man, she needed rest. "If you want to be an Alpha, you have to take care of everybody." She had no doubt Yago had visited the family already.

Allen lifted his shoulder and took a couple of steps toward her. "Like I said, that's not my job. My mate can handle that kind of crap. My job will be to run the mine and protect the pack."

"Oh, and make lots of money from the copper, right?" she asked, irritation heating her blood.

"Of course." He warmed to the subject, apparently missing her tone. "That's one of the benefits of being the Alpha. Don't you want that? I can give you a big house on the lake and everything you could possibly want."

"I can get that myself," she murmured.

She'd never understood why anybody would mate or marry for money. If money was the goal, there were plenty of ways to make it without tying oneself to another person, especially somebody like Allen.

It was time to educate him. "I don't know what you're looking for from me, but you're not going to get it," she said honestly. "We're not going to mate, and if today's fight was any indication, you're not going to be the Alpha of this pack."

He lacked an Alpha lineage, but he had definite ambitions. It was possible, but his only true path lay with mating her, and it wasn't going to happen.

"I'm not so sure you have a choice in that." He took an additional step closer to her, leaving less than a foot between them.

Her legs trembled, and it was from alertness as much as exhaustion. "You seem to have a problem with the English language, so let me spell it out very clearly." She faced him directly. "No." Then she moved toward her car.

He grabbed her arm and threw her against the vehicle. Her shoulders hit, and pain slammed down her entire back. She dropped her bag.

"I'm not messing around, and I'm tired of this." He moved in, and this time, she reacted quicker than she had last time, remembering Zelda's example.

She kicked up as fast and hard as she could, nailing him right in the groin.

Shock filled his eyes, and he stumbled back, leaning over. "What the—?" He gasped several times and then coughed, his body shuddering.

A car screeched to a stop next to Luna's Bug, and Vernon

Bushbalm jumped out. "What's going on here? Allen, are you okay?" he asked his brother.

Allen looked up, his body still hunched over, his eyes wide, and his face stark pale. He tried to say something and then coughed again.

"He got handsy, and I kicked him in the nuts," Luna said.

Vernon's eyes widened. "Allen, leave her alone." He pushed past his brother and opened the car door. "Luna, get inside."

Luna grabbed her bag off the sidewalk and jumped into her vehicle. "Thanks, Vernon."

"You bet." He pushed his brother and Allen kind of staggered to the side. Vernon looked inside the restaurant. "Is Francine covering the patients for tonight?"

"Yeah." Luna looked at the gleam in his eyes, his light smile, and then at her friend inside the makeshift hospital. "She could probably use some company."

Vernon smiled. "Maybe I'll stay." He ignored his brother. "On behalf of our family, I'm sorry my brother's an asshole. I'll talk to him when he can breathe again."

Luna grinned. "Thanks, Vernon. I owe you."

With that, she shut her door and ignited the car, noting Vernon walking right past his brother and into the restaurant, where Francine looked up and smiled. Hmm, now that was interesting.

CHAPTER 13

*E*rik's body felt like he'd reached his thousandth year on the planet as he left Jarod Randallberry's home. The parents and siblings were devastated, but he'd paid his respects, feeling their pain. Yago had spent most of the day with them, which was a good thing, except the pack wasn't protected from an attack right now.

The old wolf was in way over his head and had been avoiding Erik all day.

Jarod's family lived in an older part of the territory in a cabin away from either subdivision, and he followed their directions to Oakley Rockwood's cabin, a two-story log structure against a rock cliff with a nice wraparound porch.

Mrs. Rockwood sat on the front porch in a hard-looking chair, a cup of tea in her hand.

He approached quietly, making sure the moonlight highlighted him so he didn't scare her. She watched him draw near with no expression on her smooth face, and her body language remained relaxed. Either she was exhausted or didn't see him as a threat. Either way, he kept his voice gentle. "Mrs. Rockwood?"

he asked. Young, maybe in her early thirties, she looked like her son, with thick, brown hair and similar copper-colored eyes.

"Patty," she said softly. "Call me Patty."

"Thank you." He tucked his thumbs into his pockets and tried to appear harmless, but even he knew he looked like a killer under the moon. It was in every line of his body, and there wasn't much he could do about it. "I just wanted to check on Oakley. I didn't think he was doing that well today after being stitched up."

Patty nodded. "Yeah, I don't think he's doing that well, either." Her voice cracked at the end.

Erik didn't like the seclusion of this place, especially since the female lived alone with mainly young children. Somebody needed to create a much better security force for the entire pack. "Is he asleep?"

"No." The young mother nervously brushed at her hair. "I don't know where he is. He took off a while ago and went running, which I understand."

Erik sighed and looked down at his boots. Both he and Seth had spent their childhoods barreling through the mountains to deal with stress and pain. He could relate. Even right now, at this moment, he wished he could turn and run for days in any direction. Just run. "Do you have any idea where he might be right now?"

The female studied Erik for several long moments. "That depends. Are you here to destroy our pack or save it?"

Heat filtered through his torso. It was a fair question. Apparently, the Copper Pack wasn't as open to him taking over as he'd been led to believe—or at least they weren't as naive. While their Alpha had welcomed him with open arms, that might speak of desperation, and the pack members understood the danger he could represent. "I'm not here to hurt you," he said honestly. "I have no idea how to save you, though."

"Sure, you do," she said softly, her gaze wise.

Maybe he did. Yet even if he became their Alpha, that wouldn't change the dynamics here. The numbers were way off. He didn't know why, and he didn't know how, but he knew the pack was weak. Just finding an Alpha wouldn't save them. Yet he'd always been a problem solver and was getting attached to the pack. The kids had already dug into his heart, and Luna had her fingers on his soul. "I'm thinking about it, is all I can tell you, but I can promise I don't want to hurt anybody here."

He wouldn't mind finishing off the Ravencall Pack, however. The need to provide protection and cover sprang from deep inside him.

She nodded. "All right. Mr. Volk."

"Erik," he corrected her. "Just Erik."

A small smile almost lifted her upper lip. "All right, just Erik."

The door opened, and a little girl stumbled out. She looked to be around six with a wild mane of brown hair and sleepy brown eyes. Her tiny nightgown was pink, and her socks were a faded yellow. She moved to her mama, watching Erik. "You the new Alpha?"

Even the toddlers knew about him. "Not sure. I'm Erik."

Patty pulled the little girl up onto her lap and kissed her head. "You're supposed to be sleeping. This is Cami."

"Hi." Erik tried to smile in a nonthreatening way.

The girl just looked at him. "Where's Oakley? I can't sleep without Oakley here."

No wonder that kid didn't want to go to college. It appeared he handled an incredible amount of responsibility at his young age. If Erik took over, he'd make sure this little family stayed safe.

"Oakley is running," her mother said softly.

"Again?" Cami rolled her eyes. "You hurt your leg." She pointed at Erik's thigh, which still ached.

Erik looked down at the now-dry blood showing through

his faded jeans. "I'm okay. Guess I should put on some clean clothes." Actually, he might still need stitches.

Cami blinked. "Wanna bandage? They gots butterflies on them."

Something inside him softened. Fast. "Thank you, but I'm fine. Where's Oakley, Patty?"

Patty cuddled her daughter close. "When Oakley needs to think, he runs north. There's a nice crag in the river. He looks over a small cliff and watches it. That's my best guess. I'd go looking for him myself, but the other girls are all asleep, and I just don't want to leave them unattended right now."

"I understand. I'll bring him back." He nodded. "Night, Cami. Get some sleep, okay? I promise I'll bring Oakley home soon."

The little girl grinned, effectively stealing his heart.

Erik turned and walked north, loping into a jog. He could turn into a wolf and run faster, but he felt like staying human at the moment. So, he scented the air, caught a whiff, and turned. It took him about twenty minutes in a full-out run to reach the crag in the river, where he found the kid sitting on a log, staring down.

He approached slowly, surprised that Oakley was still dressed. So, he'd run out here in human form, as well. Erik understood that. He felt things stronger in wolf form, and if Oakley was in pain, he would want to reduce that as much as possible.

"Why are you here?" Oakley asked without turning around.

Erik crossed the area and sat on the old, weathered log, peering down at the rushing water. The snowpack had been heavy the year before, so plenty of water flowed. "I was looking for you."

"Why?"

"I figured you might need a friend."

Oakley looked sideways at him and then back at the water. "Are you my friend now?"

Erik glanced at the nearly full moon. "Why not?"

"Oh, I don't know. Maybe because you're from a different pack." Bitterness and anger tinged the boy's words, but a shit-load of pain echoed underneath.

"Yeah, I'm your friend. You can be friends with people from different packs."

Oakley shrugged, looking young in the moonlight.

"I'm really sorry about your friend," Erik said.

Oakley shook his head. "I should have protected him. He was younger and smaller, and I just didn't get to him in time."

"No, I should have protected him," Erik corrected.

"Why? You're not our Alpha."

That was true. Maybe Yago should have protected the kid. "I don't know. I'm not going to ask you what's going on with your pack because I have no doubt you all took a vow not to tell me, but I promise you, before the next moon rises, I will know everything," Erik said. "Good or bad, I will have all the facts in front of me, and I'm here to help you somehow."

Oakley snorted. "How are you going to help? I mean, I saw you fight, and you're good, but you're one guy. Unless you can turn out fifty Alpha kids that somehow grow into adulthood in three seconds, I don't see how you're going to save anybody."

The kid called it like he saw it, and Erik liked that a lot. "I don't suppose you want to tell me everything I need to know."

"I don't suppose I do." Oakley kicked out his legs.

Erik sensed pain in the air. Physical pain. "How are you?"

"Fine."

Well, good enough. The kid was walking and talking, so any injuries weren't life-threatening, and Luna wouldn't have let him out of the makeshift hospital if he'd still been wounded.

"Your mom is worried about you."

Oakley ducked his head. "I know. I don't want to worry her. I just needed time to think, you know?"

"God, do I know." Erik watched the water rush by below them. "This is a pretty place."

"Yeah. I come here to think. My dad and I used to come here. When he died, I don't know... I guess it's my place now."

"How did he die?"

Oakley shook his head.

Ah. There was obviously a big story there, but Erik wouldn't push. Not this kid, anyway. "All right. Let's talk about something else. Tell me about your friend, Jarod."

"I don't want to."

"All right. Third topic. What would you think if I did take over as Alpha?" The question emerged without Erik stopping to think about it. These people needed him. How could he turn away? What about Seth? Could Erik really change packs? If he did, he'd have to go all-in. "Oakley? I'm just asking for your opinion. That's all."

Oakley focused on him again, but he didn't turn away this time. "Are you really considering becoming our Alpha?"

Erik thought through the last couple of days. "It'll come with a ton of problems, but yeah, I'm considering it." He shocked himself with the statement because he meant it.

Oakley sighed. "I figured you came here to look for weaknesses."

"I did," Erik retorted. "But I found so many, now I might have to help."

An unwilling smile lifted the kid's lips. "That sucks, dude."

"Yeah, it kind of does." Erik moved closer to provide the kid warmth. It was a cold night. "So, what do you think?"

"Are you really asking my opinion? Like you honestly want to know what I think?"

Erik cocked his head. "I actually do. I think you're a smart kid. I think you have a finger on the pulse of this pack and want what's best for it. Plus, you have a mom and sisters to protect. Honestly, I'm asking you, what do you think?"

The kid chewed on his lip. "I think we're better off with you as our Alpha than you as an enemy."

That was a fair statement.

"And if you truly become the Alpha, then we're automatically aligned with the Silver Pack because you and your half-brother would never hurt each other, right?"

That was the definite truth. Erik nodded.

"I don't know where that leaves us with the other two packs," Oakley said thoughtfully. "Rumor has it the Granite Pack, even though they're related to your brother, wanted him or you dead."

"That's true," Erik agreed.

"And then there's the Slate Pack. I mean, weren't you engaged to the heiress?"

Erik and Emily had declared an alignment so Seth could take over the Silver Pack, but they were just friends, and both changed their minds. "Kind of," Erik said.

"Well, then they might be pissed about that," Oakley said. "So, you could bring as many problems as you solve."

Erik scrubbed a rough hand through his hair. "You're not wrong."

Oakley looked back at the water and remained silent for several moments. "All right. Considering the entire clusterfuck of a situation we have going on, then yeah. I would like for you to take over as our Alpha."

Something eased inside Erik. He didn't know what to do quite yet, but he trusted this kid, and he might not have a choice. The Copper Pack seriously needed help, and he'd always tried to save others. Plus, it wasn't like he really had a home these days. He could make one here. "I appreciate it," he said.

Oakley swallowed and drew his legs in, resting his elbows on his knees. "Now, I'd like to talk about my friend."

CHAPTER 14

*L*una rocked on her porch, staring at the nearly full moon while sipping a bourbon-laced coffee. Her mind refused to quiet, and sleep eluded her. At least her face had healed so she could remove the irritating bandage. She'd worked downstairs in her laboratory for a couple of hours until her eyes refused to focus any longer. Not that it mattered. She was no closer with her research tonight than she had been the last five years.

He came into the light, fully dressed in human form, the scent of blood wafting off him.

Her heart rate picked up, and she stopped rocking, just stared.

The raw maleness of Erik Volk stole her breath. Surrounded by ancient trees shrouded in darkness, he was still the wildest thing out there. Out anywhere.

Her mouth went dry.

He prowled toward her, graceful over the uneven ground. The blaze of his eyes cut through the mist and raked her body, sending her into fight-or-flight mode. Yet she didn't want to do either.

She finished the cup's contents in two gulps, trying to focus. Her palms dampened, and her nipples sharpened while an unreal desire clamored through her. This couldn't happen. Not again. They weren't meant to be.

He climbed the steps and towered over her before dropping to his haunches right in front of her. "You should be in bed."

Bed. With him. Where they'd spent the night before...not sleeping. She tried to speak, but no sound emerged. Was it healthy to want a male this badly? "We can't do this. Not again." Her body rioted against the words even as her brain decided to fuzz.

"Why not?" He planted both hands on her knees, sending heat down to her toes and then right back up to her core.

Why not? There had to be a reason. Wasn't there? She leaned in, drawn by the torture in his eyes. The day had hurt him. Losing the older members of the pack—and especially the teenager—had wounded him. She could see every emotion in his eyes, and he was gut-wrenched. "None of this was your fault," she whispered, cupping his hard-cut jaw with both hands. His whiskers burned her palms. She had to bite her lip from moaning.

His nostrils flared as if catching a scent. One he wanted. "It is."

She tried to soothe him, shooting her hands through his hair. Slightly growing out, she could see the blonder streaks that would be evident if he allowed it to continue. When he'd kidnapped her earlier that autumn, his hair had been a dark blond. Why had he cut it? Now, it appeared dark like his brother's. "You haven't taken the job yet, Erik. Any loss isn't on you." He'd fought like a feral wolf that day, saving almost all of them. Nobody else had come close to his body count.

"Why was only half a pack on that field today?" he growled.

She opened her mouth and then caught herself. If Yago didn't level with Erik in the morning, she would. "Erik—"

"Stop. If you're going to lie to me, then I don't want to hear a sound."

"I'm not lying—"

Then he kissed her. Fast, he swooped in, his mouth taking hers. It felt like being consumed by fire. Her body lit up, head to toe, just from a kiss. She moaned and kissed him back, leaning in and sliding her hands down to his shoulders. Passion exploded between them, still tinged with sadness and nearly saturated with fury.

She should be scared.

Instead, she pushed even closer to him, thrilled by the burn. She didn't feel like a clumsy scientist or a wounded wolf with him. No. With him, she felt all female.

Alive.

Strong.

Wild.

He swept her up and was inside the cabin in a heartbeat, his hand tangling in her hair as he set her on her dining room table. The cool wood chilled her butt as he ripped off her shirt and tossed it behind him. Then his mouth was on her breasts. Nipping and biting, he left his marks. Sparks shot through her, and she gasped.

Erik Volk had been unleashed.

He tore off his shirt, revealing still-healing wounds and rock-hard muscles. He leaned over and sucked one breast into his mouth, tearing off her jeans and kicking them to the floor. His fingers found her, sliding inside her panties, obviously finding her wet. His growl rippled from his chest into her mouth and down through her entire body.

His claws came out and shredded her panties.

She paused, stilling. Those things were too sharp. Leaning back, she balanced herself on her hands, completely nude in front of him.

His gaze kept hers, and he reached out, the claws on his right hand pinpoint sharp. He pressed all five to her clavicle and slowly drew them down over her breast and nipple.

She sucked in air, her eyes widening, more wetness spilling from her. The slight sting nearly sent her into an orgasm. Her mind blanking completely this time, she slowly looked down to see a light pink mark from his touch. That was all. No cuts. What kind of control did he have over his body to be able to touch her with claws and not harm her?

And that slight bite? She wanted more.

He traced a path down to her torso and lower, forcing her to suck in her abdomen to see. At the last second, right before she panicked, he changed his trajectory and scraped along her inner thigh.

"Now." His voice didn't sound anything near human. Rough and guttural, definitely animalistic. "I'm done with the lies." Dropping to his knees, he bit her thigh.

Hard.

She gasped, shock stilling her. Then fire lashed through her, spiraling with a dangerous edge, holding her in place.

He moved his head, right above her clit.

"No—" she whispered just as he lowered his chin and kissed her. Gently.

She yelped and then realized he hadn't hurt her. Confusion blanketed her, and a dangerous craving rippled through her body. "Erik."

"No." He turned his head and bit her other thigh.

She sucked in air, pushing toward him. What was she doing?

"Now," he said again, his mouth right above her clit, his tone stone-cold Alpha. "You're going to tell me the truth. Right?"

She couldn't breathe. Couldn't think. "I, ah—" She shrieked when he ran his rough tongue across her clit, panting upon realizing that he hadn't bitten her. Need filled her, making her ache for him. For all of him. This was so wrong.

He looked up, his eyes gleaming with an intent that paralyzed her. "That was gentle. You want me rough?"

Maybe. Not there, though. "Erik—"

He sank his teeth into her upper thigh.

Pain lashed through her, followed by a craving that truly showed she was crazy. How could she like this? The threat in him was real. He wasn't messing around.

Then he licked up her thigh, shoving his tongue inside her and swirling it around. The pleasure blew through her at a speed and with a heat that had to be unhealthy.

Her arms nearly gave out, but she tightened them to avoid falling onto her back.

He pulled out with a pleased hum. "I know if you're going to lie. I figured I'd spank the truth from you, but this might be better, no?"

"I'm not sure I like either option," she panted, chaos reining inside her.

He looked down at her swollen sex. "Liar," he whispered. Then he bit her other thigh.

She yelped. At this point, she'd wear his teeth marks all week. Thank goodness he was just using his human teeth and not fangs. "Not lying. Not completely, anyway." This was confusing. Very.

He looked up and planted his whiskered chin right on her delicate clit. Pleasure and more pain—or was that more pleasure?—cascaded through her sex. "You're trying hard to be loyal to your Alpha, aren't you?"

She was. She truly was. "I don't want to lie to you any longer."

"What if I were your Alpha?" When he spoke, those whiskers scratched her delicate flesh.

"Then I'd be loyal," she gasped. Of course.

His eyes darkened to the deep color of the river at the

bottom in still water. "What makes you think I'm not your Alpha now?"

She blinked. Good question. Fair question. He was pretty much ruling her body. She couldn't explain why this was their last night. "I'm telling you the truth. I want this. I want you. But this is our last night together." Once he understood all the facts, he'd agree.

"I can hear the truth in your tone," he said, his chin in place as he leaned over and nipped her abdomen. "But you're wrong. The truth isn't what you think." Scraping her, he lowered his chin and then sucked her clit into his mouth, lashing the nub with his roughened tongue.

Her arms gave way, and she fell back, crying out as an orgasm barreled through her, stealing her breath. Without giving pause, he forced her up again, his mouth destroying her. This time, she cried out his name as she rode the waves, her eyes shut tightly, her hands flat on the table.

He released her, standing tall between her legs. His hands went to his jeans, and he shoved them down, revealing his hard cock and bloodied thigh.

Lying on her back, spent, she could only stare at him. Then her gaze caught on his leg. "Erik—"

"Later." He grasped her shoulders and pulled her from the table, frowning at the thin edge. Holding her aloft, he looked around the living space, and satisfaction darkened his expression. "This is softer." He turned and tossed her over the edge of the sofa.

Her hair flopped over her head, and her nose hit the cushions. "Hey—"

Strong arms grasped her hips, and he pressed at her entrance. Big and strong. Definitely hard. "Say yes."

There was no other word she'd give him right now. "Yes. God, yes." She'd already orgasmed twice, and she wanted another one. She felt empty. Only he could fill her. She'd worry about that in the morning. For now, she turned her head to the side so she could breathe, shoving hair out of her eyes.

"Good." He pushed inside her with several strong thrusts, finally taking her over completely.

She stilled, forcing her body to accept him. Nerves zapped inside her, cascading around him. A roar filled her ears. Then he pulled out to power back inside, hammering into her. She shot up so quickly she could barely breathe, and then she was falling, screaming his name as electricity arched through her.

Whimpering, she came down, only realizing after a couple of breaths that he wasn't done. Nowhere near.

She dug her fingers into the sofa cushions, trapped over the back, unable to do anything but feel. A spiraling feeling started deep inside her again, curling, flashing energy into every nerve. Sucking in air, she stiffened and then detonated again, biting the cushion in a futile effort to stifle her scream this time.

His fingers tightened on her hips, and then he stiffened, his body jerking behind her with his climax.

She couldn't breathe. Her body was done. She melted into the cushions, satiated.

Chuckling, he withdrew and lifted her, tossing her over his shoulder.

"Hey." Her hair streamed down his naked body.

He smacked her ass, not very gently. "That spanking is still on the table."

The sound she made might not have been one of protest. Even so, her eyelids closed as exhaustion began to overtake her.

His chuckle strengthened. "Oh, you're not sleeping yet."

CHAPTER 15

*W*ith dawn still breaking outside, Erik strode into the conference room of the main lodge, pleased to see Yago, Butch Hollowgale, and Allen Bushbalm waiting for him. He walked to a sideboard and poured himself a cup of coffee. "It's nice of you all to show up." He'd called them early that morning and demanded an audience. "How is the pack doing?"

"Not great," Yago said, looking even older than he had the day before. Deep lines cut grooves near his temples and along his jawline, and sorrow glowed in the depths of his eyes. "I can't believe the Ravencall Pack dared to attack us like that."

"Well,"—Erik pulled out a chair and sat—"we should probably talk about that. Don't you think?"

Allen crossed his arms. He looked surlier than usual, although he had been a decent fighter the day before. "It's time for you to leave, Volk. We need to get our pack in order."

Erik ignored him. "Yago, what's going on? Why the hell do you only have half a pack, if that? I know that at least one of your kids has lost his father. What happened? What don't I know?" He leaned forward. "I am done waiting for the truth on this."

"Oh? What are you going to do?" Hollowgale asked.

"I could take out all three of you right now if I wanted to." Erik met his gaze directly. "And then I could bring ten percent of the Silver Pack and take over the entire territory." He wasn't bluffing. He could easily do those two things. He didn't want to because he was rapidly becoming attached to the members of this pack, but he was done with it. "Speak now." He looked at Yago.

Yago flushed, and both of his Enforcers shifted their weight. Considering Erik was attending the funeral of a teenager that night, he was finished being polite.

Yago sighed. "You do deserve the truth. I don't know what I was thinking, assuming we could get you into the pack without giving it to you. We've lost half our pack—actually, maybe a little bit more."

"No shit, Yago," Erik growled. "I figured that out on my own. I'm looking for details and answers."

Yago looked down at his gnarled, age-spotted hands. "About five years ago—"

Erik sat back, his mind reeling. Did he just say five years ago? But he kept his expression calm.

"We were poisoned."

"Poisoned?" Erik's jaw nearly dropped.

Yago reached for his coffee cup, his hand shaking. "During the harvest celebration, a poison that Luna has determined was partly made from rhubarb leaves was somehow inserted into the champagne fountain. We all take a glass for the toast, so every adult present ingested the poison."

"What's the harvest celebration?" Erik asked.

Hollowgale crossed his arms. "It's a once-a-year thing where we celebrate the successful mining of the copper. It's an old tradition, and all the adults partake."

Yet half the pack survived? "Some people didn't drink that night?" Erik asked.

"Some people survived the poison," Bushbalm muttered. "Not a lot of us."

"Unbelievable." Erik rubbed his temples as a raging headache tried to blow off his head. "Why didn't you tell us? Why didn't you notify any of the other packs?"

Yago shook his head. "We've aligned to protect each other from outside threats. But if I lost half my pack, maybe you wouldn't have come after us. But you can't tell me the Silver Pack wouldn't have tried to take my territory."

Erik wasn't entirely sure Seth wouldn't have tried to take the territory. He knew without a doubt that his father would've seen the weakness and taken over, and five years ago, his father had been in charge. "Okay, so let me get this straight. Your plan was to just lie low for...what? The next fifty to a hundred years and rebuild your pack without letting us know?"

Yago scratched at a burn on his arm. "I was thinking about it. I don't know. We figured if we got you in, had you become the Alpha, that would align us with the Silver Pack, no matter what. There was a risk that you might try to take over, but—"

"You hoped I'd be loyal."

Yago took a deep drink as if seeking courage from the caffeine. "I was hoping you'd consider truly leading."

"All right." Erik sat back. "Who poisoned you?"

"We don't know. We considered the Ghostwind Pack our biggest enemy at the time, but we couldn't find any proof. Then we thought about the Ravencall Pack because they make all their money from selling spices and elixirs to humans via the internet."

Allen leaned forward. "Considering the Ravencall Pack attacked us earlier, they've moved up in my view."

Yago shook his head. "The night of the poisoning was a

stormy one, so anybody could've masked their scent. Even so, I figured somebody would've noticed an enemy around us."

Shock nearly kept Erik immobile for a moment. "You haven't avenged what happened?" How was that even possible?

"We couldn't even figure out who poisoned us," Hollowgale muttered.

God spare him from idiots. Erik ignored his coffee. "All right. So, how many pack members do you have? And don't lie to me. I'm done with this bullshit."

Yago nodded. "I understand. We've got about fifty older couples still alive, all over three hundred years old. For some reason, the poison didn't affect the elderly."

"What about fighting age?" Erik asked.

"We have about a hundred members of fighting age, ranging from twenty-one to a couple of hundred years old," Yago said slowly.

Erik calculated the disastrous numbers. "A hundred? You only have a hundred fighting-age members?" No wonder the football players had jumped into the fight the day before.

"Yes, we have about two hundred kids, sixteen to twenty years old, and about a hundred children younger than sixteen," Yago said wearily.

Erik scratched his eyebrow, his wounded leg pounding like a bitch. "So, you have about five hundred members of your pack still living." That was sad. That was less than half what they'd need. It was a miracle the Ravencalls hadn't taken them out before now. "Have you been attacked before?"

"Not like yesterday," Yago said. "We've had skirmishes, but not like that."

None of this was good news. "If the Ravencalls poisoned you and knew you were weak, they would've struck before now, right?"

"I don't know," Yago said. "They were probably waiting to see if I alerted other members of the Stope Packs Coalition."

"Which is what you should have done," Erik said, fully understanding why the leader hadn't. There's a good chance he would've lost everything, including his pack's homeland.

Yago crossed his arms. "You fought well yesterday. I would like for you to become the Alpha of this pack immediately. I'm willing to step down."

Allen slapped a hand on the table. "No, that is not how this is going to happen. I'm taking over the pack. Don't make me kill you, Yago."

Erik showed his teeth. "I think you need to back away right now."

"I don't think so." Allen moved toward the Alpha.

Erik lunged across the table, shoving the threat away from Yago and into his buddy. "Back up now," he growled, letting the wolf show beneath his skin.

Hollowgale grabbed Allen and pulled him back. "Now, wait a minute here, Volk. You don't want to be the Alpha of this pack, so let's not fight about it."

"I do." Erik made the decision right then. No way would he let this asshole screw up the pack's lives. Those kids needed cover, and Luna was already his, whether she realized it or not.

"Good," Yago said, standing and glaring at his Enforcers. "The best way to transfer leadership is to plan a union in the future, but that can come later, if you want. Have you decided on Zelda or Francine?"

"I've decided on Luna." Erik met the male's gaze. Of course, he needed to court her and get her agreement. "I want Luna."

Yago brightened. "Perfect. We'll have the funeral tonight and then the transfer of power tomorrow night. Hopefully, at that time, you two can announce your intentions. There's no hurry to actually mate since you'll need to court her per our traditions —which I know you'll follow. I'm sure you'll have many fine sons."

"I can't believe this baloney," came from the doorway.

Erik pivoted to see Luna standing there dressed in dark slacks and a pretty blue sweater. He'd left her sleeping peacefully and figured she wouldn't be up for a while. "I was going to ask you for your hand first, and I guess there's courting to do," he said dryly. Though after the night before, he didn't think she'd say no.

"Well, the answer is no." She lifted her chin.

"Ha," Allen said. "There you go. Stick with your own pack, sweetheart."

"Fuck you, Allen," she said. "Don't make me kick you in the balls again."

Erik turned and pierced the male with a look. "What happened?"

"He got handsy, and I kicked him," Luna said. "That's not the point right now."

Actually, the point was, Erik was going to take off the asshole's head.

A rustle sounded behind Luna, and Vernon Bushbalm walked inside. "Hey, I heard we were having a meeting."

"Where did you hear that?" Yago asked.

"From me," Luna said. "I called him. We need to talk about this whole council idea. First of all—"

Vernon elbowed her aside, interrupting her. "Yeah. We need an accountant. Somebody who understands the numbers and knows how to grow the pack should serve on this council."

"There will be no council." Erik's voice dropped. Everybody stiffened.

"Now, wait a minute here," Hollowgale protested.

Erik kept his body between the Enforcers and Yago while calculating the distance to Luna if he needed to cover her. "No, there's no council. I'm taking over as the Alpha for this pack. I'll have two Enforcers, and they're not in this room right now. Understand?"

Yago cleared his throat. "I'd like to be some sort of senior advisor."

"That's fine," Erik said, fighting a headache again. "You can be the senior advisor."

"Thank you." Yago sat back, apparently pleased.

Erik wanted to shake them all. "Luna, stop fighting this. I don't care if you blow things up. We need to figure out how to save this pack." He wasn't entirely sure he could keep his brother from trying to take over, and he knew without a doubt that he couldn't keep Philip Nightsom and the Slate Pack from coming at them. He had to think of something and fast.

Luna took a deep breath. "Obviously, you didn't hear the whole story."

He stilled. "There's more to the story?" He looked at Yago, who was busy staring anywhere but at Erik.

"Yeah, tell him the whole story," Bushbalm said, glee in his eyes.

"What else could possibly be said?" Erik looked at her.

She gulped, her face pale. "You don't understand. Many of us died from that poison. It affected males differently in that they aren't as strong as they were, but we're hoping that comes back. Like this is just an illness, and they're still recuperating."

Erik studied Yago. Perhaps that was why the Alpha looked so old. "All right. That makes sense. What else?" Gut instinct told him there was more.

She clasped her hands together. "For the females, we haven't been able to have children. I can't have kids, Erik. It doesn't matter if I have Alpha blood in me or not. It's not going to happen." She took a deep breath and stared at him, tears in her eyes. "Francine and Zelda were both away at volleyball and football games during the festivities. They didn't take the poison. They're both fine and are better mates for you."

So *that's* why she was pushing him away. "Are you sure about this?" he asked.

"No," Yago burst out. "We're not sure about anything. It could be temporary and related to hormones, which are affected during mating. Keep in mind, wolves live forever, or it might take an Alpha like you to fix the problem."

"Which is why I'm willing to mate her," Allen spat, his face an angry red. "I think I can fix her."

Yeah, that was why. Erik shook his head. "She's not going anywhere near you, asswipe."

Allen snarled, and the hair on the back of Erik's neck rose. Oh, he couldn't wait to get the guy alone. He took a deep breath and looked at everybody in the room. "All right, I appreciate the truth. Finally." He glanced at the female he had no intention of letting get away. "We obviously have a lot to talk about."

Her shoulders slumped. "There's nothing else to say."

His chin lowered. "You're wrong about that, baby."

CHAPTER 16

*L*una walked wearily down the stairs to the basement of her cottage, her heart hurting and mind reeling. The funerals had been both lovely and incredibly painful as the smoke lifted the souls of her packmates from the funeral pyres. It was unthinkable that they had been attacked in their own territory, and it was a sad testament to where their pack had ended up.

She flicked on the lights, instantly taking comfort in the organized bottles on the shelves containing various colorful liquids, as well as the many charts on the wall. A wooden table took precedence in the middle of the room, piled high with papers and notes with cups holding pencils and pens. She kicked off her kitten heels and padded barefoot on the wooden floor, still wearing her black funeral dress.

Oh, they'd spent the ceremonies in pure wolf form, but afterward, there had been food and refreshments at the main lodge. Erik had remained slightly away from most of the group, letting everyone grieve, but his dark gaze had been watchful. She knew without a doubt that he hadn't missed anything.

Word had gotten out that the transfer of power would occur

the following night, and there were both grumblings and expressions of hope. For now, she had work to do.

She opened her laptop and booted it up, hoping the newest calculations had come through. She had written the program after testing the hormone levels of all of the females in the pack who had ingested the poison. At least those who would let her take their blood. Many people still distrusted science, which was something she just did not understand.

She sensed Erik entering the cabin before she heard him, and her breath quickened. "I'm downstairs," she called out. His heavy footsteps soon sounded on the stairs, and she looked up as he reached the bottom.

He stood tall and tough-looking in dark slacks and a white button-down shirt, apparently having removed his tie and jacket earlier. Somehow, he appeared even deadlier in the civilized clothing. "You're a little more organized than you were last time I was here."

She flashed back to the first time they'd met. Even then, he'd been compelling. Sexy and dangerous. "I was in the middle of a research study last time you were here. You know, when you kidnapped me." She meant to sound snappy, but her voice emerged breathy.

"I know," he said easily. "You were pretty easy to kidnap."

How she wished she could fight. "Gee, thanks," she muttered.

"The Silver Pack owes you for helping Mia when she needed it," Erik said smoothly. "Don't ever forget that."

She truly hadn't considered that possibility. Maybe Seth would remember that fact if the Copper Pack required assistance.

"How are you?" Erik asked, his gaze dark.

Her entire body hurt. "I'm okay. Funerals are tough, especially when there's a kid involved."

"I know. We need to up everybody's training since our numbers are so limited."

"You're going to need a pack administrator," Luna said, having given it some thought. "Yago hasn't been organized for the last several years, and things have fallen by the wayside. I recommend Francine."

Erik crossed his arms. "Are you still trying to push me toward one of those other females?"

The idea of seeing him with one of her friends hollowed out her stomach. Having him close to her in the secluded basement short-circuited her body into tendrils of need, even though she was sad and tired. She cleared her throat. "No. I recommend Francine for the job. If something romantic ensues, then that's between the two of you."

"What about you, Luna?" he asked softly, a threat in his tone.

Her entire body chilled and then heated. Fast. "I've already told you. I'm not a good candidate." She gestured toward the many charts on the walls. "I've been tracking hormone levels. They do rise and fall, but so far, I just can't find a solution. I mean, wild yams have progesterone, so if I could come up with a concoction or something...but I just don't know. We don't have any history of science to help us."

He shook his head, his gaze not releasing her. "I know. Same with the Silver Pack. We have a healer, but we've all stayed away from Western medicine for way too long."

"Human research won't help us," she said. "Our biology is too different."

He grinned, the sight more irritated than humorous. "I never thought humans would be ahead of us in anything."

She chuckled. "They are way ahead of us when it comes to science, medicine, and such. You know that."

He walked over and read the charts. "I don't understand any of this."

"I created my own system." She eyed his broad back. His strong, muscled, and seriously wide torso. "I can read it. So far, the results just don't mean anything."

He turned to look over his shoulder. "You're telling me that none of the females poisoned that night have gotten pregnant in the last five years?"

"Not one," she said, her head aching. "Unfortunately. The poisoned males have been able to procreate with uninfected females, although they lack some of the strength they once had. For now, anyway."

He turned and then walked over to the vials on the top shelf, noting the blue and green colors. "What's all this?"

"Mainly herbs I've collected and created elixirs from. Most are for healing."

"Any dangerous ones?"

Her grandmother had taught her better than that. "Not if taken correctly."

He nodded. "Good to know. So, what happens tomorrow night at this changing-of-the-guard ceremony? We don't have that in the Silver Pack."

She thought through what she'd read in the pack tomes, as she had never witnessed a changing of leadership. "There's a ceremony. It helps if there's a full moon, which there will be. That's a good thing—not that it has any effect on us. It's just symbolic."

He nodded. "I'm aware."

"The outgoing Alpha will make a speech and hand over three relics for your safekeeping, and you will accept them and make a vow to the pack."

"What relics?" Erik asked.

She didn't think she was supposed to share that information with anyone outside the pack. "They're copper," she said, having placed them outside in the forest to draw energy from the moon. Yago had dropped them off earlier in the day, asking her to hand them to him during the ceremony.

He still seemed to be trying to matchmake her with Erik, despite the good of the pack. Yago should know better.

Erik leaned over to read a chart on her desk. "I see. I need to know what laws are in place here, Luna. There seems to be a surprising lack of cohesion and organization."

"Oh," she said, brightening. Standing and hustling over to a cabinet in the far corner, she opened a drawer and pulled out a heavy blue leather-bound book. "I actually have this, too. The compilation should be in the main lodge, but I was doing some research and forgot to give it back a couple of years ago."

"These are your laws?" He accepted the book.

"Yeah. As you can tell, they haven't been updated in a while, but most of them have to do with pack security, leadership roles, and, of course, the mine."

He rolled his neck. "I'll need to take a look at the mining records before making an offer to buy it." His voice dropped.

"Not your thing?" she asked.

He shook his head. "Not even close. I don't mind mining, but record keeping, selling, and buying just aren't interesting."

"You don't have to do any of that as Alpha," she said. Should she explain the structure of the mine to him? Or was that another secret the other packs didn't know? She felt like she was treading on toothpicks and trying not to get pierced.

He didn't take note of her silence. "I'll definitely want to work in the mine. I think everybody should since it provides security for the entire pack. We need money."

She nodded. "We definitely need money."

Erik rolled his eyes. "I can't believe the disrepair this pack is in right now. Where do I get the mining records? Please, tell me some are at the main lodge."

"I assume they're all up in the mine's main office."

"Who runs that?" Erik asked.

She didn't pay a lot of attention to the mine. "I think Yago still directs the mining activities, but Vernon handles the books and all that entails. He's a decent guy and is great with numbers.

He'd also be good to put on a council if you're going to have one."

"I'm not having a council," Erik said. "There will be no such thing."

She shrugged. "Suit yourself."

"Who enforces the laws around here?"

That was a smart question. One that made sense and showed a thought to the future. "Right now, the Enforcers. We used to have a sheriff, but..." She let her voice trail off.

"He died by poisoning?"

"*She* died by poisoning," Luna said. "She was a rare female, and we all loved her, but she was also single, which was too bad. She would've made great children." Luna tapped her fingers on the table, trying to be logical when all she wanted to do was burrow into his warmth and seek safety. "We're in unprecedented times and need more pack members."

Erik took a green vial off the shelf and popped it open, smelling the contents. He reared back. "What is that?"

"Lavender." Interesting. The guy didn't like lavender.

"Oh." He corked the bottle and shoved it back into place. "I understand we're low in numbers. I'm trying to think through a solution."

This was a dumb idea. Well, a good idea, but perhaps an unrealistic one. Definitely one she didn't like. "We need to have more kids. A strong Alpha bloodline would be a good thing," she said tentatively, wondering if he'd hear her out.

He turned and faced her fully, irritation sizzling across his expression. "I'm finished talking about me being a stallion for one of your friends. All right?"

She snorted. "That's actually exactly what I'm talking about, and maybe it's for more than one of my friends."

He straightened. "What?"

Oh, she hated this idea with every fiber of her being, but

logically, it made sense. "What if you had kids with several different females?"

He shook his head as if she'd sprayed his face with water. "Are you kidding me?"

"No. It would create a strong bloodline. Several, really. We need that, and we need kids. I assume you're fertile." It helped to think like a scientist and not a horny female facing a badass male who already knew her body better than she did.

He drew back, his gaze stunned. "Luna, I'm not impregnating a bunch of females in this pack. There has to be another way."

She stiffened, her heart leaping, even though her mind knew better. "It was just a thought."

"It was a crappy one," Erik said, shaking his head. "You really are one of a kind. You know that?"

She sat back down on her stool. "I know," she said glumly. "I really do."

For the first time that evening, amusement danced in his eyes. "I'm not saying that's a bad thing. Do you really think you could share me with other females if we mated?"

"We are not going to mate," she said, her stomach cramping at the thought of him with somebody else.

"We'll see about that, won't we? Did you bug Yago like this?"

She winced. "I did. Believe me, he did not like giving me samples of his sperm. Not at all."

Erik grimaced. "You didn't."

"Of course, I did. Unfortunately, he's too old to have any viable swimmers." It truly had been regrettable.

Erik blinked as if trying to banish several unwanted thoughts. "Where do I find these courting rituals Yago was talking about earlier?"

She threw up her hands at his obvious change of subject. "It doesn't matter."

"That's okay. I'll find them on my own." He glanced at his

watch. "It's almost two in the morning. You need to get some sleep."

"I will." She looked back up at her charts. "In a little while."

He shifted as if his clothes were too tight. "I'm going for a run, and then I have a meeting at dawn."

"With whom?"

"With the leaders of the other three packs, of course." Leaving her stunned, he turned and started up the stairs. "Be prepared after the ceremony tomorrow night," he called out.

"For what?" she yelled.

"For whatever this damn courtship is," he yelled back, his footsteps heavy as he stomped across the room upstairs and then shut the door.

Courtship? With her?

CHAPTER 17

*A*fter a night running through what was apparently becoming his territory, Erik changed into jeans and a shirt and drove the seventy-five miles to the middle of nowhere. His brother was already waiting, sitting on the hood of a truck, eating an apple.

Erik surged out and crossed the muddy field to reach him.

Seth jumped down and gave him a hug. "How's it going?"

"It's a clusterfuck," Erik said honestly. "They need an Alpha, and they need one right now."

Seth tossed the apple core into the forest. As tall as Erik, his hair was a pure black, and his eyes a mix of different blues from light to dark. A scar ran down the right side of his jaw, showing life experience marked by fighting and surviving.

"So, you're saying we could take them out pretty easily. How do you feel about running a copper mine?" Seth asked.

"I don't want to take them out. Anybody dangerous has already been taken care of." Well, except for the two Enforcers he wasn't quite sure what to do about. One of them had a family, and the last thing he wanted to do was hurt Izzy or her family, but he wasn't entirely sure Hollowgale wasn't a big bully. Yet another thing he had to figure out.

"Retribution is at hand," Seth said. "They came into my territory and attacked."

"And you killed all six of them," Erik said. "Let it go. Your pregnant mate is safe. Get a grip."

Seth's eyes darkened to the color of midnight. "Watch your tone, little brother."

"Watch yours." Erik shoved him. "I mean it. Enough of this. I have real problems to deal with. There is no threat to you or Mia from the Copper Pack. You have my word. It's either good enough for you, or it isn't."

Seth growled, the sound more wolf than human.

A silver truck pulled into the clearing from a barely there forest road. Jackson Tryne jumped out. "Hey, are you two fighting? If that's happening, wait till Nightsom gets here. I want to make bets on the outcome."

Erik turned and faced Seth's cousin. Since Erik and Seth were half-brothers, Seth had a whole other family Erik didn't know. Not that Seth knew them.

Jackson was the tough Alpha of the Granite Pack, where Seth's mother had come from. A barrel of a male, he had shocking blue eyes and hair as dark as Seth's. Erik had never seen him wear anything but faded jeans and ratty T-shirts, and today was no exception.

"Jackson, it's somewhat good to see you." Erik held out a hand to shake.

Jackson shook and then fully turned to Seth. "Hello, cousin. How are things?"

Seth shook his hand. "Absolutely fine. How about you? You find a mate yet?"

"Oh, I have one in mind, as you know." Jackson winked. "Anybody want to tell me why we're meeting at the shit crack of dawn?" His bloodshot eyes took in the entire area.

"Why? Did we take you from a party?" Erik drawled.

"Yeah, you did," Jackson said, turning as a white SUV drove down the same road he'd taken and pulled up. "Well, this is interesting."

Emily Nightsom jumped out of the vehicle, her light blond hair shining beneath the newly awakened sun.

"Em," Erik said, pleasure filling him as he strode toward the female. "It's good to see you." He was glad she had attended instead of her father, the Alpha of the Slate Pack.

"You, too." She chuckled and leaned in for a hug.

Emily stood to about six feet tall and had light hair and dark eyes. She and Luna had formed an instant friendship upon meeting when they'd both been told they would have to mate somebody. "How is Luna?" she asked predictably, her kindness well known.

"She's a handful." Erik drew Emily to the other two males. "Where's your father?"

She stepped gracefully over a series of small boulders. "He's busy with something and sent me to this meeting."

"Isn't that a delight?" Jackson leaned forward, grasped her shoulders, and gave her a kiss on the cheek. "Although considering you were kidnapped a couple of months ago, I don't like you being here without protection. As far as I've heard, nobody has found your kidnappers."

She rolled her eyes. "I escaped and can protect myself, Jackson. Don't be an ass."

He kissed her cheek again. "In that case, it's lovely to see you, Em."

She gave him a half-hearted shove. "Don't mess with me today. I should be asleep." She turned to Seth. "Hi, Seth." She leaned in for a hug before stepping back.

Jackson crossed his arms. "We're supposed to mate sometime in the oncoming year. Your father offered, and I accepted. Don't you remember our exceptionally binding agreement?" While his tone remained light, his gaze had darkened.

She rolled her eyes, pink climbing into her high cheekbones. "Thanks, but no thanks."

"I wasn't asking," Jackson said.

Erik held up a hand before the two could get into a real fight. He had no doubt that Jackson would just kidnap Emily if he felt like it. The Alpha definitely played by his own rules. Frankly, it was a surprise he hadn't already made a move. Something must be going on with the Granite Pack, and Erik had enough on his hands to worry about. "Thank you all for meeting me this morning."

Emily looked down at the mud covering her designer boots. She wore black slacks and a form-fitting gray sweater with subtle gold jewelry, appearing regal even in the wild setting. "Why are we meeting in the middle of a field? Seriously, Erik. We're fairly civilized these days. We could just, you know, have coffee and breakfast together."

"You can have breakfast with me anytime, baby," Jackson said.

"You're about to get punched," Emily shot back, turning to face him.

Jackson's smile was slow. "Anytime you want to wrestle, I'm here."

Erik barely kept from lunging at the Alpha. "Would you two knock it off? Save it for later. Right now, I need to talk."

Seth chuckled. "It's not so easy being in charge, is it?"

"Actually, it completely sucks," Erik said. "I don't know how you've kept your brain for the last year."

"What about me?" Jackson asked. "I've been Alpha for a good twenty years and am only thirty-five."

Emily snorted. "You did not become an Alpha when you were fifteen."

"I did. I just had guides and Enforcers the whole damned time."

Erik shook his head. "Maybe that's why you're reliving your youth."

Emily rolled her eyes. "Yeah, party animal."

Seth glanced at his watch. "Listen, I need to get home. Erik, why are we here?"

"We're here because I wanted to announce to the three of you that I am taking over as the Alpha of the Copper Pack, effective tonight," Erik said.

Seth's jaw dropped, and he quickly shut it. "You really are?"

"What the hell do you think I'm doing these days?" Erik asked.

Seth shook his head. "I sent you into their territory to find their weaknesses, not to adopt them."

Jackson finally grew serious. "What about their current Alpha?"

Erik shook his head. "Yago is old. He's tired and wants out. He doesn't have kids, and there's only one female with Alpha blood in the entire pack."

"They didn't plan very well," Seth muttered.

Erik didn't have a response to that, so he didn't bother.

Emily looked his way. "Luna has Alpha blood." She smiled. "Are you going to mate Luna?"

"She has kindly declined so far." Erik frowned.

Seth chuckled. "Doesn't it suck when they don't just fall in line?"

"Shut up," Erik said.

"You shut up," Seth returned.

"Boys." Emily patted them both on the shoulders. "I like Luna a lot and think she would be a wonderful mate, and I could tell there were sparks between you, so what's the problem?"

Erik wasn't going to share the weaknesses. However, he

141

could use some female advice, and he'd been friends with Em for a long time. "There's too much going on to give you all the details, but apparently, the Copper Pack has some sort of courting ritual. Do any of you know anything about that?"

Seth frowned. "Courting ritual? What the hell's that?"

Emily tapped her pink nails on her bottom lip. "Fascinating. Courting rituals? I don't know anything about them."

Jackson threw his head back and laughed. "Oh, that's hilarious. I wish I could watch you try to court an Alpha female."

"There's nothing wrong with courting," Emily said dryly. "It takes creativity and thoughtfulness, two characteristics you know nothing about, Jackson."

Erik looked from one to the other. Whatever the story was between those two, he didn't want to know. "Em, I just want to make sure you're all right with this, you know, since we were kind of engaged." The last thing he wanted to do was embarrass or hurt Emily.

Emily fiddled with her bracelet, her smile genuine. "Everyone thinks I called it off, so don't worry about it. I'm really happy for you. I mean, if Luna ever says yes."

Erik almost wanted to confide Luna's crazy idea of having him impregnate several females to Emily, but he didn't want anybody to think Luna had lost her mind to that degree. "We'll see what happens. Right now, she's not exactly agreeing to anything, but I need to know that the alliances between the four packs are strong."

"Why wouldn't they be?" Jackson asked.

Erik shook his head. "I don't know. I've never been a pack's Alpha before, so I wanted to establish this. Plus, we had an attack from the Ravencall Pack the other day. I think they sensed weakness because Yago is getting older." Erik had absolutely no intention of telling the other three about the dismal numbers and the weaknesses in the Copper Pack.

"Someone came into your territory and attacked you? An outside pack?" Seth asked, his voice lowering.

"Sure, and we easily took care of the problem." Not exactly true, but Erik kept a calm expression in place as he lied. "I find it odd that you think that's weird when it wasn't strange when you were attacked within our own coalition."

"Good point," Seth said. "I'm still uncertain whether I should take out the entire Copper Pack or not."

Hence one of the reasons for having this meeting in the middle of nowhere. If Erik came to blows with his brother, he didn't want too many witnesses. "Considering I'm about to become their Alpha, you might want to give it a second thought," Erik said dryly.

Seth looked away. "All right, as long as there's no threat to us. Are you sure you want to do this?"

No, Erik had no idea if he really wanted to do this. There didn't seem to be another option if he wanted to help Luna and Oakley as well as everyone else he'd already grown attached to in the pack.

"It's not a bad idea," Jackson said. "You're an Alpha without a pack, and apparently, they're a pack without an Alpha. Plus, it's within our coalition, so you're protected. Unless there's something you're not telling us."

There was no question in Erik's mind that Jackson had excellent instincts and a decent IQ.

"I'm sure there's a lot I'm not telling you," he said easily. "But nothing that would affect the relationship between the four packs. I need you to get the word out, Seth. A couple of Enforcers making a statement with the Ravencall Pack. Are you up to that?"

"Sure," Seth said easily. "If they need a reminder, I have no problem giving it."

Jackson glanced at his watch. "Oops, I have to go. I have another meeting. This was fun. Next time, how about a conference call?" With that, he shot in shockingly fast and kissed Em right on the mouth. "You and I'll talk later."

He strode away toward his truck.

Emily stood in place, stunned irritation coloring her expression. "He does comprehend the fact that I know how to fight, right?"

Seth shook his head. "Why don't you two just get a room and get it over with?"

She punched him hard enough in the shoulder that his muscled body moved. "Knock it off."

"Sorry," Seth said.

"That's better." She kissed him on the cheek before turning to Erik. "The Slate Pack officially recognizes and supports your ascension to become the Alpha of the Copper Pack and vow our allegiance."

Now, that was how it was done. "Thanks, Em," Erik said.

She leaned in and kissed Erik on the cheek. "Say hi to Luna for me. I'll give her a call later this week and get all the details you obviously don't have or understand." With that, she turned and sauntered to her vehicle, leaving the two brothers alone in the small clearing.

Erik stared at his brother. "You need to buy me out of the silver mine so I can make an offer on the copper mine." He'd never thought he'd give up his stake in Volk Mining.

"Are you sure about this?" Seth asked.

Erik looked up at the brightening sky and then back down. "No. But I think it's the right thing to do. It's just a lot, and this result wasn't why I went into their territory in the first place." The proposed mating to Luna had started as a ruse. Now, he found himself wanting just that.

Seth clapped him on the shoulder. Hard. "Well, you'd better make up your mind before tonight."

CHAPTER 18

a knock on the door had Luna turning away from her too-empty refrigerator and hustling across the room to open it, stopping cold at seeing Gladys, Gloria, and Gwendolyn Santerbury on her front porch. Oh, the elderly triplets had mated and married eons ago and each had a different surname, but everyone still referred to them as the Santerbury sisters. They wore bedazzled caps with the Copper wolf logo on them, their ample bodies covered in various shades of jumpsuits. Gladys, the eldest by three minutes, held a garment bag in her hands.

"Oh, my," Luna said, taking a step back.

"We'd love to come in. Thank you," Gladys said, walking inside, followed by her sisters. They were short for shifters at maybe five foot eight, and each had curly white hair. Gladys wore hers cut shorter around her ears, Gloria's flipped out at her shoulders, and Gwendolyn had hers to the small of her back. Their eyes were a light brown, and their smiles wide. Between them, they had more grandchildren and great-grandchildren than anybody else in the pack.

Luna eyed the dusty garment bag. "You brought me something to wear?" she guessed.

"We did." Gloria clapped her hands, having worn bright red lipstick to differentiate herself from her sisters today. "We figured you'd try to wear jeans to the ceremony tonight."

"I was going to wear black slacks," she said lamely. Actually, they were black jeans, but still.

"No, you must dress up." Gladys shoved the garment bag into her hands. "You are facilitating the transfer of power, and I assume you'll be handing off the three relics."

Oh, yeah. She'd forgotten about the relics. They were still in the forest. "Yes. That's my plan," she said. "I really don't think I need to dress up."

Gwendolyn sadly shook her head, sending her long hair spiraling. "Of course, you need to dress up. Really, Luna, what would your grandmother say?"

It was a direct hit.

Luna shuffled her feet. "All right, I'll wear the dress." She wasn't too fond of dresses, really. It was easier to trip in them, somehow. Or maybe the tripping and falling were just worse when you revealed your panties as you fell.

"And shoes," Gloria reminded her, tugging a purse the size of Alaska off one shoulder. "Here, I brought you these." She yanked out sparkling, copper-colored heels that had to be at least five inches tall.

"I can't wear those." Luna tried to gracefully retreat.

Gloria shoved them into her hands. "You must."

Luna attempted to juggle the heavy garment bag and shoes.

Gwendolyn looked her over and tsked her tongue. "No, we're going to have to come over and get her ready. I mean, she's not wearing any makeup."

"I don't wear a lot of makeup," Luna said, her breath heating. "But since you're here, do you mind if I take blood from you?" All three of them had been present at the harvest celebration and were poisoned the same night as the rest of the pack. They and their mates were old enough, well over two hundred and fifty years old, and survived after being sick for a short time.

Gladys rolled her eyes. "You've taken blood numerous times. There's nothing else to see."

Unfortunately, it was a true statement. Luna hadn't found anything in their blood or hormone levels. But since they were past childbearing years, it wasn't a surprise.

She looked toward her kitchen and back. "I would offer you something, but I haven't really gone shopping in a while."

Gloria threw up her hands. "Neither have we. Isn't it terrible? We really must get the store better stocked. I'm hoping with Erik as our Alpha, we'll have an influx of goods again."

Luna gently laid the garment bag on the sofa back and tried not to remember what had happened there—Erik wildly pounding into her. She'd had no idea that multiple orgasms existed before meeting him.

"Oh, my," Gladys said. "You are blushing something fierce. Are you feeling okay?" The elderly female reached out and placed a hand over Luna's forehead.

How embarrassing. "Yes, I'm fine. Just got a little hot there for a moment." Luna smiled and put the dangling shoes on the table next to the sofa. "This was very kind of you."

"Don't worry about it," Gwendolyn said, waving a hand in the air. "We knew you wouldn't wear the right thing. Besides, it seems to us that Erik Volk really does want to mate you, and we need to talk to you about that."

An ache started at the base of Luna's neck. "It's okay. You don't need to talk to me. I've already told him that Zelda or Francine would make a much better Alpha's mate."

Gladys actually snorted, her papery skin moving around her mouth. "Well, that's just silly. Obviously, he wants you. So."

Luna opened and shut her mouth before saying, "The pack comes first."

"Oh, phooey," Gloria said. "Love comes first. I can tell you're falling for that boy."

Having anybody call Erik a boy was beyond comprehension. "I did proffer an idea to him that I thought might be of interest."

Gloria elbowed her sisters to the side. "Ooh. Do tell, girlfriend."

Luna blinked twice. Had the elderly great-great-great-grandmother just called her *girlfriend*? Was she in some new club now that she hadn't known about? "Well, in thinking of perpetuating the Alpha bloodline we're currently lacking, I might have suggested that Erik, well, you know..."

"No." Gwendolyn leaned forward. "That he what?" Her voice lowered to a hush.

Luna cleared her throat. "That he maybe, possibly, impregnate several females."

"At once?" Gloria reared back.

"Oh gosh, no," Luna said, trying to mentally banish the images that slid through her head. "No, no, no, no."

Gladys shook her head sadly. "Luna, we're wolves, not hooligans. You of all people should know that a mated Alpha would never look anywhere else. I mean, come on. Have you completely lost your mind?"

"Possibly." Luna nodded wildly. "It's entirely possible. Ever since he came into the territory, I think I might have lost my mind."

Gladys stared, Gloria grinned, and Gwendolyn burst out laughing. "Sounds like love to me," Gwendolyn said.

"It's not love." Luna waved her hands in the air. "It can't be love." The last thing in the world she had time for was to be in love with a male who couldn't be with her. "The pack has to come first, right?"

The three females sobered. "I think a happy Alpha is best for the pack," Gladys finally said. "The rest of it will take care of itself. It always does."

Gloria nodded.

Gwendolyn smiled. "You know, my Henry wasn't even a member of the Copper Pack when we started dating."

Luna stilled. "He wasn't?"

"No," Gwendolyn said. "He ran with a band of wolves, not really a pack because they didn't have an Alpha. And, well, I met him when I may have been running out of territory. It took a while, but we finally talked my father into letting him court me. It was quite fun."

"I didn't know that about Henry," Luna said. As far as she had known, Henry had worked in the mines since the day he was born and still took shifts, even though he was well over two centuries old.

Gloria studied her. "It's the male you have to commit yourself to, not the pack. If you don't know that right now, then you're not ready. But wear the dress tonight."

"All right, I will," Luna said, her mind reeling.

"Good. We'll see you then." Clapping her hands, Gloria turned and led the progression out of the cabin, leaving the smell of vanilla cookies in their wake.

Luna glanced at the garment bag. She almost didn't want to know until the last second what they'd brought for her to wear. She slowly unzipped the top to see copper sequins and sparkles.

Holy moly.

Shaking her head, she hurried out of the cabin and down the steps into the woods to find the artifacts. Reaching them, she paused. Crap, she should've brought a sack. Oh, well. Leaning down, she picked up a copper-bound grimoire that held the tradition and lore of the pack; a gorgeous wolf and crescent moon pendant that always remained on the Alpha; and finally, a large wolf statue figurine made of copper and glass.

Turning, she tripped on a branch and fell sprawling across the ground, hitting her chin on a rock. Tears filled her eyes, and she winced as she scrambled to her hands and knees, her gaze catching on the back legs of the copper wolf. They were broken.

Panic engulfed her. She picked up the pieces, along with everything else, and ran back toward her cabin. Nobody could ever know. What was she going to do? She'd been entrusted with these artifacts, and of course, she had tripped.

She had to have some duct tape around her cabin somewhere.

* * *

ERIK SAT at the head of the conference table in the main lodge as the sound of construction echoed from outside. He had already dressed in a suit, and the tie pressed his neck tightly, choking him. He looked up from a stack of ledgers at Yago, who sat next to Vernon. "Are you kidding me?"

Yago flushed. "I know it looks bad."

"Bad?" Erik's ears heated. "The mine is nearly bankrupt. Copper is at an all-time high right now. What the hell happened?"

Vernon tapped his phone that he'd been using as a calculator. "What happened was we lost half our workforce, if not more, and then made some bad business deals. It wasn't Yago."

"Then who made the bad business deals?" Erik growled.

Yago shook his head. "It doesn't matter. I'm the Alpha for at least another hour, so any deal is my fault."

"I would like to know who's running the mine into the ground," Erik said.

"My brother," Vernon admitted. "He doesn't have a head for business, and for quite a while, he was dating somebody from the Ravencall Pack."

Erik stilled. "Wait a minute. What? Your brother has been dating somebody from the Ravencalls?"

Vernon shoved his phone across the table. "Yes, and so we

sold copper to them with the agreement that they would work in the mine for a reasonable wage."

"And you gave them the copper upfront," Erik said, shaking his head. "You had to suspect them of the poisoning, considering their industry is creating spices and liquid vitamins. Yet you trusted them like that? Seriously?"

"Yeah," Vernon muttered. "We didn't suspect them of the poisoning until recently when they began attacking us once in a while."

Erik looked at Yago. "I'll buy you out of this bankruptcy."

"I don't own the mine," Yago said.

Erik pressed a finger beneath his right eyebrow as a migraine tried to kill him. "All right, who owns the mine?"

"The pack does," Vernon said.

Well, that didn't make a bit of sense. "If the pack owns the mine, why are some people living in mansions and others in cardboard boxes?"

Vernon winced. "Like I said, it hasn't been managed very well, and that is my brother's as well as Butch Hollowgale's fault. I didn't get involved with the books until a couple of years ago. By then, it was too late. We've been trying to crawl our way out of debt, but we need more workers. It's that simple."

"You need an influx of cash, as well," Erik muttered. "Does the pack own the mine as an LLC?"

"No," Yago said. "It's just well known that the pack owns the mine. That obviously isn't how you do it."

"No, my family owns Volk Mining." It was one way to ensure that the pack stayed strong, and also that power remained in the family. "All right. Vernon, come up with a fair figure, and I'll offer to buy the mine. I'm not sharing it with the pack. I want full control of it. You're going bankrupt if you don't sell to me."

Vernon flushed but nodded. It was obvious he didn't like that answer, but based on the figures in front of Erik, they didn't have a choice.

Erik cleared his throat. "I could let the mine go bankrupt and then buy it, but I'd rather avoid that if possible."

Yago flattened his liver-spotted hands on the table. "It's not a bad idea, but I would like to get pack agreement. I could sign it over to you right now, but we'd face opposition."

The last thing Erik wanted was to face any more opposition than he already would if he took over this pack. He looked over at Vernon. "Was your brother dating the wolf from the Ravencall Pack five years ago when the poisoning occurred?"

Vernon stared at him. "I don't like what you're implying."

"I'm not implying anything. I'm asking a question."

Yago looked at Vernon and back. "Yes, he was. In fact, I thought they were going to mate. Then the poisoning happened, and we discovered that Luna held Alpha blood in her veins."

So good ol' Allen decided he'd mate Luna instead of his girlfriend in the Ravencall Pack? Erik needed to get Allen alone and soon for some questioning.

A knock sounded on the door, and Francine Goodhouse poked her head in. Her blond hair was up in an elaborate bun, and she wore a light blue dress with pretty pink heels. "Yago, we need to get you ready and discuss the ritual. Are you guys about done?" She smiled.

"We're done," Erik said curtly. "I'll see you out there, Yago."

Yago painstakingly pushed away from the table and stood. "I appreciate this, Erik." He leaned over to whisper in Erik's ear. "This will go smoother if you mate Luna. Don't forget the singing part of the courtship." He stood all the way up before Erik could ask for clarification.

Singing? Erik needed to look into that. Later. "I appreciate you staying on as senior advisor."

Yago's shoulders went back, and he nodded. "I'm proud to do so." He clapped Erik on the arm and then strode out of the room.

"Hi, Francine," Vernon said. "Did you bring your brownies tonight?"

The female blushed. "I brought three different kinds. I couldn't decide."

"I can't wait," Vernon said with a grin.

Francine took one more look at Erik and then shut the door.

Vernon stood and gathered all his papers. "I'm sorry things are such a mess. I've done my best the last couple of years, but by the time I got involved..."

"I understand," Erik said.

Vernon nodded and walked around the table toward the door. "It's none of my business, but I really do think Zelda would make the best mate for an Alpha, especially for a pack that's in so much trouble." He kept his gaze on the floor and then looked over at Erik. "I mean, Francine is a sweetheart and all, but..."

Ah. It was like that, was it? "I'm not going to mate Francine," Erik said.

"Oh. Good." Vernon smiled. "Zelda will give you many fine sons."

"I'd rather have daughters," Erik said easily. "I didn't say I was mating Zelda either."

"Oh." Vernon shuffled his feet. "All right, then. Well, I'll see you out there, okay? I'll get you a figure of what the mine is worth as soon as I can, but it won't be much."

"I figured. I promise I'll overpay," Erik said.

Vernon grinned. "That's my hope." He shut the door, and his footsteps echoed on the other side.

Erik sat there for a moment and then shut the top file folder. He didn't want to look at the dismal numbers any longer.

His phone buzzed and he lifted it to his ear. "Volk."

"Hey, Volk. It's Philip Nightsom."

"Nightsom. It's nice of you to call." How unexpected.

Nightsom coughed. "I just had a report come in from my

contacts in the Ravencall Pack. Apparently, you didn't give my daughter the full truth this morning."

Erik winced. "I told her they attacked."

"Yeah, but you didn't tell her how terrible your numbers are. I'd like to make an offer to buy the copper mine and take over the pack."

Erik's ears started to heat. "We don't need to be taken over. We're fine."

"It sounds like you're in a complete disaster, and I'm giving you help. I understand from my daughter that you were planning on becoming the Alpha of that pack, and I'm telling you right now I want that copper mine."

This could lead to disaster. "You're going to cause civil war within the four Stope packs," Erik said, his voice going hoarse. "You know that, right?"

"Maybe, maybe not. Seth has his hands full with his pregnant mate and the problems that has created. And Jackson? I don't think he's ever really been on your side, if you want the truth," Philip said.

Erik thought through their interactions recently. "You're wrong. Blood always wins out, and he's related to Seth."

"We'll just see about that, won't we?" Philip said cheerfully. "But for now, I'm going to email you a very good offer for the mine and the surrounding territory. I'll absorb as much of the pack who wants to stay, and the rest can get out. Expect my email."

"If I reject your offer?" Erik asked, the wolf inside him rising fast.

Philip's chuckle went dark. "Then ask yourself. Are you really prepared for war?"

CHAPTER 19

*E*rik strode out onto the makeshift platform that had been rapidly created with fresh cedar that scented the air. On the south side of the lodge, he stood in front of a vast field filled with pack members. All five hundred had to be in attendance, sitting on blankets, standing, or milling about. He spotted Oakley with his mom and sisters and gave him a chin nod. Oakley smiled back.

The moon beamed down from a cloudless sky, illuminating the entire area, even without the lights strung between all the trees on the sides.

Yago approached from the other side, also dressed in a suit, looking regal. Even so, his shoulders were slightly stooped, showing his age. He cleared his throat. "It's a lovely night for a transfer of power." With that, he looked up at the full moon. "It's almost like fate interceded."

Then he focused on the crowd. "I want to thank you for honoring me as your Alpha for the last three hundred years. I wish that I had left progeny, but as you all know, my Delilah died young, and I never found another mate. However, Erik

Volk, an Alpha from the Silver Pack, has agreed to take on the job, and we need him now more than ever."

Erik scanned the area for threats, but besides Bushbalm and Hollowgale puffing cigars over to the side near a stand of pine trees, he didn't see much that concerned him. Several able-bodied pack members dotted the crowd, but none seemed overly threatening. He had no doubt the two former Enforcers would come at him at some point, and he wondered what kind of following they might have. Was he putting Luna in danger if she remained in his vicinity?

They had to know he'd kill to protect her—or anybody under his rule.

He smelled juniper berries before he saw her as she hustled up the side of the platform, and then his heart stopped cold. Dressed in a sparkly copper gown with impossibly high heels, she looked absolutely stunning. Small spaghetti straps held up the dress's bodice that narrowed to her small waist and then flared out with a slit in the side to allow her to move. He had no clue how she was walking on those spikes.

The wolf inside him reacted instantly, rearing up, wanting to go to her. The feet separating them were too many, and he didn't like it. Not at all.

She'd pulled her hair up into an intricate braid with copper accents woven throughout, and subtle makeup and pretty, peach lip gloss enhanced her smooth face. She held three items in her hands, obviously trying not to drop them.

Seeing him, she stumbled and quickly regained her balance, her gaze scanning down to his toes and back up, a pretty blush covering her cheeks. If that was the reaction he received, maybe he'd wear a suit more often.

He flashed back to the other night in her living room. She had a lot of furniture, and he wanted to break in each piece.

Whatever showed in his gaze had her gulping and holding very still. Smart girl.

Yago smiled. "Oh, there you are, Luna. All right, well, first…" He reached and took what looked like a solemn book bound in thick, copper-colored leather. "This is the grimoire of our pack. It has all the ancient legends and the current prophecies." Yago shrugged. "It's fun reading if nothing else." He turned and handed it to Erik.

The leather felt heavy and cold in his hands, and he solemnly nodded. "I accept the grimoire." He'd never understood that word. It seemed like an odd one, but he followed tradition, curious about the legends.

The Silver Pack had a similar book, and Seth used to read some of the tales to him. Many stories held the history of the pack, and Erik figured this book would teach him much about the Copper Pack. Everyone should have access to the history, not just him, but he'd deal with that fact in due time.

The crowd clapped, some people with great enthusiasm, and others with a bit of hesitancy. The two Enforcers against the trees didn't move. Erik turned and placed the heavy book on the table that had been situated on the platform.

"Next," Yago said, "I bequeath to you our copper moon amulet." He handed Erik a necklace with a copper pendant shaped like a crescent moon inlaid with the figure of a wolf.

The pendant singed Erik's fingers and made them tingle. He instinctively pulled the heavy leather cord over his neck, and the pendant fell over his heart.

The crowd clapped more wildly this time.

His chest filled with strength and purpose, and a sense of belonging started to take root inside him. One he'd missed.

Luna gave him a tremulous smile, brushing the hair away from her face, her hand visibly trembling. She must really not like crowds. "And, finally,"—Yago's voice rose—"I gift to you the ancient and protective wolf statue made of copper and finely spun glass that's older than any of us still alive."

A hush ran through the crowd, and several people angled closer to better see.

Luna handed over a foot-long figurine that Yago took with both hands before turning and extending his arms. Erik accepted the statue, surprised by its heft. It seemed like the wolf had been hidden away, and this beauty should also be enjoyed by everyone in the pack. He already felt connected to it, and he'd only been here a short time.

"As you hold the protective statue, please repeat this vow," Yago said.

Luna shuffled her feet. "You can put the statue down if you want, to say the vow, right?" she whispered.

Yago cut her a look. "No."

Erik smiled, trying to ease her panic. "It's okay," he said softly. It must be odd for her to be in front of such a large group of people.

Yago faced the crowd again. "I, Erik Volk, vow to protect this pack and uphold the noble legacy of the Copper Pack ancestors. I pledge to protect each member and each family, and I promise that we will thrive and overcome any obstacles. This I vow to you."

Erik repeated the words, his voice strong and sure. His left hand began to burn, and he ignored it. Soon, it started to blister. He cut a look at Luna, who was watching his hand and chewing on her lip. He tried to shift his grip from the back legs of the wolf to the top, but one leg felt loose.

A slight waft of smoke started to emerge from between his fingers. He squeezed them closer together to keep the smoke from being seen and bit back a growl at the pain.

Finally, Yago nodded. "You may place the wolf by the other two artifacts."

Erik did so, careful to position the figurine behind the book.

Yago held out his right hand and Erik shook it, trying to open his injured hand behind him so the smoke would go where no one could see it. The pain dug deep into his palm and climbed up to his elbow.

He gave Luna a look. She ducked her head and then turned to face the crowd. He had no idea what she'd done, but he couldn't mistake the relief in her pretty eyes that he hadn't called her out.

Trying to forget the agony throbbing in his hand, he looked out over the crowd. "I meant every word of that vow. This pack is in trouble, and we need to shore up our defenses. First, I'm going to make an offer to personally buy the mine. You're almost bankrupt. I won't do it unless everybody agrees, but if I don't, the mine will cease to exist."

A rumble started through the crowd, and several looked at Yago and the Enforcers.

"Obviously, you didn't know that fact," Erik said. "Vernon, where are you?"

Vernon raised his hand from near the picnic table where Francine was still busy unwrapping dishes.

"I want you to make the numbers available to the entire pack by tomorrow night. Everyone should know the problem we're in," Erik said.

It was weird to think that he was now part of *we*, but there was no going around it. "Second, we need a sheriff, and I would like to have applications handed in to, well, me, at headquarters by the end of day tomorrow for anybody who wants the job. We need a sheriff as well as one deputy. That's all we can afford right now. Second, we need a pack administrator who can organize all of this."

Vernon started to raise his hand, and Erik shook his head. "No. Vernon, I need you to be in charge of the finances at the mine, as well as for the entire pack. Whoever the administrator is will answer to you. We'll figure out a decent title for you tomorrow."

A pleased flush wandered across Vernon's face, and he winked at Luna before smiling at Francine.

Erik glanced at Luna. "I need you and anybody else who has any medical knowledge or experience to study the effects of the poison on everybody. Speaking of which, whoever the sheriff is, their first job will be to hunt down the person who poisoned this pack. There was no way somebody got into this territory without some help, and you need to figure out who it is, how it happened, and, more importantly, *why* it happened."

He looked over at a group of teenagers trying to sidle closer to the food tables. "There's a make-up football game this coming Saturday against that team out of Seattle. We will win it." The teenagers stopped moving almost comically and looked at him. "You can't hurt anybody, and the score has to be somewhat close, but I want you to win on Saturday."

Yago frowned, and the two Enforcers pushed away from the trees, but Erik ignored them as the kids shouted and gave each other high fives.

"Finally..."—he looked around—"anybody who doesn't want to stay in this pack may leave. You'll be given a stipend so you can make your way somewhere else. Anybody who does stay is here to work. We are going to fix everything, including the housing problem. And for now, as your new Alpha, I need two Enforcers. I am requesting that Zelda Graytail, and Oakley Rockwood serve as my Enforcers for the time being. If either of you doesn't want the job, we can discuss that tomorrow."

Zelda stood up from her place across the field. "I accept," she said, her voice strong and sure.

Oakley swallowed, looked at his mom, and then stood next to his sisters. "I accept, as well." His voice trembled a little but strengthened at the end.

"Thank you. We'll meet tomorrow and discuss our first moves." His hand was fucking killing him. "For now, let's eat, drink, and celebrate. Luna, a word please."

CHAPTER 20

*E*rik led Luna around the lodge and into the forest as the sounds of revelry echoed behind them. Finally, he turned her around, putting her back to a narrow Cottonwood. "Explain."

She winced, looking adorable. "I broke the back legs of the wolf."

"Yeah. I got that." He glanced down at his scalded hand. "Why am I burned?"

She kicked a pinecone with a ridiculously high heel. "I tried duct tape at first to fix it, but it was too obvious."

A startled chuckle burst from him. "Duct tape?"

She sighed, her smooth shoulders moving. "Yeah. So, I had no choice but to use my own mixture of cyanoacrylate adhesive, which unfortunately causes a caustic sensation when touched—but just for the first week or so."

Caustic sensation? "Meaning it burns the hell out of skin?"

She winced. "Yeah. Sorry about that. I barely successfully adhered the legs to the body in time to get here and just didn't get a chance to warn you. Thank goodness Yago just touched it for a moment to give to you." She patted his pec. "Thank you for hiding the smoke. That must've really hurt."

"It did." He planted his good hand on the tree and leaned over her. "You owe me."

Her pupils dilated. "Um. I do have a decent salve I can blend for you after the party. It'll take care of the burns. I promise." Under the moonlight, her eyes glowed a mysterious green with the blue only visible around the rims this time. "I think the pack would kill me if they knew I damaged the ancient wolf." Her tongue flicked out to her bottom lip in a nervous gesture. "You don't think it'll lead to bad luck, do you?"

If she got any cuter, he would mate her right here and now against the tree. "No. I think you're safe since you fixed it."

Her body relaxed and she nodded. "Of course. I mean, I'm not superstitious or anything, but still...it's nice we agree on this."

"What else do we agree on?" He slipped one of the tiny straps off her smooth shoulder, ignoring the pain in his damaged palm as he did so.

She stilled. "Listen. The attraction is here, obviously. And most of the time, I actually like you."

"Most of the time?"

She wrinkled her nose. "Yeah. The whole alpha-male thing doesn't do it for me."

"You're such a liar." He tugged down the other strap and pulled the top of the dress to her waist, revealing her high and incredibly smooth breasts. Except for the bite marks still showing from him. A dark satisfaction filled him at the sight.

Her nipples sharpened, and slight goosebumps rose on her skin. She looked wildly around as if worried about spectators.

"There's nobody near us right now," he rumbled, his senses tuned in from the forest to the lodge where the smell of beer and champagne dominated. He'd given clear orders to have guards on the drinks from the time they started flowing until the last drop disappeared to avoid another poisoning, just in case. "So, tell me again how you dislike my Alpha tendencies." Before she could answer, he leaned in and nipped her neck, leaving a love mark.

She gasped, and the scent of her desire permeated his senses. Juniper berries and musk—all female. All Luna. "Um. I liked your ideas about the housing for people. What, um, is your plan?" she breathed.

He traced a path from her neck up and along her jaw, kissing her until he could sink his teeth into the shell of her ear.

She yelped and clutched his suit jacket, leaning closer. "Um, plan?"

He nibbled on her earlobe, his cock so hard it hurt to move. "Plan? Buy the mine, pay off everyone fairly, and then start building houses as a pack." He kissed her temple and yanked the bottom of her dress up with his blistered hand.

"That's, ah, that's a good, you know, um, plan," she whispered, sounding like she was holding her breath.

He chuckled and slipped his fingers into her wet panties, no longer feeling any pain. In his hand, anyway. His dick was throbbing.

She unzipped his pants and reached for him, her hand so soft he groaned. "Erik. You're not wearing underwear." She sounded both shocked and aroused.

He gave a pained chuckle. "Ran out of boxers. Didn't think I'd be here for so long."

"Tell me you know how to use a washing machine." She stroked him, nearly taking off his head.

"I do but haven't had time." He slid two fingers inside her. She was ready. So, he lifted her with one arm, ripping off her underwear and then shoved inside her. Fast and hard.

She threw back her head, and several tendrils of her hair escaped the intricate braid. "Erik," she whispered, wrapping both arms around his neck.

"Yes. Try not to scream this time." Without giving her time to argue, he grabbed her ass with both hands and started hammering inside her, easily holding her aloft.

She stiffened and then relaxed against him, clasping her ankles at his back and all but piercing his buttock with the sharp heel.

He shifted his angle until he hit her clit, and she gyrated against him, little sounds of need emerging with her breaths. He powered into her harder and faster, still in tune with their surroundings, feeling her body start to tremble. She came with a soft cry, biting his lapel, shuddering wildly. Her internal walls gripped him so tightly he saw black.

Electricity ripped down his spine to detonate in his balls, throwing him into a climax that had him panting against her. When they both relaxed, he slowly leaned back. "Tell me again you don't like my Alpha tendencies."

Her eyes slowly focused. "Shut up."

"You shut up." He gently eased her down to the ground and held her until she regained her balance before pulling her dress down and her straps back up.

She let him minister to her, looking slightly dazed.

He grinned. "Now neither of us is wearing underwear."

* * *

Luna busied herself with helping Francine take care of the food and drink during the remainder of the party, hoping nobody knew what had gone on in the woods with Erik. However, based on several amused looks cast her way, she didn't feel comfortable in that thought.

Yago was doing a good job of taking Erik around and introducing him to every member of the pack, while Zelda remained close to them both.

"She was a good choice for an Enforcer," Francine said,

turning and watching as they spoke with several of the mining foremen near the picnic tables.

"I think she'll do an excellent job," Luna agreed, ignoring the raw spurt of jealousy that rippled through her bloodstream.

Francine rolled her eyes. "I think you need to stop playing hard to get." She leaned in and pulled a leaf out of Luna's braid. "I mean, not that you're playing really hard to get, but you know what I mean."

Luna covered her face with one hand and then stopped, reaching for an empty plate that had once held brownies. "I'm not. I'm just trying to do what's best for the pack."

"Let the pack worry about itself," Francine said. "I made him an offer and I meant it, and so did Zelda, but that was before we knew you were truly interested in the guy. Maybe you should make the offer, or are you afraid he'll accept?"

Luna gathered several of the coolie cups from beer and stacked them. They were empty. Why couldn't people use the same cup? She should have brought a pen for folks to write their names to keep track. "It's not that I'm afraid. It's that I'm worried about the pack. A pack without an Alpha is just a band, and we can't hold our own."

"So, Erik lives for…what? Another, I don't know, three hundred years? What then?" Francine eyed the remaining platters of food critically. "People didn't go for the deviled eggs tonight. Hmm, I wonder why."

"Because your brownies were here," Luna said easily. "You didn't answer my question."

Francine pushed some loose strands of her pretty blond hair away from her face. "Nobody knows what'll happen three centuries from now. Seriously, you can't plan your life around something that may or may not happen decades in the future. Plus, this ailment messing with your hormones might go away. You're a wolf shifter, Luna. Start thinking like one."

Vernon approached. "Ladies, do you need any help? I've

eaten my share of brownies. I should probably do something." He grinned, looking handsome under the full moon. He often seemed to be in his brother's shadow because Allen was such an overbearing presence.

Francine smiled. "I appreciate your interest in the brownies."

Yeah, right, like it was his interest in the brownies that kept him near. Luna barely bit back a snort. When would Vernon begin the courting rituals with Francine? He seemed shy, and hopefully Francine would give him some help.

Vernon looked at her. "Erik was serious about letting the football team win this coming weekend, wasn't he?"

"Oh, definitely," Luna said, her heart lifting. "Those kids deserve a win."

Vernon smiled and looked toward a group of teenagers flirting with each other near the gazebos. "I agree, but we don't want to bring attention to ourselves. It's a real fine line, Luna."

"I know," she agreed. "I'm not sure of our ultimate goal. I mean, it's nice to let them win, but they can never do their best or take the teams all the way to the championship. It's not fair for the kids to have to force themselves to lose."

Francine tossed several used paper plates into her garbage. "It isn't fair, but it's a good way for us to remain involved in the outlying communities. It's a good excuse to, you know, scout and see what's going on and keep our finger on the pulse of, well, the humans."

Luna nodded. "I'm aware and don't see another organic way to do that, absent using kids' sports. I still don't like losing, though." Not that she'd played sports, because she'd always had her head buried in a book, but she'd cheered on her friends. Now, she cheered on the kids.

Vernon patted her arm. "We'll figure it out, Luna. We always do. I have a feeling we're finally on the right track." He turned toward where Erik and Zelda moved along with Yago to meet a group of young mothers with toddlers crawling all around. Several of them were widows from the poisoning five years ago.

"They make a good pair," Vernon murmured.

Luna winced at the direct hit to her heart. Francine glared at him, but he remained watchful, obviously clueless. Francine rolled her eyes, and amusement tickled through Luna. Males really were oblivious sometimes.

Luna worked with Francine for another couple of hours, and then the party began to die down. Erik gave her a high sign that he was going into the lodge with Yago, Zelda, and both the former Enforcers.

"That doesn't look good," Francine muttered, finishing with wrapping up the remaining food.

Vernon had stuck by her side for most of the night, assisting with taking down tables and chairs for a while, then coming back to help. "Maybe I'll go in there, as well," he said, patting Francine on the shoulder. "I'm the new Vice President of Finance, you know."

"You chose a title," Luna said, brightening.

He rocked back on his heels, his smile wide. "I think so. What do you think about that? Vice President of Finance?"

"That's good. I also like Alpha Auditor," Luna said, snorting.

"That's a good one." Francine grinned. "Or how about Predatory Portfolio Overseer?"

Vernon chuckled. "I was trying to sound official, but how about Wolf Wealth Warden?"

"Ooh, the Triple W," Luna said. "I kind of like that one."

Francine nudged Vernon with her hip. "What about Pack Treasury Guardian?"

"Ooh, that's a good one, too," he agreed.

Luna laughed. "It would be nice if you were in there for some more balance."

"I know. I agree. Have a nice night, ladies." He turned and

strode toward the lodge with more swagger in his step than she'd ever seen.

Francine handed over several platters before picking up the remaining ones. "I think he'll do a good job."

Luna nodded. "He likes you."

Francine blushed. "Maybe you could pass me a note before gym class with more info." She giggled. "I'm tired and heading out. Did you drive here?"

"No. I caught a ride with the Santerbury sisters. They did my hair and makeup." The elderly ladies had gone home hours ago.

"All right, come with me. You can tell me how you're not into our Alpha." Francine led the way to the parking area, and they placed the platters in the rear of her SUV before climbing in. "I'm exhausted."

Luna jumped into her seat, shut her door, and turned on the heater. Sighing, she sat back, her body still electrified from her jaunt in the forest. She should be exhausted, but she couldn't help wondering if Erik was going to come by again tonight.

Francine drove slowly through the forest for about fifteen minutes and turned a corner around a sycamore tree that had stood in place for Luna's entire life. Suddenly, an explosion thundered, and the vehicle jumped as a tire blew.

"What the hell?" Francine shrieked.

Luna looked frantically around. "I think we popped a tire."

Another flash came from the forest, hitting the front tire. "We're under attack," Francine screamed.

CHAPTER 21

*L*una scrambled in the glove box. "Tell me you have a gun in here."

"I do. Wait. No, it's under the seat." Francine clicked the front lights to high beam. "Who's out there?"

Luna ducked and felt beneath the seat, her hand touching cold metal. She pulled out a weapon. "Please tell me these are silver bullets."

Francine swiveled so quickly she shocked Luna. "Of course, they're not silver bullets. Those were outlawed a century ago."

"You're kidding me. I mean, I know it was outlawed, but everybody has silver bullets." Panic clawed through Luna. Who was out there shooting at their tires?

"Nobody has silver bullets, Luna."

Maybe Luna was alone. Her grandmother always kept a shotgun with silver shells to protect the house, just in case. She took a deep breath. "Do you have your phone?"

"Oh, yeah." Francine scrambled for her purse in the back seat. "Why don't you have a phone?"

"Where would I put a phone in this outfit? I didn't even

bring a purse." Her bag was full of the artifacts, one of which had been broken, but Francine didn't need to know that.

Luna peered outside into the misty night. Clouds had started to gather, blanketing the full moon, and she shivered. She had been in such a hurry she hadn't even brought a coat.

Just then, someone wrenched her door open, and strong hands tore her away from the vehicle. Francine scrambled to jump between the seats to the back of the SUV.

Luna kicked and punched, aiming her spiked heel at her attacker's thigh. The back window shattered, and Francine screamed as another attacker pulled her out of the vehicle. Luna looked up to see a male much bigger than her wearing a ski mask. She shoved him as hard as she could, and he took a step back. She sucked in air and recognized the scent of a Ravencall Pack member.

The other guy dragged a furiously fighting Francine around the back of the SUV and shoved her toward Luna. Luna caught her friend and nearly fell when her heel sank into the muddy ground.

A third trespasser emerged from the forest.

Francine's head jerked back. "I know your smell. What are the Ravencall wolves doing back in our territory? You didn't learn your lesson the other day?" Her body vibrated with anger, and cuts showed down her arms and legs from being pulled through the broken window.

The first guy chuckled. He seemed to be the leader as the other two stood back. "We're here for the Alpha's mate."

Francine glanced at Luna. "What are you talking about?"

The guy looked them over. "Rumor has it, it's one of you. So, we're taking you both."

Terror rippled down Luna's spine, but she held her ground. "Do you really want to take on our entire coalition? You kidnap us and you're not only angering the Copper Pack, but the rest of the Stope Packs Coalition. Erik Volk became our Alpha tonight, his brother leads the Silver Pack, and he's related to the Granite Pack. Your measly little unaligned pack won't survive an attack by one of them, much less all four. You understand me?"

The guy backhanded her, and she flew into Francine, who tried to catch her, but they both went down. Luna landed on top of Francine, and she ducked her head to her friend's ear. "We need to shift and now."

Francine nodded and then pushed Luna off. Luna rolled several feet away, coming up on her hands and knees and shifting quickly, straining her muscles. Pain flared through her body as she shredded the pretty copper dress and dove out of the heels.

The air shimmered as Francine also shifted and they both started to run.

A boom echoed behind them as the three males no doubt shifted into wolf form. Otherwise, they wouldn't be able to catch the females.

Luna led the way, her jaw aching from the hit. Had she broken something? Her adrenaline rushed, and her mind reeled, but she knew these woods better than anybody else in the pack.

Francine kept pace as Luna twisted and turned and ran around in abrupt angles, trying to lose the three larger males. They were definitely getting closer. She glanced behind her to see their darkened forms bursting toward them, running full-out.

Francine was a lighter gold tinged with apricot highlights and glowed in the still-present moonlight. Damn it, they needed better cloud cover. Luna took a sharp right through a series of huckleberry bushes, aiming for the headquarters, even though she had to twist and turn to keep the male wolves from catching them.

One of the Ravencalls tackled Francine and she snarled, getting out from under him and scrambling toward Luna.

The smell of the remains of the party filled the night, along with all the multiple scents in the forest. Even though the clouds were finally thickening, Luna could see easily.

The male wolves advanced, coming way too close.

Luna gasped. They weren't going to make it, so she turned a corner, paused, and howled as loudly as she could. Francine caught up with her and joined in, their voices rising, hopefully loud enough to catch somebody's attention.

Two of the male wolves came around from either side of the trees, flanking them.

Luna panicked and vaulted forward, right into the third male. Francine leaped behind her, and they both hit him, rolling off and then scrambling to their feet and running away.

The males were in excellent shape and pursued quickly, all three somehow jumping in front of the females. Luna skidded to a halt, her claws digging into the ground as Francine did the same. They both stopped, panting. The male wolves were far larger and had sharper fangs. The one in charge growled, the sound menacing. Luna glanced at Francine. In wolf form, the enemy could shred them to pieces.

She need to try and talk to them in human form, but before she could make the shift, the lead wolf snarled and charged her, teeth bared.

Before he could impact her, a male wolf came out of nowhere and intercepted him, hitting him full-on and rolling them both over and over.

Erik! Thank goodness. In wolf form, he was bigger than the lead attacker and twice as ferocious.

Francine sidled up to her, and they sat as Butch, Allen, Zelda, and Vernon all raced into view in wolf form. Zelda impacted the second wolf with a sound like a bat hitting a watermelon. Butch and Allen hit the third, and the wolf yelped as they went for his throat.

Her jaw aching and paws stinging, Luna shifted back to human form as Francine did the same.

"Are you okay?" Francine reached for her.

"I don't know. My jaw hurts. What about you? You're bleeding from the glass."

Francine peered down at her bare arms that now had mud in the wounds. "Yeah, I'm going to need some antiseptic."

Vernon looked at the fighting wolves and then shifted into human form. "Are you two all right?" he asked, panic in his voice.

"We're slightly injured but not dead." Luna accepted his hand and tried to stand while pulling Francine up. She almost told Vernon to shift back into wolf form to help out, but Erik had already decapitated his prey, as had Butch and Allen. Zelda, her claws out, slashed down the belly of the final attacker before ripping out his heart.

Luna gulped, trying not to vomit.

Erik shifted back into human form first—tall, broad, and dangerous-looking under the now barely visible moonlight. His medallion, the one he'd accepted as the Alpha, glowed in the light. It would stay with him in both human and wolf form, and nobody knew how. But there it was. He stalked toward her. "How badly are you hurt?" His hand cupped her jaw.

Pain rocketed through her head. "I don't think it's broken, but it's pretty sore," she said, her voice emerging funny since she tried not to move her jaw.

He looked over at Francine. "You're bleeding."

"I was cut coming through the window," Francine said.

"We need to get her back to my basement," Luna murmured. "I can clean out those wounds and make sure they're disinfected."

Zelda and the other two males shifted back into human form. "They're from the Ravencall Pack."

"I could smell them," Erik said. He looked at her. "Suggestions?"

Zelda glanced at the three dead bodies. "I say we toss them back into their territory."

"Agreed," Erik said, his gaze taking in Butch and Allen. "Let's put differences aside. You help Zelda for the night. We can fight with each other more tomorrow."

The two males nodded, blood still on their jawlines from biting through enemy throats.

Erik looked at Zelda. "I want a full investigation tomorrow on how they got into our territory. Somebody must have helped them."

"Not only that. They were really close to my cabin," Luna said. "They know where I live. They were looking for your potential mates."

Erik growled, and his gaze hardened even more. But he looked pale.

Luna moved closer to him. "Are you okay? Did you get wounded?" She inspected his naked body but didn't see any injuries.

"I'm fine," he said. "Zelda, take care of it."

"You've got it." Zelda motioned to the other two.

Erik wiped dirt off Luna's nose. "Let's go to your cabin." He glanced at Francine. "Do you need me to carry you?"

"No," the female said. "Thank you. I'm fine."

Vernon tucked a shoulder under her arm. "I'll help you walk. If you need to be carried, I'm here for you." He glanced at Luna. "What about you? Are you dizzy? I could carry you."

"I'm fine," she said, just as Erik's eyes rolled back in his head. She lunged for him in time to grab his head before it impacted a rock, sliding onto her knees to do so.

His entire body went limp as unconsciousness claimed him.

CHAPTER 22

*E*rik awoke to find himself in Luna's bed with sunlight streaming through the windows. His head pounded like he'd taken a baseball bat to the temple several times, and his mouth felt like he'd been sucking on cotton all night. "Luna?" he croaked.

"I'm here," she said, walking into the room. Her eyes were tired, and a massive purple and yellow bruise covered the right side of her jaw. "How are you feeling?" She pressed a hand to his forehead.

He forced himself to sit and then shut his eyes when the entire room spun around him. "What the hell happened?" Had he taken a blow to the skull?

She felt his ears and then ran both of her hands along the cords of his neck. "You were poisoned."

His eyelids shot up and he focused on her. "Excuse me?" he croaked.

She shook her head. "I took your blood last night and tested it. It's the same poison that was used to kill half our pack five years ago."

Fury heated him so fast he swayed and reached for the

bedcovers. The necklace of wolf and crescent moon heated against his skin. It stayed with him always—wolf or human form. How, he had no clue. But it felt like his. "How's the pack? Who's sick? Did they get anybody else?" he asked in rapid-fire succession, his tongue feeling twice the size of his mouth.

She pushed his shoulders almost too easily, keeping him in the bed. "Everybody's fine."

"How long have I been out?" he asked, his vision blurry.

"Two days."

He jolted. "Two days? I can't be out two days."

"Nobody knows." She hurriedly settled the bedclothes back around him. "Only Vernon, Francine, and I were here the other night when you dropped. They both helped me get you into bed."

He didn't remember any of that. "I became the Alpha that night." Why couldn't he think? His entire body felt like it had gone through a wood chipper, and he looked down to ensure he wasn't bruised and battered and cut.

"We told everybody you went to speak to the members of the other Stope Packs Coalition to make them aware of your new Alpha status as well as confirm their alliance with us."

"Okay, that was a good thought." He shook his head. "You're sure I was poisoned?"

"Positive. I did a blood test. I shot you full of vitamin D and a rhubarb, huckleberry, bone broth, and pine needle concoction I created that counters as much of the poison as I can. It took me a while to create it, but it did help people quickly heal the last time. At least the ones I could save."

Erik tried to think back to the night of the ceremony but his mind was a blank. "So, you're telling me I'm the only person who was poisoned?" Relief filled him so quickly he leaned back against the headboard.

"Yes. Vernon and Francine casually met with everybody in the pack under the pretense of taking stock of their homes to see if they wanted to build something new or repair what they have after you buy the mine."

He scratched his whiskered chin, his face feeling a little numb. "That's a good ruse. So, they met with everybody. Nobody was hurt?" The night started to come back to him. "Wait a minute. Didn't we kill three of the Ravencall Pack members?"

"Yes," she said. "Zelda left their bodies in Ravencall territory, and their Alpha has called for a discussion with you. As your Enforcer, Zelda informed him that you would get to him when you had time."

"That was a good answer," Erik muttered.

"Here." Luna handed him a glass of water. "You need to hydrate."

He gratefully took the glass and downed the entire thing. Then his stomach cramped.

Luna shook her head. "I've been thinking about it, and I don't see how they could have gotten close enough to you after the ceremony without any of us scenting them. I know wolves can mask their scent, but not that well. They couldn't have come into the center of our pack and poisoned you, right?"

"I would have known it was them," Erik said, which led to a very shitty conclusion. Somebody had helped them poison him. "When does the pack think I'm supposed to return?"

"We didn't give them a date, but I'm sure they're starting to wonder. It's been two days and you had big plans. I've been worried about what to say."

His vision finally cleared, and he took in her pale face with the monstrous bruise. A growl ripped out of him.

She held up a hand. "You killed the guy who hit me already." She sounded wary.

"I wish I could kill him again," Erik said, reaching out and gently touching the contusion. "Are you sure your jaw isn't broken?"

"I'm sure. It's just sore. I'll heal quickly. I'm so glad you heard us howling when those male wolves chased us. I tried hard to get to you, but they were too fast. We weren't going to make it to the lodge."

He loved how her brain worked. "You were smart to howl for help when you could. You both were," he said. "How is Francine? She was cut."

"She's fine. She took a shower here, and I gave her antiseptic for all her wounds. She and Vernon are doing a good job covering for you, but if you're up to it, I think you should make yourself be seen later today."

"I'm up to it." He squared his jaw. "Did the guys who tried to take you say anything before I got there?" He drew her toward him and settled her on his lap.

She snuggled in and pressed her face to the spot between his neck and shoulder. "They said they wanted the Alpha's mate. They didn't know if it was me or Francine, so they planned to take us both."

"And the Ravencall Alpha wants to speak with me?" Erik asked, his temper raking through him.

"I guess," Luna muttered, her lips soft against his skin, spiraling desire right to his groin, which seemed to be working fine, unlike his brain. "They sent word to Francine, your new administrator, and Zelda responded."

Both females were turning out to be excellent choices for their jobs. "They want to confirm that I've been poisoned."

"You just said you would have known if it was one of them," Luna protested, still not lifting away from him.

He held her tightly, trying to offer comfort. "I didn't say they weren't involved. It's likely they brought the poison to whoever is working with them from our pack." He'd met tons of folks that night and had put his drink down several times. In fact, many pack members had brought him drinks, as well. It was impossible to know when he'd ingested the poison.

She sighed heavily against him. "Now what do we do?"

* * *

LATE AFTERNOON, Luna finished filling water glasses for everybody around the conference table at headquarters. Erik sat at the head of the table, wearing a dark, long-sleeved T-shirt and jeans and looking refreshed after a shower and a shave. While still pale, his eyes remained clear.

Francine and Zelda sat on one side of the table with Vernon and Oakley on the other. She fought a grin. So far, Erik's Enforcers were Zelda, who had offered to mate him for the good of the pack, and Oakley, a high school kid who required permission from his mom to skip study hall in order to attend the meeting.

Erik caught her gaze and a half smile tugged at his lips. Apparently, he was thinking the same thing.

She took her seat at the other end of the table. This wasn't a council, but it was a nice inner circle. She liked that Erik was already surrounding himself with people she trusted and understood why he'd left Yago out of this discussion about him being poisoned.

Francine's phone buzzed, and she pulled it out of her briefcase to glance at the face. "Sorry, I have to make sure nothing crucial is going on."

"No problem," Erik said.

Her eyebrows raised. "Oh, it's the Alpha of the Ravencall Pack."

"Is it, now?" Erik drawled. "Put him on speakerphone and answer."

Francine placed her phone in the center of the table and tapped an icon. "Francine Goodhouse, Executive Director of Operations for the Copper Pack," she said cheerfully.

Luna grinned. She hadn't realized her friend had given herself a new title. By the cocking of Erik's head, neither had he.

"Goodhouse, this is Quasar from the Ravencall Pack. I'm done waiting. We both know your numbers are depleted, and I'm giving you and the remainder of your pack one day to vacate the territory before we kill you all. We're taking over the mine."

Francine looked at Erik. His smile was chilling, and Luna was suddenly very grateful he'd never looked at her like that.

"Why do you think our numbers are depleted?" he asked softly.

Silence came over the line. "Volk?"

"Yep, that's me. You sure you want to come at me again?"

Quasar didn't answer.

Erik leaned slightly toward the phone. "I sent three of your soldiers back in pieces the other day. I have no problem taking the rest of you out. I've been out of town meeting with the other Alphas from our coalition, and they have all reaffirmed our alliance. I make one call, and you'll have every soldier from four powerful packs descending on you. Am I making myself clear?"

Quasar chuckled. "I don't think you're in the position you think you are."

"You're wrong," Erik said curtly. "I killed your attackers and your wannabe kidnappers. If you send anybody else into my territory, I'm coming after you. Do you understand me?"

"We'll see." Quasar clicked off.

Erik waited until Francine hit the button to end the call. "I think that should take care of the Ravencalls for a while," he muttered. "They know our numbers are weak, and they're definitely talking to somebody in the pack." He looked at Zelda. "Who's applied to be the sheriff?"

She winced. "We've had several applications, but none I want to hire. Nobody has forensic experience like I do."

"You do?" Erik asked.

She nodded. "Yeah, I attended the police academy for humans a while back. It was fun. I needed something to do."

Erik looked thoughtfully at her. "Why don't you apply to be the sheriff? We need somebody with some experience. You're strong and smart. You'd be good at it."

A pleased flush covered her angular face. "You asked me to be your Enforcer and I'm honored."

That was sweet, but she could serve the pack in many capacities. Luna smiled her encouragement. "You'd make a wonderful sheriff."

Erik eyed Zelda. "You'd be excellent at either job. Which position would you prefer?"

"The sheriff," she said instantly. "I'd really like to serve as the sheriff."

Erik grinned. "You're hired. You need a deputy. I expect you to find somebody by the end of the week."

Oakley cleared his voice. "I'd still like to be an Enforcer."

Erik nodded. "Keep in mind that I asked because I think you'll make a good one, but you're not obligated. We're going to make some changes around here, and if you want to go off to college for a while, there'll still be a job for you when you return."

Oakley nodded, his eyes sparkling. "I appreciate that, but this is what I want. I'm happy going anywhere you want to train for this job as your Enforcer, and I'm happy to stay here and train, but this is what I want." His voice was young, but strong and sure.

Erik looked at him thoughtfully, respect in his eyes. "Then you're hired. You're it."

Oakley smiled. "I'll soon be eighteen. I won't have to ask for permission to be here."

Erik chuckled. "That will be nice, and your idea of training with others is a good one. I'll train you here for a while, but I wouldn't mind if we looked at a couple of other friendly packs for you to learn from. Everybody's fighting style is different."

"Sounds like fun," Oakley said, grinning. "You do need another Enforcer."

Erik scratched a small cut on his hand and looked around the table. "Zelda, your first job is to figure out who tried to poison me and how they did it. We need to make sure it doesn't happen to anybody else."

"Affirmative," she said. "I believe the poison came from the Ravencall Pack, but we can't prove it yet. It just makes sense because of their skills with making spices and other goodies to sell to humans. We should have left one of them alive the other night."

"You're right. We should have," Erik said. He glanced at Luna. "I was a little blinded by rage."

"Me, too," Vernon added.

Erik looked at Francine. "I want you to start scheduling interviews with Zelda and me with the poisoning suspects. I have a list, and I'm sure Zelda does, too. We need to start those interviews tomorrow."

"Sounds good. I'll call everybody today," Francine said, all efficient.

Erik turned to Vernon. "All right, so what do you have for me?"

Vernon shoved a stack of papers across the table toward Erik. "I determined everybody's percentage of mine ownership based on their positions and the time they spent working there. I gave more points for senior positions than newer ones. In addition, I calculated the time of everybody who's retired, and for those who are widowed, and gave them credit for their spouse's time."

"Good," Erik said. "I like that."

Vernon flipped a page over. "So, here's what each person would have percentage-wise. I still don't know what you want to pay for the mine, but I valued it at a fairly decent price. I conducted a detailed financial analysis that included an assessment of projected future earnings, operational efficiency, and a review of our reserves."

He looked down at the papers still in front of him. "There are also costs related to labor and new technology that needs to be purchased."

"All right," Erik said. "Give me a ballpark."

Vernon tugged on his tie. "I would say twenty-five million, basically because we're near bankruptcy."

Erik nodded. "All right. I'll make an offer to buy the mine for fifty million. Unfortunately, the bulk of that needs to go back into the mine, and I think we can only afford to pay out pack members maybe ten million."

Vernon nodded. "That's about what I was approximating, figuring you'd double it since you said you'd take care of everybody. That will help many folks, and their payments will range from five thousand to a hundred thousand. It's a good start. Then, if the mine is up and running again, we can increase wages."

Erik nodded. "Do the retired folks have retirement funds?"

"No."

Erik pinched the bridge of his nose. "All right, we'll have to take some money as soon as we can and create a retirement fund for those pack members so they have an income."

"Agreed."

Erik looked at Francine. "I need you to determine the needs of the people in relation to a working town. When Luna's not creating a doctor's office, hospital, or at least a trauma center for the pack, maybe she can help you."

Luna sat forward. "I'm creating a trauma center?"

"How about a small doctor's office or something where people can actually come by during regular hours unless there's an emergency?" he asked.

She clapped her hands together once. "I love that idea." She'd been trying to get Yago to do so for years, but he'd ignored her.

"Good," Erik said. "I'd like for you to consult with healers in the other packs and share information and knowledge. It's time we stopped pretending that we don't need doctors and possibly Western medicine." He was pale again, but she didn't say anything. After he had supper, she'd give him another injection of the elixir she'd created to deal with the rhubarb leaf poison.

Erik looked at Vernon. "You're doing a good job on this. I would like to see the amounts that are going to each of the pack members, and then I assume you have a list of whose homes we need to update or build first."

Vernon nodded.

Erik flattened his hands on the table. "I want this to be a pack project, meaning that anybody who can help build does so. We don't have the money to hire anybody, not that we'd let humans in. So, everybody's going to take ownership in working to get these houses up."

Luna grinned. "No handouts from you, huh?"

Erik shook his head. "No. Everybody works for what they get, but they receive fair compensation, and I think that building these homes together from cutting the wood to painting the interiors will be good for the pack overall."

"Agreed," Francine said, smiling brightly at him. "That's a great idea."

"Thanks." He read his watch. "All right, everybody get to work. We'll return here tomorrow to see what we've come up with. Anybody have an idea who I can hire as another Enforcer? I'd love to find somebody who is old enough to vote."

CHAPTER 23

*A*fter meeting with all able-bodied adults in the pack, Erik arranged for a security detail to circle the residential areas for the pack at all times. He had gotten enough volunteers that he didn't have to strong-arm anybody into doing so. They each reported to Zelda, who would alert Erik of any problems.

He quickly dialed Oakley.

"Hi," Oakley answered. "You need me?"

Erik should be letting the kid do his homework. "Not right now. I just had a quick question about this courting ritual of your pack. Yago mentioned something about my having to write a song?"

"Yeah. It should be about Luna. There are a couple of other things, I think, but I haven't paid a lot of attention to courtships yet, you know? I think there's something about baking and bending a knee or something goofy like that, and I think it's more important for you to do it all right because you're the Alpha. You should ask an adult, though. I'm still figuring out this dating stuff."

Erik felt like a dumbass. "Thanks, Oakley. Talk to you later."

He clicked off and made his way back to Luna's cabin, where she shot him full of the medicine she'd created. The burn on his hand had nearly healed. They quietly ate supper together, but she kept yawning.

"Why don't you get some sleep?" he asked, his skin itching to be outside. "I'm going to run for a while in wolf form and try to regain some of my strength."

She shook her head, her eyes wide. "I can't believe how strong you are already. Even for the people who survived the poisoning last time, it took weeks for them to be upright again. That Alpha blood must have some real juice in it."

"That's me. I'm juiced," he retorted, enjoying her smile. "Get some sleep, Luna. I'll be back in a few hours."

She nodded. "Sounds good."

He stood and carried the dishes to the sink, feeling an overwhelming urge to kiss her on the forehead before he left. They hadn't discussed their relationship any further, and right now, he needed a run. Even so, he gave in to the temptation and kissed her before heading out the door. Yeah, he enjoyed the surprised look in her eyes.

He tore off his clothes on the porch and jumped, none too gracefully, onto the ground, noting that he should probably fix her railing when he got a chance. Then he was running, slowly at first, then quicker as he regained strength, his blood pumping more normally through his veins.

Without really seeking a destination, he headed north and soon found himself in Silver Pack territory. The rotating guards caught wind of him almost immediately. A couple of them gave him a nod as he ran by.

It felt good to be closer to family again, although he had a new family now. A large one of five hundred people, for whom he was now responsible.

He reached his brother's home—the newly reconstructed-after-a-fire home—and barreled past it to Lost Lake and around to the far side where Gena Stone, Mia's mother, sat on her back porch. They'd become friends quite a while ago. He in wolf form, she in human, and she had no idea that he was actually Seth's brother.

She gleefully jumped up and down, her fifty-something-year-old face lighting. She'd highlighted her hair to a nice light blond recently, and her eyes were happy. "Wolf, I've missed you. Where have you been?"

He padded up the stairs and sat, letting her scratch behind his ears and feeling her delight.

"Oh, you're still so handsome. I've missed you. What have you been doing?"

He panted and tried to smile in wolf form.

She rolled her eyes and sat. "I thought maybe you'd found yourself a girl wolf."

He gave one short nod.

"Oh, you have? I'm so glad." She kissed his nose. "It's about time. You deserve a nice girl wolf."

"Gena, get in here. Dinner's ready, and I am going to burn it if you don't hurry up," Gena's sister, Dotty, yelled.

Gena's face fell. "She's been cooking all day, you know. I need to go in. You'll come back though, won't you?" When he nodded, she scratched his ears again. "Oh, I've missed you. I'm so glad you're back." She stood and hustled inside the cabin.

It was nice to be loved.

He turned and ran back around the lake, this time heading straight for his brother's house and halting outside before shifting back into human form. He walked up the stairs and paused before knocking. He'd grown up in the house because it had been his father's, and yet now he had to knock. Or at least he should.

"Come on in," Mia called out.

He scraped his bare feet off on the rug and opened the door. "Hey, it's Erik. I'm naked," he called out.

"When aren't you naked?" Mia returned from what sounded like the living room. "Go grab some clothes from your brother before you come in, would you?"

"Sure." Erik ran upstairs to the master bedroom and yanked on a pair of his brother's jeans before returning downstairs. Mia sat in the living room on a sofa, looking like she had a nice little baby bump going on. "Wow, you have a cute little belly," Erik said and then winced.

Mia looked up and laughed. "Smooth as ever, aren't you, brother?"

He grimaced. "Yeah, sorry." He leaned over and kissed her forehead.

Mia Stone, or rather soon-to-be Mia Volk, was one of his favorite people on the planet. A tough FBI agent, she'd fallen hard for his brother and now worked as the sheriff for the Silver Pack.

"How's it going?" She gestured to a chair for him to take.

He sat. "I was poisoned the other night, so not great."

Her eyes widened. A clip secured her long, brown hair in a cute ponytail, and the green of her eyes glowed through the night. Her scent of vanilla and lilacs filled the room, and Erik found comfort in it. He'd never had a sister, and he quite appreciated this one.

"Are you kidding me? Somebody poisoned you?" She started to push herself off the sofa.

"Whoa, wait a minute." Erik leaned over and gently placed a hand on her shoulder. "I'm fine. Sit down. Take a breath." The last thing he needed was for this baby to come early because he'd startled her.

"Take a breath? Someone poisoned you. Does Seth know?"

Erik kicked back. "No, he doesn't know. I came to talk to him. I can handle things myself."

She crossed her arms and stared at him. "Well, you do look okay. Have you mated Luna yet?"

He grinned. "She hasn't said yes."

"Have you asked her?"

"Not really. They have some sort of courting ritual that needs to be followed, but I'm not certain I have all of the requirements yet." He'd been a little busy with defending the territory from interlopers, stopping a kidnapping, and getting poisoned, but he really should get on that whole courting thing.

"Is she the one for you?"

He thought through the question. It was a serious one and deserved a thoughtful answer. "Yes."

Mia blinked. "Yes? That's it? Yes."

He shifted in the chair. "You asked me a question and I gave you the answer."

"Well, yeah, but tell me something romantic. Tell me you can't live without her. Tell me the good stuff, not just yes," she muttered.

Erik sensed his brother approaching the home before the door opened.

"Hey, Erik," Seth called out. "Please, tell me you put clothes on and didn't scare my wife again."

"Of course, I went looking for some pants," Erik muttered.

Mia winked. "You wouldn't have if I hadn't asked you to."

That was probably the truth. As a wolf shifter, he was accustomed to nudity, and Mia wasn't quite there yet.

Seth walked into the room, looked at him, and moved over to pick Mia up and place her on his lap as he took her seat on the sofa. "Those are my jeans."

"They look better on me," Erik retorted.

Seth kissed Mia's neck and then studied his brother. "No, they don't. They look a lot better on me."

Mia rolled her eyes. "I swear you guys are ten years old when you're together." She placed her hand over Seth's heart. "Did Erik tell you somebody poisoned him?"

Seth lost all expression of amusement. "Excuse me?"

Maybe this had been a bad idea, but he'd wanted to see Mia as well as his brother. "Yes, somebody poisoned me. We believe it was somebody from the Ravencall Pack, and I do not know how they got into the territory or who's working with them, but somebody is." He laid it all out there, and even now, his gut hurt. Slicing pain cut through his brain, but at least he was upright.

Seth listened quietly, holding the love of his life. "I think maybe it's time you told me the full truth," he said.

Mia looked from one to the other. "I'm going to go reheat an apple pie." She kissed Seth on the nose and stood awkwardly, her hand on her belly. Then she walked over to Erik and kissed him on the cheek. "It'll be ready when you two are finished chatting." With that, she walked from the room, both males watching her go as she shut the door.

"She looks well," Erik said.

"She isn't sleeping great sometimes because she's uncomfortable, but it's pretty exciting. You either trust me or you don't, and I want the full story."

Erik sat back and studied his brother. "I do trust you." With that, he finally started at the beginning and left nothing out, finishing with more truth. "They're my pack, Seth. My loyalty is to them. Tell me you're with me."

* * *

Luna's phone jarred her from a tumultuous sleep, and she fumbled for it. "Hello," she mumbled, glancing over to see the other side of the bed empty. Not that they'd agreed that Erik would move in with her, but she'd figured he'd return to her cabin after his run.

"Luna, it's Zelda. I need to find Erik."

The urgency in the female's voice had Luna sitting up in bed and rubbing her eyes. "He went for a run hours ago and hasn't returned. I have no idea where he is. What's going on?"

Zelda was silent for a moment. "Well, I could use you, too. You're the closest thing we have to a doctor. Come out to the west side of Moonlight Pond, would you?"

"Sure." Luna pushed out of the bed. "Do I need a medical kit? Do we have problems?"

"You don't need a medical kit, but please bring me clothing. We definitely have problems, and if you have a weapon, bring it with you. I have to go." Zelda clicked off.

What did that mean? Luna dashed to get dressed, threw her hair up in a ponytail, and grabbed her grandma's shotgun before running out to her car. In the after-midnight hour, the clouds had dissipated, leaving the moon high and bright. It easily illuminated her way, even without the headlights.

She arrived to find Zelda standing near a series of birch trees, naked in the moonlight. Jumping out of her vehicle, Luna grabbed the bag of clothes and hurried toward her friend, wincing from the piercing wind. "I did the best I could, but you're a foot taller than I am." The sweatshirt had been left by a male patient eons ago.

"Anything will help." Zelda accepted the overlarge sweatshirt and pulled it over her head. The arms fit, but the rib area was still too big. Sighing, she accepted the black leggings that looked like normal capris when she pulled them up. They were full-length on Luna.

"I had nothing in the shoe department," Luna said. "There's just no way."

"It's okay. I have pretty tough feet."

Luna looked around, her heart beating. "Why am I here? What's going on?"

"This way." Zelda turned and led the way between thigh-high bushes toward a secluded area on the rocks at the pond.

Luna followed her and then stopped short. "Oh, my God."

"Exactly," Zelda said. "We're about twenty-five miles north of Ravencall Pack territory."

Bile rose in Luna's gut as she looked at the dead male on the ground. Creeping closer, she angled her head to better see his face. "Oh, no. That's Butch Hollowgale."

Claw marks showed in almost every inch of his naked body. His ribs poked out, broken and destroyed, along with his breastbone. His heart was missing.

"Butch failed to report in from his security detail, so I traced what should've been his path and found him here," Zelda said, her tone hard.

Luna crouched to better study the body. "He must have been in wolf form when he was attacked." While having a rudimentary medical knowledge, she had never studied forensics, not that she needed to. There was no doubt that at least one wolf, if not several, had taken out the shifter.

"Tell me Erik will be here soon," Zelda said. "I'm not exactly sure what to do."

"I texted him but haven't heard back," Luna murmured, brushing Butch's hair back from his mangled face. She hadn't liked the guy, but nobody deserved to die like this. She sniffed the air. "I know that smell."

"It's the Ravencall wolves," Zelda confirmed.

Yeah, Luna had learned it well the other night while being chased by three of them. "Do you have any idea what time this happened?" The blood still looked fairly fresh but had congealed around the body.

Zelda sniffed the air. "It's been at least two hours, but probably no more than that. He was out on patrol, and since our numbers are so slim, I had to send a few of our better fighters solo. I didn't think anybody could take Butch down like this."

"Me, neither. But if they had a kill squad of at least three wolves, even Butch couldn't have fought back." Luna gently grasped his hand and rolled it over. "I have no way of knowing without his claws extended if he got in any good hits during the fight."

"Of course, he did," Zelda said. "He was a fighter. And what would the blood tell you? Nothing. I'm sure he fought back, but they won. If they're going to try to take us out one by one, we need to make sure all security details have at least two, if not three, wolves. But we don't have those numbers, Luna."

Luna pressed a palm to her head. How would she tell Haney and the kids that Butch was dead? She still didn't know what kind of marriage they'd had, and it really hadn't looked good, but it would still be a difficult discussion.

"How many people do we have to bury this month?" Zelda asked sadly, looking around, no doubt scouting for threats.

"I don't know."

"Did Butch have any family other than Haney and the children?" Zelda asked. "I don't think he did, but there are a lot of connections in this pack."

"No," Luna said, shaking her head. She'd conducted a full genealogy chart of the entire living pack members when she researched the poison and tried to figure out why some people died, and others hadn't. The death count seemed arbitrary after all her work.

A rustle sounded through the brush and then Erik padded into view as a wolf. He took in the scene and then shifted into his human form.

"Is that Butch Hollowgale?" He looked closer.

Luna reached into the pack that had held clothing for Zelda and tossed over Erik's jeans. "Yeah. I figured you'd come in wolf form if you received my text."

He quickly stepped into them and walked closer, dropping to his haunches to study the body. "Looks like it was one hell of a fight." Fury darkened his cheekbones to an angry red. "The Ravencalls came into our territory again."

Zelda nodded. "We need to let the family know, as well as the pack. If they're going to come in like this, nobody's safe."

"Agreed," Erik said, looking around. "We'll have to load his body into your trunk, Luna. It's all we have. Then let's go make the notification to the family. Please, call whoever you think might be helpful to stay with Haney and the girls afterward."

Luna hadn't thought to bring plastic sheeting. "All right."

Erik looked at the new sheriff. "Zelda, get Allen Bushbalm into my office, conference room, or whatever that room is. I want him locked down until I can figure out the best way to respond to the Ravencalls. I don't need him going off half-cocked and also getting killed."

"On it," Zelda said, tearing off the clothing and tossing it back at Luna. "I'm going to run in wolf form if you don't mind."

"I don't mind, but help us with the body first."

Zelda looked down at her nude body. "I guess I could have waited a moment," she muttered before walking over and grabbing the shredded mess of Butch's legs. "I'll take the ankles. You take the shoulders."

Erik grabbed the shoulders and, together, they lifted the male and started carrying him through the forest. Luna ran ahead and opened her back hatch. She didn't have a tarp or anything to deal with the blood, but she'd worry about that later.

As they stored the deceased male inside, having to pretty much fold him in two, her heart hurt for Haney and the girls. "I'll come with you to speak with Haney," she said, looking at Erik. "You shouldn't have to do that alone."

CHAPTER 24

*E*rik drove Luna's rig toward the main headquarters, with Zelda in the passenger seat. Haney had become so distraught that Luna had decided to stay the night with her.

"That sucked," Erik said grimly, his blood pumping sluggishly again. He'd survived the poisoning better than most, but maybe he didn't get a full dose of the toxins. Or perhaps it was his Alpha blood or even the concoction Luna kept shooting into his veins. Either way, he needed to regain all his strength sooner rather than later.

Zelda nodded, looking out the window. "I know. I think their marriage also sucked, to be honest, but I didn't want the guy dead. I just wanted him to get a grip."

Erik avoided looking at the dead body in the rear of the vehicle. He'd only been in the territory for less than a week and they'd already had multiple funerals. "We'll need another funeral pyre."

"I'll take care of it," Zelda said wearily, looking out at the trees flying by.

Erik peered up to notice the sun coming up over the mountains. "This probably isn't the right time to ask, but what are the courting rituals for this pack?" He'd looked through the grimoire without much success and just needed a game plan.

She turned to him, her dark eyes sparkling, and a slight smile on her lips. "It's definitely not the time, but somebody should tell you."

He glanced at her and kept driving. "Well?"

"Oh, they're silly, but I guess it's good to make intentions known," Zelda murmured. "There are three elements to courtship within the pack. The first, you have to prove you're a good provider and thus bring food to her that you have prepared. Food must include berries, baked pies, and home-made ice cream."

He looked at her. "Are you serious?"

She shrugged. "I don't know. It has something to do with a contest years ago, and now it's considered bad luck if you don't bake pies and make ice cream. It's silly, but it is what it is. You need to present her with all of those on the same night, and you have to sing a song you've written for her at the same time. Publicly."

"I've heard. What kind of song?" Erik asked, wishing for a good fight right now.

"Something slow, like a ballad."

"I can't sing," Erik muttered.

Zelda leaned forward and turned up the heat in the SUV. "That's too bad. That's the deal, and it's more important for you as Alpha. Since you're the strongest wolf in the pack, you have to show you can bend a knee to your mate. You have to wear a loincloth, as well. At least you don't have to be naked since kids will be present."

For fuck's sake. "Fine. What else?"

"Then you have to present her with a hand-designed copper bracelet. I've seen plenty of guys burn their fingers trying to maneuver the metal. You'll have to go up to the mine and heat the material. The good news is, there are molds up there you can use for a nice design."

"I'd rather do that than sing and hand out ice cream publicly," Erik said, shaking his head. "This is ridiculous." It was too bad the Silver Pack didn't have courtship rituals like this. It would've been hilarious to see Seth go through such obstacles to gain Mia's trust. "How come the female doesn't have to do anything?"

Zelda waved a hand in the air. "These are old traditions. What do you want? I didn't write them."

He pulled up to the main lodge to see the lights blazing from inside and several rigs in the parking area. "We'll talk about this later." He jumped out of the vehicle and strode up the steps with Zelda on his heels. They walked inside to where Yago sat at the conference table, next to Allen Bushbalm. Vernon Bushbalm leaned on the counter, pouring himself a cup of coffee, and Oakley stood at the far wall, his arms crossed, looking way too young to deal with any of this.

"I got everybody here," Oakley said, his voice cracking.

Erik had a momentary pause. What was he doing having a seventeen-year-old kid be his Enforcer? His expression must have showed because Oakley stood taller.

"I'm in all the way," he said, his young voice sure. "You need me at your back."

An unfortunately true statement.

"Why did you insist we meet?" Allen asked, his voice a low growl. "It's dawn, and I'm about done with this. Your junior Enforcer here insisted we come down."

Yago clasped his hands together on the table. "I appreciate being included, but it is awfully early."

Zelda stood by Erik's side and faltered before looking down at her feet.

"What's going on?" Vernon asked.

"You might want to sit down," Erik said quietly. He had no idea if both of the Bushbalm brothers had been close to Butch, or if just Allen had. If nothing else, Vernon had probably known the dead shifter his entire life.

Vernon turned more fully to face him, putting his coffee mug on the counter. "I don't need to sit down. What's happening?"

Erik swallowed. "We found Butch's body a few hours ago in the woods."

Allen jumped to his feet, clenching his fists.

Vernon wildly shook his head. "No, that can't be. Butch is one of the best fighters in the whole pack. What do you mean, you found his body?"

"He was killed, slashed open, and the scent of the Ravencall wolves was all around," Erik said.

"This is bullshit," Allen burst out. "That's it. I'm taking the fight to them." He moved toward the door.

Zelda immediately blocked him.

"Get out of my way or I will hurt you," Allen hissed.

"Hold it," Erik said, his voice lowering to pure Alpha. "We will get retribution, but we're not going to be stupid about it. They're waiting for us to do something dumb and probably have multiple traps set for us. We need to think, Allen, not act."

Allen's hand shook as he pushed it through his thick brown hair. "He was my best friend. I should have been with him. We shouldn't have been scouting the poorer areas of the pack."

"We protect all areas," Zelda said quietly. "Now, sit down."

Allen glared at her but took a seat.

Oakley swallowed, and relief filtered through his eyes.

Erik turned to Yago. "Yago, you're senior advisor. Advise."

Yago sat back in his chair, looking older than he had even the day before. "I don't know. My solution was to get you into the pack, and it sounds like you've had some good ideas to help so far."

"I need more," Erik said. But the only thing he'd come up with was something no one would like. Still, there wasn't much of a choice. "Listen, I saw my brother earlier today, and the Silver Pack is willing to greatly expand their security details to cover our northern side."

There was a good one hundred and forty miles between the Silver Pack and the Copper Pack headquarters, and it was kind of Seth to work his people that hard. "But it's temporary," Erik added. "Unfortunately, the Ravencalls are on our southern border. As you know, the Slate Pack is south of that, and they're making threats, as well. Seth is going to give Philip a call, but he sounded mighty determined. We need protections in place, and we need more bodies now."

Allen stared at the table as if in a daze, and shock and sadness wafted from Vernon.

Erik looked at Yago. "I can only think of one way. Well, there are several ways, but only one I like. We can either join another pack, which means I'm out, and who knows what'll happen to the mine or the current members, or—"

"Or what?" Oakley whispered.

Erik took a deep breath. "There are several bands of wolves grouped to the east of us. They don't bug us, and we don't bug them. They aren't a pack because they don't have an Alpha. We can ask them to join us."

"Join us?" Allen's head jerked back. "Are you kidding me? We can't have an influx of a bunch of different wolves." His fist slammed into the table.

"We don't have a choice," Erik said. "Your grand scheme of waiting a hundred or two years and rebuilding the pack isn't going to work. We've got the Ravencalls killing soldiers, and we have the Slate Pack all but declaring they want the copper mine.

I could force an internal war between the four packs in our coalition, but there's no guarantee we'd win, and what then? It's chaos. I'm telling you, we need to rebuild our pack, and we need to do it now. If you don't like it, you can leave."

He showed no softness or mercy.

Zelda cocked her head. "You know, it's not a bad idea. More males than females died from the poisoning, and most bands around this area are heavy in males. We could start a dating service or something like that."

Erik was more interested in security, but matings and marriages sounded like a good incentive. "All right."

Zelda's nostrils flared. "We still haven't figured out who helped the Ravencalls poison us. I would like to start an investigation right away, but we've been kind of busy with everything else." She looked at Allen. "But you're here now, aren't you?"

He reared up, his face turning a mottled red. "What are you saying?"

"I'm saying you were dating a female from the Ravencall Pack, back when we were poisoned. Right?"

Allen slowly began to stand.

Yago grabbed his arm and tried to tug him down. "Allen, just answer the questions."

Allen glared at Zelda and then at Erik. "I can't believe you're accusing me of something on the night my friend died."

Zelda walked over and poured herself a cup of coffee, placing a hand on Vernon's shoulder as she went. "I'm not accusing you of anything. I'm asking you a question. Were you or were you not dating a member of the Ravencall Pack five years ago?"

"I was," Allen snapped. "Her name was Ursa, and I liked her. I mean, it was nothing serious, and as you know, I fully intended to mate Luna." His gaze remained hard as he looked at Erik. "Still do."

Something sharp and dark rose within Erik and he set his stance. "That's not going to happen."

"Oh, we'll see about that. It's up to her, isn't it?" Allen asked, kicking back with his upper lip curling.

"Yeah, we'll just do that," Erik muttered. "Was Ursa with you the night of the poisoning?"

"I saw her earlier that day, and she didn't give me any poison. She did not attend the get-together. She's not that kind of person, man. She had nothing to do with it."

Vernon frowned and leaned in as if focusing for the first time. "What happened to your neck?"

"Nothing," Allen said.

Zelda stepped closer, even though Allen was across the table, and angled her head. "You have scratch marks."

Erik looked closer and noticed a bruise on Allen's clavicle. "What happened to you?"

"Fine," Allen said, exploding. "I met with Ursa earlier tonight and we got together. We both like it rough. God, it's none of your business. None of you."

"I'd like to speak with her," Erik said tersely.

Allen blinked. "Whatever. I'll bring her in tomorrow, but don't tell Luna. Though, her Alpha probably won't let her come into our territory, considering they just killed one of our soldiers." His voice cracked on the end.

It'd be nice to interview Ursa, and Erik wasn't opposed to a kidnapping. They had to figure out where the poison was derived from before it got used on anybody else. He still felt like crap, and he was stronger than most males. "Have her here tomorrow by four p.m. I don't care what you have to do." He glanced at Zelda. "You and Vernon can get Butch's body prepared for the funeral tonight. Please, spread the word."

"Another funeral," Yago said sadly, shaking his head. "There have been far too many."

That was the sad truth. Erik jerked his chin toward Oakley. "You ready for a road trip?"

The kid straightened even taller. "Yeah. Where are we going?"

"We're going to go find new members for the pack," Erik said grimly.

"Okay, but I'll need a note to get out of school."

CHAPTER 25

*L*una finished placing the wreaths of flowers around the newly constructed funeral pyre and then straightened, stretching her back. "I think this looks nice, Haney."

Haney nodded, her face pale in the morning light. "It'll make for a good send-off." She dusted dirt off her jeans and crossed around to stand next to Luna. In her oversized blue plaid shirt with her hair pulled back, she looked even younger than usual.

"I'm really sorry about Butch." Luna slid an arm around her friend's waist.

"Thanks. I am, too," Haney said. "He wasn't the nicest, but we had four kids together, and a part of me will miss him. I always figured he'd get better, you know? Maybe when Allen became the Alpha, which obviously isn't going to happen now."

Luna sighed and tugged her friend closer. "I always thought maybe he'd become a little nicer, as well. He never hurt you, did he?"

"No, not physically," Haney said. "But like I said, he wasn't the nicest of guys to be around. I am going to miss him, though."

She gingerly touched one of the small branches that had been woven together to create the platform.

Friends would bring the body in later tonight. Right now, it was being held somewhere cool down by one of the ponds.

A truck barreled to a stop in front of the lodge, and Allen Bushbalm jumped out. He scanned across the expanse of parking area and then steeled his shoulders, heading their way. Today, he wore a green flannel tucked into black jeans with his battered boots. "The pyre looks nice," he said softly when he arrived.

"Thanks." Luna kept ahold of Haney.

Allen shook his head. "I'm so sorry. I should have been with him. I can't believe anybody took him down." He stared at the empty platform.

Luna wanted to offer comfort, but considering she'd kicked the guy in the nuts just a couple of days ago, she didn't move.

Allen reached out to gently place a hand on several of the branches. Purple bruises marred his cracked knuckles.

"What happened?" Haney asked.

"I punched a couple of trees," he said, looking over his shoulder at them. "It didn't help." He turned to fully face them. "The new sheriff is on me about my relationship with Ursa and the poisoning. You know I would never poison this pack, right?"

Luna studied him. She didn't think he would, yet he had really wanted to be the Alpha. Taking out half the pack had certainly left them weakened and susceptible. If Erik hadn't agreed to step up, Allen very likely would have become the pack leader. She kept those thoughts to herself.

Haney shook her head. "We know you didn't do anything. Are you going to bring Ursa in to talk to the sheriff?"

"Yes. I sent word. She should be in our territory later tonight." He studied Luna. "She and I are over. You know that right?"

Luna forced a smile. "You and I are never going to happen. You know *that*, right?"

His face darkened. "Luna, I don't care that you're damaged."

"Damaged?" she said, drawing back. "There's nothing damaged about me." Sure, she might not be able to have kids, but that didn't mean she was damaged. "I promise you, Erik and I will figure out our future." Right? He had to have feelings like she did.

She wanted Alpha blood in the bloodline more than anybody else, but modern science might be able to help there, as well. "If you and this Ursa have a chance, you should take it." She meant every word. Perhaps the right person could file off Allen's rough edges.

He rolled his eyes. "I swear, I don't know what's happened to this pack. Half of us are gone, the best soldiers are dead, and Erik Volk has become the Alpha. I'm not going to let this stand." He glared at Luna. "My brother thinks you're just an angel. You and that Francine Goodhouse. I think neither of you cares about this pack. This is what you wanted all the time. You wanted the power."

Luna cut a look at Haney. Power? Yeah, that's the last thing she wanted.

"It's been real nice seeing you, Allen," Haney said softly. "Have a good day. We'll meet up tonight for the funeral."

He glowered but turned on his boot and stomped back to his truck.

Haney shook her head. "I can't wait to meet this Ursa."

"Come on, let's grab some coffee in the lodge." Luna took Haney's hand to walk across the clearing to the front steps and up inside to the quiet conference room. "It's not always the freshest of coffee, but if you add a sprinkle of cinnamon, it isn't bad." She poured them two cups.

Haney fell into a chair. "It was nice of the Santerbury sisters to watch the kids today since none of them wanted to go to school."

"I don't blame them." Luna slid the coffee toward her friend before taking her seat.

Haney leaned forward. "Is it true that Erik has gone out to seek more members to join our pack?"

Wow. Word really got around, didn't it? "Yes, it's true. We need numbers, and it would be nice to have an infusion of new blood, don't you think?"

Running footsteps sounded outside and then through the lodge as Izzy barreled into the room, her hair a wild mess and her eyes wide.

Haney stood and pulled her daughter in for a hug. "What are you doing?"

Izzy shook her head. "I just heard the news that Erik went out to get us all mates. Is that true? Do we have to mate people from other packs or bands?"

Luna coughed. "No, that's not true." She shook her head. "I can't believe the rumors that get started in this place sometimes."

Izzy's gaze caught on the coffee. "Ooh, fresh coffee." She hurried toward it.

Her mother frowned. "Since when are you drinking coffee?"

"Every chance I get." Izzy filled herself a cup and took a place at the table as if she belonged right there. "I have to tell you, that is a huge relief. I did not want to be handed off to some dude from a band from the middle of the state."

Her mother dropped back into her chair, her mouth agape.

Luna covered a smile and tried really hard not to laugh. "Did you really believe that nonsense?"

Izzy took a deep drink of the coffee and pleasure lifted her lips. "I don't know. Erik's done some unconventional things, and we do need numbers. Everybody will be happy to know they don't have to mate somebody."

"Oh, my goodness." Luna put her fingers to her eyebrows and pushed. "Izzy, that's insane. We are hopefully getting some new people into the pack—if anybody says yes—which will give us strength in numbers and more workers for the mine. We need to dig ourselves out of this hole, and copper is doing well right now."

Izzy cupped both hands around her mug. "I heard that Oakley didn't go to school today because he was actually serving as Erik's Enforcer on this trip. Is that true?" The girl's eyes sparkled.

Ah, a young crush. How lovely.

"Yes, it's true," Luna said. "Oakley's become very important to the protection of the Alpha. I think he has a lot of training to undergo, but he sure seems to want the job."

Izzy bit her lip and looked down at the table. "I like that about him. But I also heard a rumor that Erik was going to let us go off to college or trade school for a short time. Is that true?"

Luna would love for the kids to have exposure in the human world. "I haven't heard any concrete plans about that, but I know that his former pack is in the process of creating avenues for wolf shifters to attend college or trade school or even apprenticeships for four years before returning to the pack. I'm sure Erik would entertain a similar program if all of you are interested."

Izzy shrugged. "I don't know. I feel like I might be interested, but right now I'm not sure. I have time to decide."

Haney took a drink of her coffee. "Is Yago okay with all of these changes?"

Luna tapped her fingers on the table. "I'm not sure, but they're all needed. We really do need to enter the new century, and we're in dire straits. If we don't get our numbers up, we'll be attacked again and again until there's just nothing left of us. And the mine has real value. We just have to work it right."

Haney nodded. "I agree. I'm not quite sure what I'm going to do now that Butch is gone."

"We'll figure it out." Luna patted her hand. "I promise. I'm sure there'll be some sort of benefits from the mine, and who knows, perhaps we'll start opening businesses again if we get enough people into the pack. It's an idea."

Haney rolled her eyes. "I don't know what I'd do. I'd have to think about it. I'd need a couple more years to make sure all the kids are in school, I think."

"Mom, you're a great artist," Izzy said. "I don't understand why you don't paint more. I mean, you don't have to sell your paintings and drawings just to pack members. We do have the internet these days, you know?"

Haney brightened. "That's true. I'm not exactly sure how to do that."

Izzy waved a hand in the air. "Don't worry about it. You just paint and draw, and I'll create a website for you."

For the first time, Haney's eyes started to sparkle like they had years ago. "Your father didn't like me working as an artist."

"He's gone," Izzy said abruptly. She glanced at Luna and paled. "I mean, I'm sorry he's gone because he was my dad and I loved him, but it would be nice to see my mom succeed." She looked at her mother. "You are an amazing artist. We've studied art in school, and I'm telling you, we could make a ton of money with your paintings. Plus, you don't even have to go anywhere to sell them. We'll just do it online."

Haney pursed her lips. "It would be nice to have something positive to focus on, wouldn't it?"

"It would," Luna agreed, her mind moving to thoughts of Erik.

How was he? She had given him another syringe full of the elixir to shoot into his leg, but she didn't have a lot of confidence that he'd remember to do it. His strength had returned much faster than she would've expected. It was impressive, really. Even so, he and a seventeen-year-old kid were going into what could possibly be enemy territory, just the two of them. She couldn't help but worry.

"Luna?" Haney asked.

Luna jolted. "What? Oh, sorry. I was lost in my head."

Izzy snorted.

Haney cleared her throat. "Yeah, I thought so. I asked you about Erik. Are you finally going to give in and date the guy?"

Heat climbed into Luna's face. "You know I want to do what's best for the pack."

"Oh, shut up," Izzy said, and then the girl caught herself. "I'm sorry, I didn't mean to say to shut up."

"No, shut up," her mother agreed. "Come on. It's obvious that you have feelings for him. He definitely has feelings for you and isn't hiding it. Stop worrying about the pack. Don't be foolish."

Izzy nodded. "Seriously, he's hot. If you don't grab him, somebody else will."

"Izzy," her mother admonished. Then she looked at Luna. "But she's not wrong. Plus, he needs somebody here, somebody just for him, and I think that's you. You know you love him. I can tell."

Luna gasped. "What do you mean? He's only been in the territory for a week."

"But he kidnapped you months ago," Izzy objected. "We know you've been back and forth to their territory to see Mia, and we know you've seen Erik, too. I may be young, but I'm not stupid."

Luna grinned. "There's a lot to think about."

"No, there isn't. There's just the two of you," Haney said. "Believe me, life changes way too quickly. Don't miss out on it."

Luna swallowed. It was a good point, and she definitely had feelings for Erik. Strong ones, and right now he was most certainly in danger.

CHAPTER 26

Smoke still hung heavy in the air as Erik and Oakley made their way into more central Washington.

"Whoa, the forest fires were bad this year, weren't they?" Oakley asked as he jumped out of the truck.

"Yeah," Erik muttered, stepping out and noting the large gate to the Thunderhoof Corporation. It was good cover in case humans scouted around. "Something feels off." He shut his door.

Two males met him before they could walk through the gate, both tall and broad with blond hair and smelling like fresh grass. Interesting scent for wolf shifters.

"Can we help you?" the first guy asked, his tone polite.

"I'm Erik Volk. I'm here to see, I believe, Konrad Vix. Is he still in charge of this corporation?" Konrad was the only name mentioned in the state database.

The first guy nodded. "Erik Volk as in Volk Mining?"

"That would be me." Erik met the guy's gaze directly.

His buddy shrugged. "Come on in. If you're here to steal more from us, it's going to be a sad day."

Erik paused. "Steal from you? What are you talking about?"

"We were attacked," the first guy said. "Half our cattle were stolen, and the majority of our apple trees were burned down. That's not even close to the full damage." His shoulders slumped.

"By whom?" Oakley asked, stepping up to Erik's side.

"We don't know. Best guess is it was the Ghostwind Pack. They've been trying to move into our territory for years, and this time they succeeded," his friend said grimly. "Come on, then. We have a truck over here."

Erik nodded to Oakley, and they walked over to the truck, stretching into the back seat. "Tell me about your operation," Erik said.

"I'd rather not," one of the blond guys muttered.

"Fair enough." The feeling of desolation was digging into Erik's skull, and he wondered about the wisdom in making this approach.

They drove by acres of fields with few cattle and then several torched orchards before reaching a steel building that looked more like a shop.

"Welcome to headquarters," the first guy said wearily.

Erik tuned into his surroundings and didn't feel one ounce of threat. This place was downright depressing. He exited the truck and walked to the front entrance, knocking on the metal door.

"Come on in," a male voice called out.

Erik looked at Oakley, who just quirked an eyebrow. So, he opened the door and stepped inside a large garage-like area with a couple of desks pushed to the corners, and farm equipment sprawled across the ground.

A man looked up from putting an engine together, sitting on a tarp on the ground, grease on the side of his face. "Hi, who are you?"

Erik looked around, surprised that he didn't see any Enforcers. "I'm Erik Volk."

The guy reached for a wrench. His hair was a light blond, and his eyes were a piercing black. "Volk, as in Volk Mining?"

"Yeah, I get that a lot," Erik said. "Word might not have reached you yet, but I just became the Alpha of the Copper Pack."

"No kidding? I'm Konrad Vix, which you obviously know already." The guy sat back on his haunches. "How did one of the silver mining Alphas end up with the Copper Pack?"

"It's a long story," Erik said. "But I'm here to make you an offer."

Konrad stood, a good six-foot-five and broad like a farmer. His face was rugged, and his jawline hard. "An offer? For what? Burned-out orchards and a few dairy cattle? I accept."

Erik leaned back. "I'm not kidding."

"Neither am I," Konrad muttered. "You can give me the money. I'm buying weapons. You can have the land, and I'm going after the Ghostwind Pack."

Erik had never dealt personally with the Ghosts. "Are you sure they're the ones who attacked you?"

"Yeah, they took out most of our holdings and slaughtered our cattle. I've heard rumors that they and the Ravencall Pack are going to combine. If that happens?" Konrad shook his head. "We don't have the resources to fight them. We just don't."

"What do you have?" Erik asked, noting Oakley scouting the building and then positioning himself near the only door. The kid had great instincts as an Enforcer.

"Does it matter? We're done. We're moving somewhere else. Maybe we'll learn to fish." Konrad tossed the wrench down near the engine.

"Our pack was cleared out about five years ago and we're at half the number we need to be," Erik said suddenly.

Konrad blinked. "That's a weakness you probably shouldn't brandish around here, Volk."

"No shit, Konrad," Erik retorted. "Like I said, I'm here to make you an offer."

The male wiped his greasy hands off on a rag and then shoved it to hang out the back pocket of his jeans. "This just got interesting."

Erik liked him immediately. "We'd like for your band to join our pack."

"Why, you need worker bees?" Konrad drawled.

"I do," Erik said. "I also need soldiers and bodies. We have acres upon acres in our territory to the north that could hold both cattle and dairy cows, which I believe you'd like. In addition, we have plenty of land for apple orchards, wheat production, and even potatoes. It's my understanding that if you can grow the feed for the cattle and the dairy cows, we can make a lot more money."

Vix cocked his head. "Somebody did their research on my operation. We had a good little co-op going here. You have enough money to invest in this grand scheme of yours?"

"I do," Erik said. "I'll be broke afterward, almost completely because I bought the mine, but I will hire you and anybody else you want, and give you a good working wage. We can create what you had here. But you will be full pack members and take an oath to that effect."

Konrad slowly nodded. "You sure you have the space to do all this?"

"I'm absolutely positive. Space is what we've got. People is what we don't."

"What's the catch?" Konrad asked.

"Full loyalty," Erik instantly said. "You're currently in a band, not a pack led by an Alpha because either you and your followers were not team players or because you grew up outside the packs. I don't care. But in the Copper Pack, we're a team, and there may be some fighting with the Ravencalls, and apparently, the Ghostwind Pack, coming up. So, training will be key. What are your demographics?"

Konrad studied him for a moment and looped his thumbs in his pockets. "My demographics? Got about a hundred able-bodied adults, and fifty to sixty older folks who have a lot of wisdom and knowledge but aren't able to help much in the fields. And the rest are kids, maybe sixty of them. It's a good group of people, but we never really considered joining a pack."

"Yeah. Well, this is a full invitation," Erik said. "No strings. I'll set you up, give you a good wage, and your people can integrate fully in the businesses and the pack in the future."

"If we do that, I want part ownership of all farming, ranching, and harvesting opportunities," Konrad said. "I'm bringing the knowledge and a few good assets while you're buying the rest. Twenty-five percent for my group."

Erik studied him. "That sounds fair." He reached out a hand, and they shook.

"All right," Konrad said. "I need to speak with everybody in our corporation. I'll let you know who's joining. Not everybody will."

"I'll take what I can get," Erik said honestly. He cleared his throat. "Any chance you have anybody who'd make a good Enforcer?" He glanced at Oakley. "The kid could use some backup."

* * *

It TURNED out the farming group had already begun preparations to leave the area, many sensing that another attack was imminent. So, Erik and Oakley stayed and helped load the remainder of what they could, using trailers, flatbeds, and trucks. It was sad that an entire community's belongings could be boxed and shipped so quickly, but when the enemy was breathing down your neck, there wasn't much of a choice.

Konrad separated the beef cattle and dairy cows into multiple trucks and then gathered what chickens and sheep they had left. It wasn't many. He approached Erik. "The sprouts and everything we'll need for new fields will be in another truck, and any farming equipment we still have will come last."

Erik nodded. "We don't have houses built yet, but everybody who wants one can design their own. We'll build them together as a group."

"I like that, but many of us don't want to be in the middle of a town."

Oakley snorted. "Like we have a town, dude." He paused. "I mean, we don't have a town. Many people live in cabins scattered throughout the territory or in a couple of subdivisions."

Erik nodded. "I plan on building two more subdivisions, and then I would like to keep the smattering of cabins within a contained enough area that we can patrol. They don't have to be too close, and you don't have to see your neighbors, but I figure you and most of your workers will want to live near the farmland."

Konrad nodded. "Exactly. Though we have many members who have no interest in farming. They might want to work in your mine or in some sort of security detail after they learn how to fight. Only a few of us really know how to fight now."

"That's next on the agenda." Erik noted the apples and seeds being piled into another truck. It'd be nice to have an apple orchard. Even the Silver Pack didn't have that.

Movement sounded, and a female walked around one of the trucks, her hands full of ledgers. "Konrad, I have most of the records for the last five years, but I can't find anything before that."

Erik stilled. "Emily?"

The female jerked and looked at him. "Excuse me?"

She was the spitting image of Emily Nightsom. Well, except Em was a good six feet tall, and this female had to be five-six, tops. But the wild, curly blond hair and sparkling black eyes were the same. The bone structure was shockingly similar, and even their scents were close.

Erik blinked again. "I don't understand. Who are you?"

The female shifted the binders in her hands. "I'm Nadia Hodge. Why?" She frowned and looked at Konrad as if seeking answers.

"I'm Erik Volk, the new Alpha of the Copper Pack." He studied her again, trying to find an answer.

"We've been told who you are." She took a step back. "Why are you looking at me like that?"

He couldn't look away. "Because you're the spitting image of Emily Nightsom, one of my good friends."

"Ex-fiancée," Oakley said helpfully.

Erik shot him a look. "Not really. We're just friends."

Oakley shrugged. "She's hot, dude. Well, she's not as pretty as Luna." He scratched his chin. "That's not true. They're both freaking gorgeous."

Erik watched him. "Are you done having a conversation with yourself?"

Oakley flushed. "Oh yeah, sorry." He straightened as if remembering he was the lone Enforcer in the area. "You do look just like Emily." He smiled.

Nadia shifted her stance on dirty white tennis shoes. "I don't know Emily, and I don't know why I would look like her. Everybody has a doppelganger, correct?"

Erik had absolutely no idea, yet even this female's voice sounded like Em's. If they were on the phone, he might not be able to tell the difference. "This is definitely a mystery to be solved."

"There's no mystery." Nadia turned back toward the trucks. "I'm in the green truck, and I have all the records I can find. We're still missing a few."

Konrad pressed a hand to his head as if a headache were

trying to kill him. He rubbed his right temple. "A lot of the records were in the western barn that burned down. At least you have those. We'll know how to crossbreed what we have left. Thanks, Nad."

"You bet," she said. With one last distrustful look at Erik, she turned and sauntered back toward the already waiting trucks.

"She even walks like Emily," Erik whispered tersely to Oakley.

Oakley shook his head. "Let's get out of here. I feel something on the wind."

"So do I," Konrad said grimly. "I don't suppose you brought backup for this trip of yours to return home."

"I brought him." Erik gestured toward Oakley.

Oakley grinned.

"Great," Konrad muttered.

CHAPTER 27

*L*una missed Erik. The guy had only been gone for the day, yet she felt like she needed another cup of coffee. It was as if the energy in the pack had waned. Sighing, she reached for her still half-full mug on the conference table.

"You okay?" Vernon asked from her side, stacks of papers in front of him.

"Yeah, I'm fine. Just, I don't know, a little down. Must be the weather."

Francine snorted across from Vernon. "Yeah, it must be the weather." She made a notation. "It looks like we have the order necessary to build or repair houses with the schedule organized by need." She scratched her chin. "I suppose we'll tweak it a bit when Erik gets here with the Thunderhoof folks."

"Copper Pack folks," Vernon corrected. "They're part of us now."

"Not yet. They have to take an oath," Luna reminded him. "But you're right." She scrutinized the inventory text Erik had sent with how many trailers the new members would bring. "Where is that sheet showing our remaining empty cabins?"

Vernon rifled to the bottom of his stack and pulled out

some handwritten notes. "Here we are, and I've created a little bit of a map. We've already offered these to current pack members, and none of them wanted to move that far out. Plus, these are closer to the proposed farming and ranching areas. I assume many of the new members will want these."

"There are only ten homes," Luna said. "We should probably head out there and see what kind of shape they're in."

Francine nodded. "I'm already organizing cleaning crews with the kids from the school. I'd like to be able to pay them something, but we don't have any money."

Luna sighed. "I think Erik has looked at the mining records, but he hasn't reported in to me. In fact, you're the one he'll probably speak with."

Francine looked stunning today in an oversized sweatshirt and ripped jeans, with her blond hair falling around her shoulders.

"That's a pretty sweater," Luna said.

"It really is," Vernon agreed without looking up from his papers. He jolted and then glanced up, blushing before looking at Luna. "You look pretty today, too, Luna."

"Gee, thanks." She tried not to laugh, having dressed in her regular jeans and a blue sweater that brought out the blue in her eyes. Not that she'd worn it for Erik. Nope, not at all. She glanced at her watch.

"He's probably an hour away." Francine reached for a pencil. "Remind me to ask Erik if there's any extra money we can use to pay the kids a little bit. They deserve to make something for their time and effort."

Luna glanced at the to-do list in front of her friend. "You don't need me to remind you. You have a list."

"Yeah, I know, but if I say it out loud, it helps me remember," Francine said.

Luna glanced toward the window at the darkened day.

Hopefully, Erik would beat the storm coming their way. "It's snowing." She caught sight of the few flakes drifting down.

"It's about time," Francine agreed. "The winter has been slow to come."

"It's coming in with force." Vernon glanced at his phone. "The weather app says it's going to snow all week."

Luna shook her head. "Like we need a weather app for that." Every wolf could sense the changes in the weather.

Vernon paused and lifted his head.

A fissure of awareness ticked down Luna's spine.

Francine frowned and looked at the doorway. "What's going on?" she asked as if trying to read the atmosphere.

A thumping sound echoed from outside, and then a wave of presence rippled through the oxygen.

"Oh, crap." Luna pushed out of her chair. "We have a problem." She ran through the lodge to the front porch as her friends followed and then watched as a sleek gray helicopter descended onto the parking lot.

"Did Erik say he was flying home?" Vernon asked slowly.

"No." Luna thought through the weapons in the lodge. They had a few guns, but nothing impressive. "Vernon, why don't you hit the gun safe?"

"You've got it." He turned and barreled back into the lodge.

"I sense more than a helicopter," Francine said, just as multiple squads of wolves ran into the clearing.

The force of their collective energy pushed Luna back a step. Huge and dangerous-looking, they ranged in color from a light blond to a deep black. She sniffed the air, recognizing the scent. "The Slate Pack is here."

As the craft quieted, two males jumped from the front of the copter, and both hurried to open the back door. Philip Nightsom stepped down, looking tall and broad in the swirling snow. Luna had met the Alpha years ago at an all-pack meeting where she had tried to seek out other healers. It had taken her two weeks to talk Yago into allowing her to accompany him.

Nightsom took in the scene and then walked across the distance to the porch with the two males from the copter flanking him. They were dangerous. Without question.

Luna gulped.

"There are about one hundred and fifty wolves in our fricking parking lot," Francine muttered under her breath.

"I hope Vernon's calling for backup," Luna said, her voice trembling.

Francine wrung her hands. "We don't have this much backup."

"Good evening. Where's your Alpha?" Philip's voice carried through the strengthening storm. His gray hair still held on to a few strands of blond, and he looked powerful in a fancy beige-colored suit with a red power tie.

How kind of him to dress up before he invaded their territory.

Vernon emerged with three weapons in his hands and immediately set them aside. The guy wasn't stupid.

A truck careened into the parking area, nearly hitting a couple of the wolves, who scattered, snarling. Yago Yassi jumped out of the passenger side with Allen Bushbalm stepping warily out of the driver's seat. Fury darkened Yago's gaze as he stormed up to Philip, looking even older than he had the day before. The poisoning had affected him more than Luna liked, and he'd never quite recovered.

"What the hell are you doing in my territory?" Yago spat.

Philip smiled. "I warned Volk I was coming. This is no longer your territory." He looked at his assembled wolf pack. "I brought some of my best fighters, and we both know you don't have the numbers to beat back any sort of assault. So, how about we go inside this nice, warm lodge, get out of this storm, and hammer out an agreement? I'm prepared to offer you a somewhat decent sum."

Fury flashed through Luna so quickly her throat felt burned. This was an insult of epic proportions. "We have an alliance." Rage vibrated down her legs. She was two seconds from shifting.

Philip faced her. "I understand your anger, but you might as well accept the truth here. Some of you will be welcome to stay. Some will be asked to leave, and that's me being nice."

"What about the alliance?" Yago asked, his hands on his hips.

Philip shrugged. "Seth is busy right now, and I don't think Jackson would lift a finger to help anybody. I'll handle them both once the territory is mine."

"We're not going anywhere." Luna reached for a gun.

Philip's tallest Enforcer started toward her.

"Wait a minute." Yago held up both hands. "Luna, put down the weapon. You can't shoot all of them."

"No, but I can try," she said grimly, holding the weapon with the barrel pointed down. "However, I really only need to aim at one target, don't I?" She stared directly at Philip as she issued the threat.

"I like her," Philip said congenially. "You are Luna McElhanney, aren't you?"

Luna blinked.

"Oh, I've done my research. We could use a good healer. You are welcome to stay."

The words that lingered on Luna's tongue would probably send the Enforcer straight at her. "Erik Volk is the Alpha of this pack now," she said. "You're absolutely crazy if you think his brother won't back him up. The Silver Pack has already been notified of your infiltration." She eyed Vernon, who gave her a slight nod. Good.

Movement sounded up the road, and wolf after wolf of her pack ran toward her. Everybody from the high school kids to the elderly hurried in their direction through the now-blasting snow, teeth bared and snarling. It was an impressive number, if not an impressive force. However, Nightsom had brought fighters and soldiers.

Luna only had elderly folks and kids, with a few fighting-age adults tossed into the mix. "You are making a mistake." She prepared to shift.

Another wave of energy, heated and raw, burst through the misty, snowy day.

Luna turned, along with everyone else, as Erik ran into the parking area from the other forest in wolf form, along with two hundred or so wolves she'd never met. They snarled and bared their teeth, flanking the wolf shifters from the Slate Pack. Between Luna's people and Erik's new friends, they outnumbered the soldiers.

The fight would be bloody.

Erik shifted back into male form, fury darkening his skin as he stalked toward Philip, buck-ass naked.

"Clothes," Luna whispered.

Francine nodded. "I think we have some in the lodge for this sort of occasion." She glanced at the glowering wolves in every direction. "Well, maybe not this occasion, but you know what I mean." She turned and hurried into the lodge, returning with ripped, faded jeans and a torn black T-shirt. "It looks like we're low on extra clothing."

"Erik," Francine called out. He looked at her, and she threw the clothing at him.

"Thanks." He snatched it out of the air.

It was nice and polite how everyone waited until he'd pulled on the jeans and T-shirt before continuing.

Luna shook her head. "We have a bit of a problem here, Erik."

"I can see that." Erik moved closer to Philip, whose two Enforcers instantly flanked him, both with their teeth bared.

Erik ignored them. "I told you not to come. Did you not understand what I said? Philip, I'll kill you. I don't want to because your daughter is one of my best friends, but if this thing evolves into a fight, I'm telling you right now, I will take you out."

Philip turned and looked at the two groups of wolves surrounding his soldiers. "My money is on my males."

"You're going to bleed," Erik muttered.

A golden wolf over to the side instantly shifted back to human form, becoming a stunning blonde with dark black eyes.

Luna gasped. "Emily?"

"No." The female threw up her hands. "I am not Emily." Naked and truly gorgeous, she walked through the white snow toward Erik.

"Crap," Francine said. "Just a sec." She turned and bustled back inside the lodge before returning with a red cotton dress. "It's all we've got," she said. "Excuse me, female who looks exactly like Emily?"

The female turned. "I'm Nadia."

"Nadia, hi, I'm Francine." Francine tossed the dress at her.

"Thanks." Nadia slowly pulled the dress over her head. It was loose-fitting but long-sleeved and hung to below her knees. "This was made for someone tall," she muttered. "I should be taller."

Nightsom stared at her with his mouth open. "I don't understand."

"It looks like you've been busy," Erik drawled.

Nadia shook her head. "I'd like to avoid a problem here. You're my father, by the way. Not that I care at all.

Erik stared at her. "You said you'd never heard of Emily Nightsom."

Nadia flicked a glance at him. "I lied."

Erik pressed his lips together and nodded. "Respect. You're good at it."

"Thanks." Nadia smiled.

"I don't understand," Nightsom said.

She lost the grin, facing him. "My mom was Gladys Santerbury."

Philip's eyes widened, and his jaw dropped. "Oh."

"Yeah, oh. I believe you had an affair with her before you became mated and married," Nadia said.

So, this female was actually older than Emily. They could be twins except for the height difference.

Luna cleared her throat. "I'm Luna, and I'm friends with Emily. You should meet her. You'd like her."

Nadia's expression didn't alter. "Maybe. I don't really care."

Nightsom obviously calculated the situation. He couldn't back down, but these circumstances presented a decent escape avenue for him. Luna wondered if he'd take it.

He brushed snow off his shoulder. "All right. We'll withdraw for today if you come with me. I'd like to know my daughter."

"Fuck, no." Erik pivoted.

"Wait." Nadia held up a hand, looking at the still-snarling and bristling animals in every direction. "I'll go. I don't mind. I've actually been curious."

Erik stepped even closer to Nightsom, and his Enforcers tensed. "You'll guarantee her safety?"

"Of course." Nightsom drew himself up.

"I don't exactly trust you," Erik said. He looked at the new wolves. "Nadia is one of ours now, and she'll be protected as such. Konrad, do you mind sending two of your best fighters with Nadia?"

A wolf near the front, a big, dark one, shifted into human form. A tall one. "Yeah. No problem."

"Oh, for Pete's sake." Francine headed back into the lodge and brought out a battered cardboard box to drop onto the wet deck. "Here are the clothes we have at the lodge. If anybody else

shifts to human, we're down to purple cargo pants after these."
She threw a pair of black jeans at Konrad.

"Thanks." He caught them and gracefully stepped into them.
Francine grinned.

Luna had averted her eyes, mostly, and he was something to
look at. Handsome in a rough type of way.

Erik's anger swelled through the storm. "Okay. Nightsom,
get your soldiers off my territory. All of them. Now." Full Alpha
fury lowered his voice. "My people will shift back so you and I
can discuss this like reasonable people before we have a funeral,
to which you are not invited. Then my newest members will
take their vows of allegiance." He bared his teeth. "But if you
ever even think about coming into my territory uninvited again,
I'll rip out your jugular so fast you'll watch your neck flop on
the ground as you die."

CHAPTER 28

*E*rik patrolled the pack territory all night to ensure that Nightsom and his Slate Pack soldiers hadn't dared to return, all while working on his damn song to court Luna.

He was not a songwriter.

Finally, with morning light guiding him, he padded to what seemed to be the main street in the small town.

The sheriff's office looked like something out of an old Western. He stood in the snow in front of the two-story building, noting it wouldn't take much to get it back into shape. The bottom floor showed a wraparound porch beneath a patinated copper awning with three windows above it. Three trusses protruded above those windows, with the middle one a couple of feet higher than the other two, sporting a large copper star at its center. It appeared the building had been neglected for about five years, with some of the paint peeling and parts of the railing missing, but it remained in fairly decent shape.

He looked up and down the street that had apparently once held various businesses, including a large diner-style restaurant. All were vacant now and showed signs of neglect, but they wouldn't be too difficult to start up again.

He walked up the warped steps and directly into the station. Dust instantly assailed his nose, and he sneezed, noting a large reception area with a few wooden chairs scattered about.

Crossing around a lone and battered desk, he continued into the interior of the building, seeing offices and a couple of cells at the rear.

"In here," Zelda called out.

He turned right and moved through an open doorway to what apparently served as an interrogation room.

Zelda sat across the table from Allen Bushbalm, who looked like he'd just come from the mine in dirty overalls. It was customary to change clothing when leaving a mine, so Zelda must not have given him a choice.

"This looks comfy," Erik drawled.

"This is an outrage." Allen slammed his fist down on the metal table, leaving a dent.

Zelda shook her head, dressed in jeans, a white shirt, and a black blazer with a new shiny badge at her belt. "This is necessary. You said that Ursa, your lady friend from the Ravencalls, would be meeting you last night."

"She didn't show up." Allen shrugged. "She's a chick. I don't know what to tell you. They're notoriously unreliable." He winked at Erik. "Except for Luna. She's always there when you need her."

Erik showed his teeth but otherwise didn't move. If this moron thought he could piss him off, well, he was probably right, but Erik had more important things to worry about. "Tell me about Ursa," he said, leaning against the doorframe.

"What? She's a hot piece of ass. She's cute. She's blond. I think her eyes are blue or green. Or, I don't know, maybe brown. But we dated, we had some fun. It was what it was. That's it."

"You brought her into our territory?" Erik asked.

Allen snorted. "Our territory? Oh, you really do think you're the Alpha, don't you?"

"Pretty damn sure of it," Erik said. "Answer the question."

Allen kicked back, his shoulders wide in the flannel beneath the overalls. "I don't know. She is a member of the Ravencall Pack. She works at a store. She doesn't have any Alpha blood, and like I said, she's fun. We had a good time. I think she wanted something more, but she was never going to get it."

Erik really wanted to punch this guy, but now wasn't the time. Well, probably. It could be the time.

Zelda must have caught wind of his expression because she shook her head. "To your knowledge, does Ursa have any, I don't know, affinity with poison? Is she a pharmacist or healer?"

"Hell if I know," Allen said. "I mean, their whole pack is well known for creating concoctions. They get all their money from the natural herbal blends they build. That company must make a fortune."

Erik had looked into it, and it did make a fortune. They used all-natural ingredients found in forests or that they farmed and had begun selling those to the human market years ago. Their online business was freaking impressive. It was unfortunate they planned to expand their holdings by a hostile takeover of the Copper Pack. He admired their ingenuity with their business, but trying to take out an entire pack with poison was just cowardly.

Zelda crossed her arms. "Tell me about the night of the poisoning, when all the champagne was contaminated."

Allen paled just slightly, but it was enough for Erik's interest to pique. "All right, so we were having the party, and she wanted to attend. She was willing to do almost anything. So, we got it on in the forest for a while, and then I brought her to the festivities. I didn't think anybody would care."

"Did she have access to the champagne fountain?" Zelda snapped.

"Probably." Allen looked away and then back. "But she's not the type to poison a bunch of people. Really. I mean, she's not that bright."

"Could somebody else have sent her?" Erik asked.

Allen grinned, and the sight wasn't pretty. "Well, I suppose. She's a submissive little thing, so I mean, I guess. I didn't see any poison vials on her or anything like that. But after we finished in the woods, it's not like I paid a lot of attention."

A clanging started at the base of Erik's neck. He'd never named a headache before, but Bushbalm was about to become a migraine. "What happened after the party?"

"Nothing. We got it on again, and she went on her way. Folks didn't start to become ill until the next day, so honestly, I never even thought about it."

Erik breathed deeply, calming his temper. "How sick did you get?"

Bushbalm lifted a shoulder. "I was sicker than a dog but recuperated fast. I'm tougher than most."

Right. Or he had known only to drink a small amount of champagne during the toast.

Footsteps impacted the wooden floor outside, and then Oakley came into view, along with Konrad. "Hey," Oakley said. "I got out of school early, figuring there was Enforcer business to do, and this guy was waiting outside."

Konrad stood to about six foot seven, dwarfing Oakley, who would probably be taller than that within a few years. Today, Konrad wore clean black jeans and a white T-shirt, even though the air had chilled to freezing outside. Snow dotted his hair.

Oakley brushed some flakes off his shoulders. "Another storm's coming," he said cheerfully.

Erik stepped outside the interrogation room. "What's up?"

Konrad scanned the area. "So you need another Enforcer. I'm it." His voice was hoarse and rough.

Oakley looked at him. "Cool. Have you been an Enforcer before?"

"No," Konrad drawled. "I've never been part of a pack before. Somehow, I ended up leading a group of farmers who needed protection, and I did learn about ranching, but it ain't my thing."

Erik looked him over. "You can fight?"

Konrad's chin lifted. "Yeah, I can fight. Spent my whole life fighting, actually. I promise I'll cover your back and protect this pack now that it's mine."

Sounded good to Erik. Everyone from the Thunderhoof band had willingly taken the Copper Pack oath the night before.

Oakley's shoulders relaxed. "It'd be nice to have another Enforcer. It ain't easy keeping track of this guy all the time."

Konrad scoffed. "Agreed. We should probably get two more bodies and do a rotation of four."

"Oh yeah, that's a great idea," Oakley said. "I'll get the word out."

"Wait a minute," Erik said, lifting his hands. "I don't need..."

"You're the Alpha now," Zelda called out from the interrogation room. "Not an Enforcer. Learn the difference."

Maybe the headache was turning into a Zelda migraine. Erik pressed on his temple with one finger, trying to drive away the pain. "All right, but I'd like to get somebody on Yago, as well."

"Why?" Oakley asked. "He's not the Alpha anymore."

Erik couldn't get the leader's fragility out of his mind. "Yeah, but if somebody takes me out, they'll take him out at the same time."

"Nobody's going to take you out," Konrad said, his voice rough.

"Still, I want a rotating guard on Yago." Erik yanked his phone out. He already had Konrad's contact info. "I'm texting you the name and phone number of Francine Goodhouse, who's the administrator for the pack. Have her send out word and get applications. You can interview who you want to do the job, both of you."

"Sounds good," Konrad said, while Oakley nodded.

Erik's phone buzzed, and he lifted it to his ear. "Volk."

"Hey, Volk. It's Francine at headquarters."

"Hi, Francine," he said. Of course, she was at headquarters. He knew where she worked. "My Enforcers will be calling you soon."

She cleared her throat. "All right. For now, we just had a call come in. Fishermen found the body of a female out near Swankies Pond. They said she smells like a Ravencall member."

Erik looked at Oakley. "Where is Swankies Pond?"

"It's toward the eastern side of the territory," Oakley said. "Not much to it. A bunch of ducks live there, but there's some decent fish if you don't mind moving through sticker bushes."

"Eastern?" Erik asked. "So, between us and Ravencall territory?"

"Yeah."

Fucking great.

* * *

AFTER AN HOUR of driving through the territory on rough, barely cut-in roads, Erik stood over the body of a young female with his Enforcers at his back, Zelda at his side, and Allen Bush-balm across from him. The female was nude, having obviously come into the territory as a wolf and then shifted back to human. Her throat had been ripped out, leaving her head barely attached. She had light hair and was fit with several tribal tattoos down her left arm.

"Ursa?" Erik asked.

Allen nodded, having lost his usual cocky expression. "Yeah." He dropped to his haunches. "Who found her?"

"A couple of males out scouting for winter fishing," Zelda

said. "I'll interview them, but they're a couple of old guys I can't imagine hurting anybody."

Erik leaned down and touched the female's arm. It was cold, and she was stiff. She'd been dead for probably a day, if not longer. "I need you to account for your time the last twenty-four hours," he said to Allen.

Allen looked up, his gaze hard. "I wouldn't have killed her. Seriously. Like I said, we had a good time."

"Were you supposed to meet?" Erik asked.

Allen lifted his shoulder. "No, I just told her to come into the territory, and she agreed. I figured she'd show up last night, and she didn't. Considering we're at war with her pack, it wasn't a huge surprise. I didn't even think to go looking for her." He swallowed.

Erik couldn't tell if he regretted that action or not. He lifted his head and scented the air, but the kill wasn't fresh enough for him to identify the attacker. Plus, it had snowed all night, and the area smelled of wet pine needles and winter.

He grabbed his phone and pressed it to his ear, calling Francine.

"Hi. Did you find her?" Francine asked.

"Yeah, we found her. Her name's Ursa, and she's from the Ravencall Pack. I need you to get me a contact number for their Alpha so I can make a notification. He called your phone the other day, but I didn't take down his number."

"We are not meeting with the Alpha," Konrad said.

Erik wouldn't mind staring into the eyes of his new enemy. "We'll see."

"Okay, give me a second," Francine said. Rapid typing came over the line, and then she cleared her throat. "All right. I'm sharing his contact info with you. He's probably still alive after the attack the other day."

"He wasn't here," Erik said. "I would've sensed another Alpha. Thanks, Francine."

"Sure thing." She ended the call.

Erik tapped his screen and dialed.

"Quasar," came a curt answer.

"It's Erik Volk, Alpha of the Copper Pack. I sent several of your wolves back in body bags the other day."

Quasar growled. "What do you want, Volk?"

"I'm calling with a notification. We have a dead female here. It's Ursa from your pack."

"Ursa's dead?" Quasar asked. "You killed a helpless female?"

Of course, not. What a moron. "No, I didn't. I only kill if I'm attacked. We found her body on the outskirts of our territory. I have no idea who killed her. Do you know why she was here or what she was doing?"

"I had no idea she was in your territory," Quasar snapped. "We want the body."

That was fair. "Of course," Erik said reasonably. "I'll ping you where we are, and you can come and get her. You and two Enforcers and nobody else. I don't want another fight, but I'll take it. I don't know if you've heard, but we've vastly expanded our numbers."

"I hadn't heard. I'm trying to expand mine, as well."

Erik shook his head. "You don't want war with me, buddy. It won't end well for you."

"What does that mean?"

Why did he have to continually spell things out for people? "It means if you send another force into my territory, I'm coming for you after I take care of them." He let the full Alpha growl drop into his voice. "That's a fact. Stick with your herbs and spices and your conglomeration that's making you a fortune. You don't want a piece of this."

"I don't take kindly to threats."

"I couldn't care less. Since I'm issuing them, as soon as I find out who killed Butch Hollowgale, I'm finding them and ripping off their heads."

Quiet ticked for a moment. "Who the hell is Butch Hollowgale?"

Anger raced through Erik. "He's the shifter killed near our border with the smell of Ravencall all around him."

"I have no clue about any Copper death near the border."

Erik forced his shoulders to relax. "Sounds like you don't have a very good finger on the pulse of your pack." Maybe Erik would do the entire pack a favor and take this guy out. He sucked at being an Alpha.

"How did Ursa die?" Quasar asked abruptly.

Erik stared somberly at the body. "Her throat was slashed, definitely by a wolf. If it was one of my people, I'll find out and let you know. If it was one of yours, I expect the same."

"Nobody from my pack would've killed her," Quasar said.

Erik couldn't say the same because he didn't know his new pack very well. "What did Ursa do for your pack?"

"She worked at the pharmacy. She was one of the two pack members instrumental in creating several of the spice blends coming out during the holiday season. Why?"

"Who's the other member?"

Quasar growled. "None of your business."

Erik motioned for Oakley to grab a blanket to cover the body, and the kid ran back to the truck to fetch a heavy covering. "Somebody poisoned half this pack five years ago, and I think you know that."

"Yeah, I do know that. But it wasn't me. It wasn't on my orders, and I didn't have anything to do with it. That's just cowardly, and not how I'm taking over your territory." The ring of truth echoed in Quasar's tone.

Interesting. "Would Ursa have had access to ingredients to make a poison?"

"Oh yeah, and frankly, she was our chief chemist. She could have created anything she wanted."

Damn it. Erik had really needed her alive. "Why would she want to murder half my pack if not on your orders?"

"I don't know, and I don't really care. I'll ask around. But she was a quiet little thing who basically stuck to her job. I'm not even sure she had many friends."

"Great," Erik said. "All right, I'm pinging you now." He did so and then ended the call. "How badly did you want to be Alpha, Allen?" he asked quietly.

Allen shot to his feet. "Not that badly." Fury sharpened his gaze.

"We'll see about that," Zelda said. "Come back to the station. This is going to take a while."

CHAPTER 29

*L*una shivered in the interrogation room as she sat on a hard wooden chair.

"Sorry about that," Zelda said, sitting across the table from her. "We have the heat working now, but it's going to take a little while to warm up the building."

"No worries." Thank goodness she had worn a heavy wool sweater. The sky had opened up again, pelting snow to cover the world. What had she been thinking, wishing for winter to come the other day?

Zelda opened a file folder and pulled out a legal pad before reaching for a pen. "Luna, you understand why I need to ask you some questions, don't you?"

"Of course." Luna crossed her legs. She'd worn heavier jeans today, along with her brown boots, so at least her feet remained warm. "I'm the healer for the pack, and I often create elixirs and medicines. I could create a poison if I wanted."

"You certainly could," Zelda said. "This one was, I believe, created from rhubarb leaves?"

"Yes," Luna said. "When I examined a sample of the champagne a few days after people started getting sick, I found rhubarb, along with some other ingredients that I just couldn't identify. I mean, it's not like I have a real laboratory. I assume if we sent a remaining sample to one of the medical labs in Seattle, we could get a full comprehensive view, but Yago wouldn't let me."

Zelda frowned. "I think it's a good idea, don't you? I mean, if we know exactly what was in it, maybe we can help solve the remaining problems. The males really aren't as strong as they used to be. Their strength is coming back, and even though no female has become pregnant yet, I am hoping that comes back, as well."

Yet, it hadn't.

Zelda stared down at her paper. "I'm so sorry about that, Luna. It doesn't seem fair that the males can still procreate."

"No, but they are weaker," Luna murmured. "Plus, only two males have impregnated females who weren't poisoned. That's a pretty small sample to know for sure."

Zelda tapped her pen on the paper. "Did you create a poison to kill half the pack?"

"No, I did not," Luna said. "If I had, I certainly wouldn't have drunk the champagne myself."

"We don't really know that you did, do we?" Zelda looked up to meet Luna's gaze.

Luna's jaw opened, and then she pressed her lips together. "Well, huh. Interesting. No, I guess you don't. I told everybody I was sick because I was, but I still tried to help other people. I guess I could have faked that," she said thoughtfully.

Zelda blinked. "I think you mean to say that you were sick and did take the poison."

Luna waved a hand in the air. "Of course, I was sick. Honestly, I didn't poison anybody. I would never do that, Zelda. You know that."

"I still have to question you," the sheriff said quietly.

Luna nodded. "I get it. Yes, I could create a poison. No, I

don't know what was in that poison aside from rhubarb leaves. Yes, I drank the champagne and got sick and now cannot have children. Finally, no, I don't have any idea who else would've done it." That seemed to be the litany of answers required for this interview.

Zelda started making notes.

"What would my motive be?" Luna asked curiously.

"Maybe you want to be the Alpha."

Luna burst out laughing. "The last thing in the world I want to be is the Alpha of a pack." She couldn't imagine trying to manage such a dangerous group. "I do not want to be Alpha, and if I just wanted to kill Yago, it'd be easier to take out one person than an entire pack, don't you think?"

Zelda's eyebrows lifted. "Have you thought about killing Yago?"

Luna's head rolled back as she tried not to shake it. "No. I haven't thought about killing Yago. I like Yago a lot. I'm just saying there's no motive for me to have poisoned everyone."

Zelda shook her head. "Sometimes, motives aren't apparent until later. Maybe you're a serial killer."

"Huh," Luna said, nodding. "I guess that could be a motive, but it wasn't me."

"I know it wasn't you," Zelda said.

"You're doing a really great job at this, though." Luna leaned over, setting her elbows on the table. "You really are."

A pleased expression wandered across Zelda's face. "Thanks. I'm excited Erik hired me to be the sheriff."

"Have you found a deputy yet?"

"No," Zelda said. "Erik mentioned approaching that Frostland band of shifters near Seattle. Since one of the members of the Thunderhoof group became one of Erik's Enforcers, I'm waiting until he brings in the Frostland group. If they want to join the pack, maybe one of them wants to be my deputy."

Luna clapped her hands together. "That is an excellent idea.

If we integrate them into positions of power, their groups will feel part of the pack right away."

Zelda nodded. "That's what I'm thinking."

Luna tried to rub warmth into her fingers. She should've worn gloves. "Any news about who killed Butch?"

"Nothing. I interviewed the guys who found him, talked to his family and friends, and so far, it does seem like he fought with a Ravencall wolf or a few. The death occurred close to their territory. So now, I'm not sure what to do."

No way would the Ravencalls give up one of their own. "It's too bad Allen didn't go meet Ursa that night. What a jerk. I hope he's feeling guilty," Luna muttered.

"I doubt it." Zelda clicked her pen. "Did you know her?"

Luna nodded. "A little bit. She was a chemist and a healer, and a bunch of us try to stay in contact about medical issues, even if we're at war publicly. Or if we shouldn't talk publicly."

"Did she seem like she'd want to poison people? That she could?"

Luna thought back through their few interactions. "I really can't say. She seemed kind of spacey to me but had a knack for making the spices for their pack as well as different medicines." An idea began to form. "She worked with another female named Elsa, who I've consulted with about other matters. I reached out to both of them after the poisonings, but they wouldn't respond."

"That's not surprising. Speaking of the poisonings, how are you feeling?"

Luna shrugged. "I'm good. I've been checking my hormones, which haven't changed, so no news on that front."

"What about you and Erik?" Zelda asked.

Luna swallowed. "Is this part of the interrogation?"

"Interview," Zelda corrected. "And no. This is me asking as a friend."

Luna exhaled. "I don't know. I've tried to explain to him how important the pack is, but we can't seem to stop..." She let her voice trail off. Even the mention of his name flared intrigue and need through her body.

Zelda snorted. "Yeah, I caught that expression. I could smell him all over you."

Luna frowned. "I've been wearing my orange spice scent like crazy. You can still smell him?"

Zelda laughed outright this time. "Yeah, he's an Alpha. You're not keeping a secret here."

"Oh, well, I'm sorry about that because I know you liked him, too." Now that she'd had him, the idea of him with another female felt like a sharpened claw to the heart.

Zelda scratched a couple additional notes on the paper. "Not really. I mean, I barely know the guy. I like him, but we don't have the connection you obviously do."

Luna felt like a dork. "I don't know what to do. He takes over everything. It's just his natural personality, and I feel like I can't think. I don't like it."

"Don't you?" Zelda asked.

Luna rubbed her chilled arms. "No, not really. Well, maybe a little, but he's also in a dangerous position. I've lost everybody, Zelda. When my grandma died, it crushed me. I can't imagine losing somebody like Erik."

Zelda nodded. "I understand that. I figured that was holding you back a little bit, but is it worth not living? I mean, come on. Life is short. Are you really going to let fear keep you from happiness?"

"What about the pack? What about the Alpha bloodline?"

Zelda shook her head. "I think you'll figure it out. We can talk Erik into sending that poison sample to a human lab to get some answers. I think you'll find a cure, and if you don't, then you don't. Live the next three to four hundred years. The pack will take care of itself. I can tell you have totally fallen for him."

Luna had never been able to hide her feelings, so that observation didn't surprise her. "Are you about done grilling me about my motivations for murder? Francine is outside waiting for her turn. She appeared pretty excited to be brought in for questioning." This wasn't a television show, for goodness' sake.

It made sense that Zelda wanted to speak with the somewhat leaders of the pack.

Zelda nodded. "I have a full day."

That begged the question. "Why isn't Yago here?"

"I talked to him first," Zelda said. "He claimed innocence."

"Shocking," Luna murmured. Of course, Yago hadn't poisoned himself, along with all of his followers. He loved them all.

"One more question, girlfriend," Zelda finally said. "What are you planning to do with Erik Volk?"

That really was the question, wasn't it?

* * *

ERIK DROVE AWAY from the copper mine, his brain reeling with facts and figures as snow bombarded his truck through the already darkened night. It had been a long damn day. "You've done a good job trying to organize the books," he said to Vernon Bushbalm, who sat in the passenger-side seat still thumbing through ledgers.

"Thanks. It's not a matter of supplies, equipment, or product. We just need more workers. I met with several of the ranchers and farmers, and that's what they want to do. That's what we need them to do. So, we still need bodies, Erik." Frustration coated Vernon's words.

"I know. I'm going to reach out to the Frostland group tomorrow, just so we can have more people here. I'm not entirely convinced the Ravencalls won't try to hit us again."

Vernon nodded. "It sounds like it. They blame us for their female's death since she was found on our property. I don't blame them." He shook his head. "I can't imagine Allen would hurt her, though."

"Can't you?" Erik turned his head and pierced him with a gaze.

Vernon fidgeted. "I don't know. I just don't know."

He didn't want to know. Erik had no doubt Allen could cause serious damage if he wanted, and it seemed he did. "Can you think of any reason your brother would want to poison this pack and get Ursa to help him?" He asked the question straight out.

Vernon drew back. "Of course, not. I mean, my brother can be a jerk to the ladies, but he's not a serial killer." Shock and then anger sizzled through Vernon's eyes. "I know that he has an interest in Luna, but you can't let that cloud your judgment. My brother's a bully, not a murderer."

That might be true, but Erik wasn't convinced. He pulled the copper bracelet out of his pocket since it was still hot and burning him. Some of those molds were pretty cool. He figured while he was at the mine looking things over that he would prepare for this crazy courtship ritual, and he'd actually enjoyed creating the bracelet out of copper.

"It's a pretty band." Vernon tugged his out of his briefcase. "But I like mine better." He'd eagerly jumped in to create his own bracelet. Apparently, he and Erik's admin were doing well.

"I like mine." Erik's had three roughly delicate strands of copper twining around a silver one that would look beautiful on Luna's wrist. "When are you going to start this whole ritual thing?"

Vernon's was one solid, thick line with stamps inlaid on it.

"I'm thinking Christmas," Vernon said. "What about you?"

"I'm thinking tomorrow."

Vernon laughed. He shook his head. "I thought Alphas were supposed to be patient."

"Ha. I don't think anyone's ever called any Alpha I've ever met patient," Erik returned.

Vernon carefully placed the copper band back in his case. "Do you mind dropping me by the sheriff's station? Zelda was going to interview Francine earlier, and I want to know how it went. Plus, I believe Zelda wants to interview me."

"I doubt Francine stayed at the sheriff's station all day." Erik glanced at his phone. "I think she returned to headquarters."

"Nope," Vernon said. "She said she was going to hang out and try to clean up the place and get it all organized for Zelda. Maybe she'll want to grab dinner." He glanced at his watch.

Erik had texted Luna earlier but hadn't heard back. Maybe she was helping, and that was why.

Vernon finally shut the ledgers. "Well, it's the best I can do." He rolled his shoulders. "I'm glad you're going to get more fighters. I heard it didn't go well with the Ravencalls when they picked up Ursa's body."

"It wasn't pretty, but nobody fought. So, my gut instinct says they're coming at us and soon." Erik pulled up to the sheriff's station and exited his truck, wondering why Luna hadn't responded to his texts. Even if she were busy, that was unacceptable, and apparently, he needed to explain that to her now.

Vernon gathered all his books and ledgers together and hustled through the snow. Erik opened the door for him. "Thanks." He moved inside, where Francine instantly spotted them. Her hair was up in a bandana, and dust covered her nose.

"I think I have this place almost set to rights." She shook her head. "It'll be nice to get a deputy in here, and I think we need somebody to manage the front desk."

"Fine by me," Erik said. "We'll just have to figure out a way to get people paid." His bank accounts were empty after buying the mine and the farming operations.

"Hi, Francine," Vernon said.

She blushed a pretty pink. "Hey, Vernon."

"Who's Zelda with?" Erik asked, noting the closed door to the interrogation room.

"She's with some of the older members of the pack, just trying to get some history. So far, nothing." Francine wiped a smudge off her left hand.

Unease settled into Erik's gut. "Where's Luna?"

"I don't know." Francine busily began dusting one of the bookshelves, her face averted.

"Francine?" He lowered his voice into a pure Alpha growl.

She winced as she lifted her gaze. "I really don't know where Luna is."

"Speak now," he said.

She looked at Vernon, who shook his head. "I don't know what's going on," he said.

Francine's shoulders slumped. "Luna got a crazy idea. I tried to talk her out of it, but you know Luna," she said. "Why don't you try calling her again?"

"Where is she?" Heat flashed down Erik's torso.

Francine gulped and looked away, twisting the dust rag in her hands. "She went to meet with her contact in the Ravencall Pack."

CHAPTER 30

A waning moon glowed through the trees, giving the forest an ethereal look in hues of aqua, indigo, and navy blue. Luna waited patiently on a fallen log, rolling her neck as the chill of the night swept over her bare skin. She'd run in wolf form and now didn't have clothing, but that was nothing new for her people.

The atmosphere swelled before Elsa walked into the small clearing, having obviously just shifted from wolf. She smiled.

"Hello, my friend." Luna stood. "It's good to see you." She studied the healer.

Elsa had lived for at least two hundred years and had long, grayish-black hair and light gray eyes. She looked fit. "Good evening."

"Thank you for meeting me."

"Of course." Elsa moved closer and cast a worried look around. "Though we're being hampered quite a bit. Our freedoms have been tamped down lately by Quasar."

"Yeah, good old Quasar. What was he thinking, attacking us?" Luna truly didn't understand his motivation.

"I don't know. He's obsessed with gaining more territory and money, and the copper mine could be incredibly lucrative."

"That's true," Luna whispered. "But we have a new Alpha, and he has issued a threat if your Alpha makes another move into our territory. I don't think ours is the type of male to bluff."

Elsa stretched out a hand and wiped dirt off her fingers. "I understand, but there's not much many of us can do. Quasar's brother is a good male, a smart one, although a bit nerdy. We'd like for him to challenge Quasar, but I don't know if he could win."

Luna swallowed, trying to think of the right words. "I'm sorry about Ursa's death. I really am."

Fire flashed in Elsa's eyes. "As am I. I'm shocked that your new Alpha would allow anybody to murder an unarmed and unaccompanied female."

"I don't think we did," Luna retorted instantly. "I don't know who killed Ursa, but it certainly wasn't Erik or anybody he sent."

"What about the male Ursa loved?"

Oh, the grumpy Allen Bushbalm. Luna looked down at the myriad sticks on the ground. "I don't like Allen, but I don't see him murdering Ursa. I don't think he loved her, though." She grimaced. "I'm sorry to say that. You do know that many of us were poisoned years ago?"

"Yes. I've recently heard that fact. Your diminished numbers are now public knowledge."

Wonderful. If Ursa had given Allen the poison five years ago, could he have killed her now to keep her quiet? Luna instantly banished that thought. While Allen was a jerk, no way would he take out half his pack. Plus, he had been incredibly ill after drinking the champagne five years ago. She remembered having to shoot him full of her treatment elixir several times. There was no way he could have faked that.

Luna sighed. "Do you know anything about the poison that took out half our pack?"

"I do not," Elsa said formally.

Luna waited patiently, knowing that sometimes silence was the best track to take.

Elsa's shoulders slumped. "Ursa could have created such a poison. So could I. So could you," she hastened to say. "All I know is that she loved that Bushbalm fella with everything she had, and she would've done anything he asked her to do for him."

"Even create a poison to kill everybody?" How unfathomable.

Elsa stared down at her feet. "I just don't know, Luna. I've looked through her entire kitchen and lab, where she created all the spices and medicines. I found nothing that would indicate poison. I did find rhubarb."

Of course. Luna had plenty of rhubarb around. The plant had excellent healing properties. That didn't mean anything. "Is there anybody she would've confided in?"

"No. If not me, then nobody." Elsa shook her head. "I wish I knew something. I really do. But I couldn't even find a journal."

So much for that idea. Luna ground a palm into her eye. She had hoped there'd be a magic cure somewhere so she could have children, but she'd have to keep looking on her own. Perhaps time would heal their bodies, as it often did.

Elsa glanced back toward the darkened forest. "I have to go, but if I find anything, I'll be in touch."

"Same," Luna said.

A stick cracked, and then two males walked into the clearing. They were fully dressed so they hadn't shifted.

Elsa gasped and jumped in front of Luna. "Bert, John Lee, what are you doing here?"

"We followed you. Quasar has somebody on you at all times." The first guy, a huge blond, smiled and revealed several gaps where teeth should be. "We have instructions to take whoever you meet with." His gaze caught on Luna. "It looks like we won the jackpot."

His buddy chortled. "I would've bet anything you wouldn't have dared leave the territory, Elsa. I guess I was wrong."

Luna hadn't even smelled them. Sure, they were downwind, but she really needed to work on her olfactory senses. "Listen, we have a new Alpha, and he has clearly stated that if anybody comes into our territory uninvited, he's going after your leader."

"Let him try and then die," the first guy said. "For now, you're coming with us."

* * *

FIRE LIT Erik from within as he bounded into the clearing with Vernon at his side. They hadn't had time to call in his Enforcers. He could not believe Luna was here. He shifted into male form, not giving a shit that he was nude. "I'm going to give you one chance to get the fuck out of my territory, or I'm killing you both," he said, angrier with Luna than he could ever be at these morons.

The first one, a mammoth blond, smiled. "Oh, man. We take out the Alpha of the Copper Pack and we're heroes."

His buddy was shorter but wider and had impressively roped muscles. The guy must work manual labor often. He smiled and had more teeth than his companion. "Yeah, let's take him."

They both rushed Erik, and Vernon, still in wolf form, intercepted the dark-haired guy, who shifted fast. The blond instantly shifted, and Erik did the same. Leaping forward, they impacted in the air and spiraled down to the ground, landing hard. Air whooshed out of Erik's lungs, and he rolled to the side, coming up on all fours. The other wolf did the same. He was even huge in wolf form. He snarled, and now he had a full set of teeth. No wonder the guy had shifted. His fangs were impressive.

He leaped for Erik, who feinted back, let him twist to the side, and then charged, hitting him with his head and knocking him onto his belly. Faster than a second, Erik clamped down on the guy's jaw and ripped as hard as he could, pulling out tissue and a bone. Blood sprayed everywhere. The wolf beneath him yelped. Erik bit again, completely decapitating him. He spat out more blood, tasting bourbon.

He turned to see Vernon fighting furiously with the other wolf. He wanted to jump in, but he waited. Vernon slashed his thick claws down his prey's belly. The wolf yipped and tried to back away, striking out with claws and tearing them across Vernon's maw. Erik winced, looking over to make sure that Luna and the other female were safe by the tree. They watched the fight with wide eyes.

The other wolf bit into Vernon's shoulder, and Vernon howled before knocking him off, turning, and striking with his jaw to the other wolf's eye. The other wolf shrieked, the sound almost more human than animal. Without pausing, Vernon bit down and ripped out the other wolf's jugular before turning and spitting it all out. The wolf flopped wildly. Vernon took a shuddering breath, turned, claws out, and ripped through the remaining neck tissue to decapitate his enemy.

Erik nodded. It was a good fight. He shifted back into human, his bones aching, and his new wounds bleeding. Vernon did the same, bent over, shuddering and coughing.

"You good?" Erik asked.

Claw marks bled freely across Vernon's jaw. "I'm good."

"You need to shift back and heal on the way home," Erik said.

"Yeah. Got it. You sure you're okay here?" Vernon looked from him to the females.

Fury burned like a live wire in Erik's gut. "I'm good."

"Okay," Vernon said tiredly, shifting slowly back into wolf form, his bones creaking. He turned and padded leisurely away, pain echoing from him.

"I have to go," the older female said to Luna.

Erik pierced her with a gaze. "I gave your Alpha one warning. He didn't heed it. Tell him I'm coming for him soon."

Gulping, her eyes wide, she nodded and ran back into the forest.

Luna clasped her hands together. "Um."

"Oh, there's no *um*, baby," he said, his breath heated. "We're going to settle this right now." So much for courtship. His mate needed to learn her new reality. Immediately.

CHAPTER 31

*L*una's legs trembled, and she retreated a step.

Blood coated Erik's chest and jaw, and raw muscle showed in every line of his powerful body. The moon highlighted him, showing him in human form with the animal morphing beneath his skin, barely contained. Wanting out. Wanting her.

She swallowed. "I—"

"No words." The guttural tone of his voice pierced the silent night, slamming against her freezing skin.

She shivered, out of her element. Her heart raced, her lungs stuttered, and a fluttering sensation whipped through her, igniting her form. "I think—"

"I told you no words, and you obviously *didn't* think."

Awareness of a new kind crashed through her. Yet she had to explain. "Elsa and I have met up secretly through the years like most healers are forced to do. I thought she could help me. That I could figure out how to have kids. Maybe mate."

"You just can't help but disobey, can you?"

Her head jerked. Did he just say that? Honestly? "Listen—"

"No." He stepped closer to her, an Alpha covered in blood,

fury blazing a cerulean blue in his eyes. "I'm done with this mating *maybe* crap. We are mating. It's a fact."

She automatically stepped back, and her bare butt hit the bark of a tree. Worse yet, desire slammed from the back of her neck to her breasts and straight down to her already pounding clit. "We need to talk," she breathed.

"Done talking." He took another step, bringing heat and a burning energy with him. "First punishment. Then mating."

Her eyes widened and her chin dropped. "Punishment?" What did that mean? Why couldn't she breathe?

One nod. Just one short nod came as his hard-cut jaw tightened. "Yeah. This was dangerous and stupid. I promise that you'll never do it again."

Instinct took over, and Luna pivoted to the side, turning to run. She knew better than to shift into wolf form because there was no way she could outrun him like that. However, he was slightly injured, barefoot, and he didn't know these woods like she did.

She cut left and leaped over a series of bushes that she had practiced on before when working on agility and grace.

He remained silent behind her, but she could almost feel him breathing down her neck. She turned right suddenly, barreling through a series of sycamore trees before pivoting through some birch and cottonwood. She glanced over her shoulder to see him also rounding the trees.

He didn't seem to be running or panting, but she burst ahead. She ducked her head and increased her speed, excitement, delight, fear, anger, desire, and anticipation all flowing as freely through her veins as did the adrenaline. Running naked through the woods was nothing new, but she stepped carefully so as not to hurt her feet. The trails were barely there, but she knew them even with her eyes closed.

Turning again, glancing over her shoulder, she didn't see him.

Triumph filled her as she kept running, startled to see him waiting up ahead.

She switched directions and ran toward more familiar ground. Soon reaching her special place, he once again was already there. She skidded to a stop near the cliff, panting wildly. How did he beat her to the pond?

He smiled and walked toward her, still bloody. She couldn't go anywhere. She looked frantically around for an escape. He planted one hard, warm hand on her chest and pushed.

She yelped and fell back into the air, her arms and legs kicking until she hit the water. An echoing splash soon came from her left. Gulping, she dove deep and swam underwater, frantically trying to reach her small ledge.

There was an extra—unknown to anybody but her—trail that veered off to the other side, and if she could get there, she could escape him.

He caught her before she reached the ledge, one of his hands clamping her nape. She tried to struggle, but he held her in place. The water was warmer than the cool air, and her hair floated all around. She kicked back, nailing him in the thigh.

His growl echoed through her entire body, and then suddenly she was flung up onto the outcropping, landing hard on her bare butt.

Realizing he'd freed her, she turned, trying to get onto her hands and knees, but he swung up to sit next to her. She coughed out water and looked at his cut body. The blood was off him at least, but the fury still glowed in his eyes, as did a determination that pretty much stole any breath she'd ever had.

"Now, Erik—" She yelped when he grabbed her nape again, flinging her across his bare and wet knees.

She stilled, face down, and realized that he'd fisted her hair to prevent her face from impacting the rock. Then, at odds with the rest of his movements, he gently twisted her head and pressed it down so her cheek rested safely on the hard ledge.

She started to struggle, and he flattened one hand on the small of her back, effectively immobilizing her. She kicked out, but it was no use.

"Don't ever go into the forest by yourself at night to meet somebody from another pack," he said grimly right before his hand descended on her ass.

Hard.

The slap echoed through the entire area surrounding the pond. She heard it before she felt the pain.

It exploded throughout her butt and down her thighs. She yelped and tried to slide both hands onto the rock, but he held her in place.

He spanked her again, setting up a hard rhythm that soon had her whimpering. Her entire butt was on fire. Even heat slid into her face, which was pressed against the cool rock. Tears gathered in her eyes. He was not messing around. Soon, the pain spread into a desperate pleasure. Hot and wild.

Finally, he flattened his hand over her entire butt, keeping the heat flared inside her. "Do you understand me?"

Gulping, she tried to nod while planning his death. Kind of. Sure, she was turned on, but this was unacceptable. Although she had a brain and wouldn't challenge him.

Not right now, anyway.

He rubbed her abused rear end, nearly making her orgasm right then and there. "What are the rules?" he asked, his tone implacable.

"No more venturing to meet other healers on my own," she sobbed, her body on fire with both pain and a need she would never be able to explain. She tried to move to brush her pounding, aching, desperate clit against his leg, but he didn't allow her. It was impossible to be aroused, pissed off, and in pain at the same time.

Yet, here she was.

The slaps had turned from painful to something heated and

dangerous with an edge. She had never wanted anybody so badly. How could she want to both kill him and ride him like a prized pony?

He smacked her again.

She hissed. "What?"

"I'm not kidding, Luna. I can't lose you. Don't take a risk like that again." The words were sweet. The hand on her ass was not.

"I understand," she whispered as he lifted her to straddle his legs, facing him. This time, his erection was hard against her. He smoothed back her hair and wiped her tears off with his thumbs.

The anger had fled from his eyes, leaving an intense determination. "Nothing can happen to you. You're everything to me."

The words dug deep into her heart.

She rubbed against him, needing relief. His mouth descended on hers, kissing her hard, taking what he wanted and giving so much more back. His fingers fisted her hair, and he kissed her deeper, one hand sliding down to tweak her nipple.

Her sex pounded with need. She moaned and kissed him back, throwing her arms around his shoulders. He deepened the kiss and then leaned back to let them both breathe.

She blinked. "I'm probably going to get you back for this."

His grin was quick but fleeting. "Can't wait. My rules are clear, and you will follow them."

They'd see about that. She'd never been much of a rule follower.

He kissed her again. "I want this, Luna, but it has to be your decision."

The enormity of the question struck deep into her soul. He meant it. Even if she couldn't give him children, even if she couldn't continue the Alpha line, he wanted her. "But—"

"No buts. This is just you and me. We'll figure everything else out later. I promise."

Gulping, she nodded. She'd loved him since the first second she'd seen him, and she'd been lying to herself to think otherwise.

His gaze missed nothing, and he held nothing back. "Are you sure?"

"I'm sure."

He kissed her again, laying her on the ledge and then nipping and biting down her body, taking time with both breasts and then reaching her core, where she desperately needed him. Two swipes of his rough tongue, and she was off, crying out his name as an orgasm took her hard. He used his fingers the second time, and she was sobbing by the time she came down afterward. Yet it wasn't enough.

It was nowhere near enough. "Erik," she said, reaching for him.

"Yeah." He grabbed her hips and flipped her over.

"Oh," she gasped, catching her balance on her hands and knees. He poised at her entrance, hard and throbbing. She sucked in air, holding her breath.

He shoved inside her with one hard, determined, powerful thrust.

She threw her head up, and her entire body jerked as her back arched. She cried out as the pleasure and pain mixed into something delicious and frightening. She would never be able to understand it.

Then he was moving—hard and fast and wild. He hammered into her, taking her over until all she could do was close her eyes and feel Erik Volk in every cell of her being. She started climbing desperately, pushing against him, her head down, and her hair brushing the ledge. There was no feeling in the world like this. She needed more. She needed him.

She caught her breath as time stopped, and she hung suspended in that desperate void between pleasure and pain.

Then she fell over, shrieking his name as a climax took her somewhere else.

Pain slashed into her shoulder as his teeth found their mark, claiming her, marking her, taking her over for all time.

The orgasm whipped through her like a whirlwind, head to toe and centered where they met, and she sobbed, taking more of him, riding the waves and finally coming down.

He jerked hard with his release behind her, his fingers bruising her hips, his mouth still on her neck. Slowly, his fingers retreated, and his teeth retracted, leaving her entire shoulder on fire. He licked the wound once and leaned down even more to kiss her cheek, putting his heated mouth right to her ear.

"Mine," he whispered.

CHAPTER 32

ate morning arrived with snow still pounding the ground. Something inside Erik's chest had finally settled, eased, and calmed. Things were set with Luna, and they could start their future now. He rubbed the permanent bite mark over his heart that she'd given him last night in her bed. Marking him as hers for all time. He liked that. A lot. He walked out onto her snowy front porch and buckled his belt as a truck pulled up, containing both of his Enforcers. Oakley and Konrad jumped out.

"You called?" Konrad asked.

Erik kicked snow off his boots. "I need you to up the patrols around the entire territory for the next several days."

"Why is that?" Oakley asked, wisdom in his young eyes. The kid was seriously impressive.

"I'm meeting with Quasar from the Ravencall Pack as soon as I can get there." Late-afternoon darkness would arrive about the time he reached their territory, which would be perfect.

Konrad crossed his muscled arms over his wide chest. "Meeting?"

"I gave him a warning, and he came into our territory," Erik said. "I can mask my scent. You can't. I'm going to go take him out."

"You need your Enforcers with you," Oakley protested.

Erik shook his head. "This is an Alpha-to-Alpha fight. I'm not sneaking up on him. I'm not coming from behind. I'm going to knock on his door, and we're going to have it out. If I don't come back, you'll need to make provisions for a new Alpha."

Konrad lifted his chin and sniffed the air. "I smell Luna on you."

Erik didn't say anything.

Oakley's eyes widened. "Dude, you can't mate her and then run off and die."

"Don't call me *dude*. I'm not going to die," Erik growled. "But I'm also not going to send sneak attacks into their territory like they've been doing to us. I'm going to end this once and for all."

It was how it was done, and he was tired of these games the Ravencalls were playing with him. Plus, after speaking with Luna, he'd discovered there might be a better Alpha to take over the Ravencall Pack. One that perhaps he could work with, or at least with whom he could reach a treaty.

"You're not going alone." Konrad shook his head.

Oakley's lips firmed. "Agreed. We became your Enforcers because we know how to do the job. We're coming with you."

The door behind Erik opened, and Luna slipped out. "I agree," she said, tapping her foot impatiently.

He looked over his shoulder at her. "I appreciate that, but..."

"It's all good." Konrad held up a hand. "We already increased the patrols. We're covered for at least the next week until we need to get to work with the farming land and the mine. By then, we'll have the Frostland band in place."

Erik tugged his T-shirt farther down because it was caught up around his neck somewhere. "We've reached out to them and need to have a meeting face-to-face in a couple of days. If something happens to me, I expect you to follow through with it. This pack needs the numbers."

"We'll follow through," Konrad said somberly. "But nothing's going to happen to you."

Erik scented the air and could smell a couple of his males close. Good. He wanted Luna's cabin patrolled continually, and it was good that people were following orders. "All right, then, let's go. We can take the truck most of the way there since you won't be able to mask your scents."

There was actually no reason to change into wolf form until he reached Ravencall territory.

Luna grasped his arm. "I think this is a bad idea."

He turned to face her, lifting her chin with two knuckles. "It's my job, and it's one of the reasons you all sought me out." He kissed her on the nose. "Try to behave yourself while I'm gone."

With that, he turned and walked down the stairs, noting again the destroyed railing. He really needed to fix that. He slid into the passenger seat of the truck while Oakley jumped into the back and Konrad drove. They made it in silence for about three hours before Oakley cleared his throat.

"Man, you really have to do the courting ritual. You're going a little backward about it, but it still has to be done. It's important to the pack."

"I understand." Erik settled his body to get ready for a fight as the sun went down behind the mountains. He was still a little sore from his multiple skirmishes lately, and he hadn't quite come back from being poisoned. He needed a good month until he reached full strength again.

Konrad turned down yet another dirt road now covered with slushy snow. "Yeah, I've been hearing rumors about the Copper Pack rituals, and that cooking a pie is as important as the song is. Have you created a song about her yet?" His lip turned down like the idea was distasteful.

"I'm trying," Erik said. "I've been a little busy."

Konrad snorted. "Well, at least I got a couple of people to admit that the loincloth isn't really necessary."

Erik turned his head. "That's excellent news." The idea of walking through town to reach her publicly in a stupid loincloth had irritated the crap out of him. He'd rather go naked.

"Well, you have to wear boxers," Oakley chimed in. "Just not a loincloth, since we're past that."

Konrad nodded wisely. "Oh yeah, definitely boxers. But at least you don't have to make something out of leaves."

"Leaves?" Erik muttered. "I'm the Alpha now. Isn't there any way I can change this tradition?"

"You can't change a tradition," Oakley said from the back seat. "Come on. You have to do things right if you truly want to be part of this pack."

"Enough," Erik said. "We'll discuss this later or not at all."

He hadn't come up with a decent song because nothing rhymed with Luna. How could nothing rhyme with the female's name? He would never figure out a good song and he wasn't lyrical. He sang once in the shower years ago as a kid, and Seth had threatened him with death if he ever did it again.

Konrad looked outside as they clearly entered Ravencall territory. "This is odd. There's nobody here to greet us."

"Keep driving," Erik ordered.

Oakley quieted in the back seat and slid over, no doubt to look through the window for threats. They made it to the interior of the Ravencall territory and its stone-and-wood lodge headquarters building. One by one, people came out of the forest and from behind the lodge, where soon a tall male who had to be about six foot eight with long, black hair strode out, his swagger obvious.

"Ah, crap," Konrad muttered. "We're surrounded." He rolled down his window.

The male smiled. "I'm Quasar. We heard you were coming."

Erik exited the vehicle and slammed the door. "Obviously. How about you stop sending kidnapping squads into my territory?"

"It's not going to be your territory much longer." Quasar stomped down the stairs, flanked by four dangerous-looking soldiers.

Erik crossed his arms. "It is. We have our numbers up, and I'm tired of this."

"You're not going to survive the next ten minutes," Quasar offered.

"Then you're a coward," Erik said congenially.

A muted gasp went through the crowd. Konrad and Oakley instantly jumped out of the vehicle and flanked Erik.

"This is a bad idea," Konrad said under his breath.

"Too late now," Oakley said, almost cheerfully. "You can't just kill us." His voice rose. "Erik Volk is the Alpha of the Copper Pack. His brother's Seth Volk, and we have already reaffirmed our alliance within the Stope Packs Coalition. You kill us, or at least him, and all four packs will descend on you like rabid dogs."

Erik glanced sideways at his young Enforcer. "Nicely said, Oakley," he murmured. He turned and met Quasar's gaze. "However, I'm here for you, so how about you stop worrying about numbers and you and I have it out right here? What do you say, or are you a coward?"

No gasp went through the group this time, but everybody stilled. Even the breeze seemed to pause.

"I'm more than prepared." Quasar clomped down the remaining steps, his cowboy boots sharp with silver tips. "I've been training, Volk. Rumor has it you're not quite up to par."

No, he wasn't. He could still feel the poison in his veins, but it hadn't stopped him earlier.

Quasar's gaze raked him. "And I see a few swipes from a recent fight. Where are my males?"

"They're dead," Erik said. "They came into my territory, and they tried to take my mate. They died hard. I warned you what would happen, and if you gave a crap about your people, you wouldn't have sent them." His voice went full Alpha, and several people in the accumulated crowd started to shift uneasily on their feet.

"You want to do this in wolf or human form?" Erik sounded bored now.

"I'm good with human," Quasar said.

"Yeah, no shit." Erik could heal faster in wolf form, and the poison wouldn't bother him as much, so he'd be weaker as a human. "Before we get to this, how about you tell me why you sent poison into my pack five years ago and then more recently."

"Wasn't me," Quasar said, his smile more of a sneer. His eyes were as dark as his hair and his jaw was wide, as was his face.

A male cleared his throat and stepped out of the crowd, one who looked like a slimmer version of Quasar. "We could just reach a treaty and not fight to the death here."

Ah, that must be the brother.

"Oh, no. We're fighting to the death." Quasar removed his jacket. A light snow began to fall.

"Sounds good to me." Erik cracked his neck. "You two, step back." His Enforcers looked at each other. "Now." They both unwillingly took a step back. "I have your word that no matter what happens, these two are free to leave and return to our territory."

"You have my word," Quasar said. "They can take your body with them." With that, he charged.

* * *

LUNA WORKED HARD in her basement for most of the day, searching for a difference in her hormone levels after mating.

But so far, nothing had changed. It was just an idea and one she hadn't been sure about, but she planned to keep track.

Her phone buzzed around suppertime, and she answered, "Hello?"

"Hey, it's Francine. Rumor has it Erik went to fight the Alpha of the Ravencall Pack. You sure that's a good idea?"

"No, I don't think it's a good idea," Luna burst out. "But he didn't listen to me."

"I'm sorry," Francine said. "I'm baking cookies and plan to watch a movie. You want to come over and have a girls' night, like we used to?"

Luna swallowed. Erik could be hours, and all she was doing was worrying about him. "Yeah, I would love to. Can I bring anything?"

"Do you have anything to bring?" Francine asked, laughing.

Luna thought about her empty fridge. "No, but I can stop by the store."

"No, I've got everything. I even have some wine. We'll have cookies and wine."

That sounded somewhat delicious. "All right, I'll be right there."

Luna quickly changed into jeans, a clean shirt, and light snow boots before digging out an old bottle of wine from the back cupboard. It was a good vintage, so she could contribute at least a little bit.

She wanted to call Zelda, but Zelda was in charge of rotating the guards all night, so she wouldn't get to have fun for a while. They really needed to bring new blood into the pack so they could all relax. She hustled out to her SUV and jumped in, driving through the now-snowy night to reach Francine's cute cottage right outside the main subdivision by the lake. The snow was getting thicker, and it covered her head and shoulders even as she ran from the vehicle to the home and knocked on the door. Francine opened it, and instant warmth and the smell of butter cookies wafted out.

"Oh, it smells delicious," Luna said.

Francine pulled her inside. "Get in here. It's freezing out there." She took Luna's coat, hung it up, and Luna kicked out of her boots, handing over the wine.

"Ooh, this is a good one," Francine said with a smile. She lived in a cute home with an open floorplan, and the kitchen was readily visible. The walls were a light green, and the countertops a sparkly white marble.

Luna glanced at the plush sofa that fronted a roaring fire with a TV above the mantel. "I love your place."

"Thanks. Me, too. Baking those goods and selling them to humans has helped me make a little money. Yago was always against my creating a virtual storefront, but I'm thinking that's going to be okay soon."

"I think so, too," Luna said happily. She loved the changes Erik had proposed.

Francine leaned in and gave her a hug. "Stop worrying. He's tough, he's strong, and he's determined. Either he'll reach a negotiation and a truce with the Ravencalls, or he'll make sure they never come onto our property again."

Luna gulped. From what she knew of the Ravencall Alpha, there would be no negotiation and no treaty. Not to mention, Erik had decided to kill the guy.

Francine lifted her head and sniffed. "Oh, my," she said. "Somebody is mated."

Heat flared into Luna's face. "I know."

"When?"

"Last night. It was sudden, but..."

Francine blew out air, her cute face relaxed. "Sudden? Give me a break. You've been head over heels for that guy since he kidnapped you in September."

It seemed like everybody knew that fact but Luna. She shook her head. "I guess so. I'm still worried, you know?"

Francine drew her into the kitchen and handed her a cookie. "You need to stop worrying. Things work out the way they work out, right?"

Luna took a bite. The treat melted on her tongue, and sweet sugar slid through her body. "I don't know how you do it. This is wonderful. Like heaven mixed with good cheer."

Francine hopped. "Do you like it? I put a little extra nutmeg in it this year."

"It's delicious." She smiled at her friend.

Francine's blond hair was up in a ponytail, and her eyes sparkled. Without makeup, she looked about eighteen years old. "Excellent. I'm bringing this recipe to the late-November get-together at the lodge to celebrate the snow finally arriving."

It was one of their fun annual traditions, and Luna loved seeing the kids play in the snow during the festivities. She took a seat on one of the embroidered stools. "So, tell me, what's up with you and Vernon?"

Francine crossed around into the kitchen and began opening the wine. "We've gone on a couple of dates, and he's a nice guy. He's smart. I like that."

Luna nodded and reached for another cookie. "I like that, too. And he's in an important position now, as vice president of pretty much anything mathematical. It seems like he's ready to settle down."

Francine poured them two glasses of wine. "It does seem like that, doesn't it?" Her smile was sweet.

A loud pounding on the door had them both jumping, and then it was kicked open. Snow and the wild wind blew in, right before Allen Bushbalm marched his way inside, fury on his face. He looked tall and wide as well as darkly dangerous. "You two are coming with me," he said. "Now."

CHAPTER 33

Quasar slammed into Erik, throwing them both up into the air and down to the ground. Snow scattered in every direction, and pain lanced Erik's spine. He shoved the shifter off him and rolled over, flipping to his feet. Quasar did the same and instantly charged with a spinning roundhouse kick. Erik ducked, barely avoiding a devastating impact.

In a heartbeat, Quasar surged forward in a front kick, nailing Erik beneath the jaw. His head jerked back as pain clashed through his skull. He stumbled and then regained his balance, his boots sliding across the icy ground.

So, this guy was a kicker, definitely well trained, and not just in wolf combat.

Quasar smiled and then kicked again. Erik instantly lifted his leg and met the kick with one of his own, clashing boots.

He jabbed into Quasar's gut with a left and followed with a right that hit the shifter hard enough that he staggered back.

Quasar returned with an instant chop blow to the face, throwing Erik to the side and almost down. He came back up just in time to duck two more roundhouses. This guy was faster than Erik had expected. He stumbled back and then righted himself.

Just as Quasar kicked up again, Erik grabbed the male's ankle before his foot connected with his face, fury zinging through him.

Quasar jumped on one foot, twisting the kick. Erik pulled back, holding the guy's other ankle as he let him fall to the ground. Then he knocked him down again with a hard punch to the jaw.

Quasar turned around, grabbed Erik's arm, and flipped him over his shoulder.

Erik hit the ground and rolled, sliding across the snow and ice, pain ricocheting across wounds from earlier as he regained his feet. Rage grabbed him, and he paused. Luna came into his mind. Her sweet smile and kind heart. He went stone-cold, feeling the rush of the Alpha pour through his veins.

Quasar kicked him in the knee and knocked him onto his back before jumping on top of him. Air whooshed out of Erik's lungs. He levered his knees up beneath Quasar's groin to flip the male over his shoulders, following and landing on the bastard to punch him several times in the face.

None of the crowd moved or tried to help—or even made any sound. It was odd. Quasar punched Erik in the neck, and he flew several feet to roll in the snow before coming up to stand just as Quasar did the same.

Quasar's claws emerged from both hands. Now, the crowd did murmur, nobody moving forward. Both of Erik's Enforcers angled closer, and he motioned them back. It was cheating, but now it was fair game for him, too. He allowed the claws on only his right hand to extend.

Quasar swiped out and hit Erik in the jaw, then slashed down his torso. Erik jumped back just in time to keep from being disemboweled. His clothes were shredded. He kicked Quasar in the jaw, and Quasar slashed again with the claws.

Erik pivoted to the side and grabbed Quasar's arm to force it behind his back, wrapping his leg around Quasar's neck and rolling them both to the ground, keeping hold of the hand with the claws.

He set his knee on Quasar's stomach, but Quasar's legs were too fast, and he wrapped them around Erik and turned them both over. Erik shot an elbow back into Quasar's gut and rolled away, coming up on his feet as his enemy did the same.

Quasar charged, and Erik slammed his claws into Quasar's neck all the way through and then sliced both ways. Quasar's head slowly rolled off his body.

Everything inside Erik hurt from head to toe, but he remained standing and then faced the assembled crowd, looking for threats. Nobody moved. His Enforcers stepped up on either side of him, prepared to defend.

Finally, the male who looked like Quasar moved forward out of the crowd.

"Who the hell are you?" Erik asked, blood dribbling from his mouth.

The guy stared down at the body, no expression on his face. "It looks like I'm the new Alpha. He was my brother."

"Are we going to have a problem?" Erik asked, the claw marks down his torso feeling like someone had rubbed salt in them.

"No, no problem. I'm Forrest, and it looks like you just made me Alpha of this pack." The guy looked up, his eyes serious. "You won't have any more problems from us. We just want to live our lives, make our spices, and get rich."

Apparently, people hadn't liked Quasar much. Erik couldn't blame them. "I can agree to that."

"I would like to find out who killed Ursa. She was one of ours," Forrest said.

Erik understood. "If I find out anything, I'll let you know." The cold was starting to seep into his bones, and he needed to get into the warm truck to heal. He remained standing and showed no pain, however. "How did you know we were coming?" he asked Forrest.

Forrest looked down at his dead brother and then up at Erik. "Fair enough. We got a phone call. I only heard part of it because I wasn't really involved in my brother's business. But it was somebody from your pack named Bushbalm."

Erik stilled, and then flames burst through him. "We have to go. Now."

* * *

LUNA JUMPED off the stool and stood, facing Allen Bushbalm.

Fury darkened his face as he entered the room.

"You kicked open my door." Francine strode around the counter. "What in the world is wrong with you?"

"Like I said, we're leaving, and we're doing it right now." Allen lumbered toward them. "I'm not messing around. Let's go."

Luna braced, ready to fight. She truly hadn't wanted Allen to be a bad guy, but he was making this move now that Erik was gone. "I mated Erik. It's too late, Allen."

Allen's eyes widened, and his lips firmed into a line. "Even so, you're coming with me. We can talk about it later." He looked behind him at the broken doorway. "Now."

Were the patrols near? Luna searched for a weapon and motioned toward the knife block. Francine nodded and backed away toward it.

"Come now," Allen said urgently. Headlights came through the window, and he clenched his fists. "Fuck."

Relief swept through Luna. The patrols had come. Thank goodness. "Go now, Allen. We can forget all about this."

Footsteps sounded as Vernon ran inside. His gaze took in the scene. "Are you okay?" he asked the females, his gaze taking in them both. His eyes were wide, and his jacket was covered in snow. He looked much smaller than his older brother.

"We're fine," Luna said. "Allen was just leaving. This doesn't have to be a bad thing. Take your brother and go. Perhaps we can forget all about this." What had Allen's intentions been, anyway? Kidnapping them? "Allen. You need help." There was a nice place called Lost Asylum that could possibly assist him.

Allen angled to the side. "I don't need help."

Francine hustled to Luna's hip, a knife in her hand. "It's over. Let your brother take you."

A fight between the two would be disastrous for Vernon. Luna tried to keep her voice from shaking. Where were those patrols? Would they see the two rigs outside and investigate, or figure the females were safe? "Allen. Please, let us help you."

Allen turned to face his brother and then angled his body so Vernon couldn't reach them to help. "We're leaving, Vernon. This isn't going to happen. Please, just get out of my way. Leave here and forget all about this." His voice turned pleading.

"Allen, leave them alone." Dark circles stood out beneath Vernon's eyes. "I don't understand why you don't just go."

"I can't," Allen said, looking at Luna.

Luna sighed, her heart hurting for the guy, even though he was there to kidnap them. "Allen, I told you it was never going to happen between us." Maybe he had more mental problems than she had realized. What had he done to other females? "Did you kill Ursa?" Was he a killer?

"Of course, I didn't kill Ursa," he snapped. "No one's listening to me. Why don't you come now, Vernon? We can leave the ladies alone and just go talk. You and me. Like brothers." The pleading tone now held a note of desperation.

Luna frowned. What was he talking about?

"No." Vernon pulled a gun from the back of his waist and pointed the barrel at his brother.

Luna gasped, panic heating her breath as she yanked

Francine closer to her side. "That's not necessary. Honest. Allen isn't going to hurt anybody, right? Vernon, don't shoot your own brother." Her sweet friend would never recover from that.

Red splashed high across Vernon's cheekbones. "I'm done with you interfering, Allen. You're a rotten brother, and you're going to leave her alone."

Francine edged toward Vernon. "I'm fine, Vernon. He didn't do anything. Let's call Zelda. She can take him in. I'm sure we can all come to a good resolution here. Nobody has been hurt yet."

Vernon glanced at her and then looked at his brother. "I don't think so." He fired three times, hitting Allen center mass.

Luna and Francine ducked in unison, throwing up their hands to protect their heads.

Allen flew back into the island with a loud crash. The plate of sweets broke, scattering cookies and shards of ceramic in every direction.

Francine gasped and put her hands to her mouth. "Vernon, what did you do? You didn't have to shoot him!"

Luna turned and rushed to Allen, grasping his shoulders and easing him down to the ground. Blood bubbled from his mouth and ran down his chin. His eyes widened, and he gasped several times. She shoved his coat out of the way and lifted his shirt to see three bullet holes with black rims. "He needs surgery now. Were those silver bullets?" Shock cascaded through her, and she turned to look over her shoulder at Vernon.

"Of course." Vernon stared dispassionately down at his brother. "What else would I use?" He turned the barrel of the gun to point at Francine.

Luna froze. "What are you doing?" She slowly stood and turned to face him.

"Vernon?" Francine asked, her eyes wide and her pupils dilated. "What are—?"

He fired. The bullet hit her in the stomach, and she fell back against one of the stools, her eyes wide in shock as she slid to the floor next to Allen. Blood burst from her abdomen, and she placed both hands over the wound, shuddering wildly.

Luna tried to rush toward her, but Vernon raised the gun and pointed at her. "You're not going anywhere, Luna."

She couldn't grasp what was happening. "Vernon, what did you just do?"

His smile didn't look like him. "I just cleared the path for us. Now, come quietly, or I'll shoot you in the leg, and then you'll come quietly. We have to go. Right now."

CHAPTER 34

Shock kept Luna in place until Vernon grabbed her arm and started dragging her through Francine's home. "Stop." She struggled as hard as she could, pulling away and trying to kick his knee. "We can't leave them like this. You shot them with silver bullets."

Even now, Allen had fallen unconscious while Francine lay still staring up at the ceiling, her hand over her stomach wound.

"They shouldn't have gotten in my way." Vernon hauled her toward the door. "Stop fighting me or I'll shoot them both in the head."

She stopped.

"Let's go." He pulled her through the doorway.

Her feet slid on the frozen front porch into the snow. "I need my boots."

"No, you don't." He continued to tug her down the chilly sidewalk with snow covering her feet until he pushed her into his car. "Hold still," he said, fastening her seat belt over her arms.

She could easily get out, but he kept the gun pointed at her as he slammed her door and walked around the vehicle to the driver's side, settling in his seat.

"This isn't going to work," he said.

Was he coming to his senses? She tried to keep her voice calm. "I know. Let's get help to your brother and Francine right now. Vernon, we'll figure this out." Her head reeled, and she could barely catch a thought, but she still tried to reach him.

"No, that's not what I meant." He opened his door and stepped out, motioning her toward the driver's seat. "You drive so I can keep the gun on you."

Fear made her hands tremble as she zeroed in on the barrel of that gun. Fumbling, she crawled over the center console and sat in the driver's seat. The car was running, so really all she had to do was put it in reverse.

He pointed the gun at her temple. "I will shoot you."

She paused, screaming inside. What could she do?

"Put your hands in your lap," he ordered, his voice higher than normal.

She did so. He fastened the seat belt over her arms and then slammed the door, still keeping the gun aimed at her through the window and the windshield as he crossed around the front of the vehicle and slid into the passenger side.

Then he aimed the gun at her. "Okay, you can free your arms."

She easily pulled them free and placed them on the steering wheel.

"Drive now."

Gulping, hoping her friends weren't dead inside the house, she pulled the car out of the driveway. "Where are we going?"

"North. Head toward Seattle. We have to leave the territory," he muttered.

Her hands shaking, she turned down the quiet road and then looked at him. "Vernon, I don't understand. What are you doing? I thought you and Francine had something good going on."

The snow in Vernon's hair was melting, and he brushed the wet, dark strands away from his face. His eyes blazed an unholy hue in the small cab. "No, I never had feelings for Francine. I hung out with her lately as I figured this romance between you and the stupid Silver Pack member would wane. I was giving you space and time and figured you would finally come to your senses." He gestured with the silver gun as he spoke, and every time the barrel aimed at Luna's neck or head, she cringed. "You haven't seen me for years," he said. "For years, I've been waiting for you."

She'd had no clue. Sure, he asked her for a drink once in a while or to go to lunch, but she'd figured it had been as friends. "Why are you doing this?"

"Because I love you," he burst out. "I've loved you since we were kids."

What in the world? Shock nearly had her easing off the gas pedal. "You never said anything."

"I have. You just haven't listened. I've talked about the future of the pack, and the future we could have and how important it could be, and you just haven't listened." His voice turned to a whine.

She had never seen him or even thought about him as anything more than a friend.

"Drive faster, Luna." He gestured with the weapon.

She sped up. Where was Erik? Was he hurt? Had he beaten Quasar in the fight? Would he be back soon? She frantically searched on either side of the quiet road, looking for any of the patrols in the tree line.

"I know where they are," Vernon said, sighing. "There's nobody near here right now. Keep driving, Luna. Even if somebody saw my car, they wouldn't think twice about it."

It was unfortunately a true statement. She shook her head. "How could you shoot your own brother?"

"He was in my way. He discovered everything I'd done. I guess the old guy wasn't as dumb as I thought." Vernon chuckled. "He actually came to rescue you tonight; to get both of you free before I got there. Can you believe that? Like he's a hero."

Guilt swamped Luna for a second. If they had just listened to Allen and gone with him, then Vernon wouldn't have shot Francine or his brother. "I thought he killed Ursa," she said dully.

"No, that was me," Vernon said, almost casually.

Luna jolted and let off on the gas.

He shoved the barrel of the gun into her arm. "Drive faster," he spat.

She sped up. "Why did you kill Ursa?"

He didn't answer, and her mind calculated all the facts she knew. There was only one conclusion to make now, and she could barely believe it. "Wait a minute, did she give you the poison five years ago?"

Vernon eased back in his seat, his hand shaking slightly on the weapon. "Yeah, she gave me the poison. I convinced her that if we took out many of the mating-aged males, Allen would become the Alpha. Her big goal was to mate him and become the Alpha female of the pack, and so she went along with a pretty good plan."

Luna's jaw dropped, and she flicked on the windshield wipers as more snow began to bombard the vehicle. "Are you insane?"

"No. It was actually a nicely calculated, logical plan," he countered. "Well, kind of."

She looked at him. "You killed half our pack. You weakened the males, and you made it so the females can't procreate."

"Yeah, that was an unfortunate side effect. Honestly, Luna, none of that was supposed to happen. The poison was supposed to spare the older people, and the kids were safe because they didn't attend the harvest celebration. It was only supposed to affect the males and make them infertile."

"So, you didn't mean to kill everybody?"

"I knew some people would die," he said, his tone unconcerned. "She told me that was a risk, but not as many as who did."

"You're evil," Luna said quietly.

He snorted. "No, I'm just a male in love."

Just how terrible a person was he? "Why did you murder Ursa?"

"Didn't have a choice. She wanted to tell Allen the whole truth." Vernon grinned, looking like her boyish friend again. Yet the glow in his eyes was new. Maniacal.

Bile rose from Luna's stomach. Her brain reeled. "What about Butch?" she whispered.

Vernon chuckled, the sound gross. "That moron came to me, all concerned that Allen had poisoned everyone. Dumbass. He wanted to help his friend—thought Allen had psychological issues. So, I had to kill him, and he was not expecting it. At all. Didn't see me coming."

Luna swallowed. "You figured that if Butch went to Allen, then Allen would figure out it was you?"

"Yeah, probably." Now, he seemed to be bragging. "I had a couple of Ursa's old sweatshirts that I spread around the trees near Butch's body so the whole area smelled like Ravencall wolves. You all fell for it and thought he'd been killed by the enemy."

She gagged. This was sick. "So, you poisoned Erik last week, as well."

"Of course, I poisoned Erik. Stupid Alpha blood. He should be dead with the amount I made sure he drank that night. I can't believe he's still even standing. The good news is I warned

Quasar that Erik was coming tonight, so he's dead now. You might want to move on pretty quickly."

Pain pierced Luna's chest. Erik couldn't be dead. She turned and looked sadly at who she'd thought was an old friend. "Vernon, I thought I knew you."

"Eh, nobody knows anybody," he said softly. "People are very easy to manipulate. I convinced Allen he'd make a better Alpha than anybody else and that he needed you to do it, and I convinced Ursa to give me the poison to help Allen. Really, the only goal I ever had in mind was you and me, Luna. I love you."

"I mated Erik," she said, her heart aching.

"Yeah, but he's dead. Now, it's just you and me. So, you might as well get on board. You don't really have a choice, do you?"

For a moment, the moon cut through the clouds and glinted off the silver weapon in his hands. She had to figure a way out of this, even if he shot her.

God. Erik had to be alive. She loved him so much, and she'd never even told him. She needed that chance. Even if taking it might get her killed.

* * *

IN WOLF FORM, Erik tracked Luna to Francine's house and nearly panicked when he saw Allen's truck in the driveway. He barreled through a broken front door with his Enforcers on his heels and then skidded to a stop, his claws scraping across Francine's wooden floor. What the hell?

He shifted instantly back into human form and rushed toward Francine, whose eyes were closed, her hands covering a bloody wound in her stomach. The coppery smell of blood permeated the entire house, along with a hint of sugar cookies.

"Francine," he said, gently rubbing her shoulder. "Francine." He removed her hands and looked at the wound on her abdomen. It was definitely a bullet hole, and black rimmed the entrance wound. Somebody had shot her with a silver bullet.

Konrad and Oakley both shifted back into their human forms.

"Get me a knife," Erik ordered. "A sharp one."

Oakley jogged around the counter to the kitchen while Konrad went to check on Allen.

"Francine, wake up," Erik snapped.

She murmured something, and her eyes opened, filled with tears. She tried to speak, but blood seeped from her mouth.

"Here you go," Oakley said, handing over a wicked-looking steak knife.

"This is going to hurt," Erik said. "Hold her down."

Oakley gulped and pressed down on Francine's shoulders.

Erik slid the knife as gently as he could into the bullet hole. Francine cried out and struggled, but Oakley held her in place. Erik slipped a finger in and felt around, finding the bullet. The silver burned him instantly. Using the knife and his finger, he forced the projectile from her body. The bullet flipped up into the air and fell onto the wooden floor, rolling end over end toward the sofa, leaving splotches of blood along the way.

Francine gasped and shuddered.

"Go find bandages," Erik ordered, pressing his hand to the bleeding wound.

Oakley, his face pale, jumped up, looked frantically around, and then ran in the other direction.

"Francine, you're going to be okay." Erik brushed hair back from her face and then wiped away a tear sliding down her cheekbone. "You're okay. I got the silver out. What happened?"

"Luna," she croaked out. "Vernon took her."

"Vernon?" Erik leaned in closer. "Did you just say Vernon?"

Blinking tears from her eyes, she nodded. "Yes. He shot us both and took her." Shuddering, she passed out.

"Here you go," Oakley said, running so fast he dropped and slid on his knees.

"Thanks." Erik gently placed the bandage over Francine's wound. He'd gotten the silver out in time so she would heal, but it would take a little while. "Press on this for a few minutes." He took Oakley's hand and placed it over the bandage.

"No problem," the kid said, stark pale.

Erik then moved over to Konrad, who shook his head. "He took three silver bullets to the heart. He's gone, man."

Allen's eyes opened, and he sucked in air.

"Holy crap," Konrad said. "He didn't have a pulse."

The guy tried to speak.

"No, be quiet. Let me get these bullets out. This is really going to hurt," Erik said.

Allen shook his head. "Luna," he whispered. "Vernon took her. You have to go get her now. He is crazy."

Everything in Erik stilled, and he paused, torn for a moment.

"I've got this." Konrad grabbed the weapon out of Erik's hand. "I'll get the bullets out, you get Luna."

"Don't let him die," Erik said curtly.

Konrad gave a short nod.

With that, Erik turned and shifted back into wolf form before clearing the doorway. His entire body hurt, but nothing mattered but getting to Luna. Apparently, he owed Allen for trying to save her. What had he missed with Vernon? The guy had seemed congenial and nice. Everything he'd done had been in an effort to get closer to Luna?

Erik's paws tore up the snow-covered road as he tracked her scent. They'd mated, and he could follow her anywhere, but her scent was getting fainter. She was traveling quickly to the north.

Blood still flowed from his wounds as he ran faster into the wind, and more snow beat mercilessly down in the freezing-cold night. Winter had arrived in full force.

He tried not to panic as fury burst through his veins, giving him added speed and strength. How had Vernon gotten under his radar? He'd even set up and then tried to kill his own brother. There was no doubt in Erik's mind that he would kill Luna if he thought he was losing her.

About an hour out of the territory, he caught sight of tail-lights, and his adrenaline sped up. He only had one chance to make this work and keep Luna from getting shot. Thank goodness the wind was pushing against him. He ducked into the forest and ran alongside the vehicle, seeing Luna in the driver's side. If he failed, he'd lose her forever. He didn't care if he took a bullet. The only thing that mattered was Luna.

So, he ran about a mile ahead and found a turn that she'd have to make to stay on the road. Crouching, he waited behind a rock, and when she turned the corner, he leaped up, teeth bared, claws out, and dove right through the car's windshield on the passenger side.

Glass ripped his side open.

Luna shrieked, and Vernon bellowed. The gun went off, and pain burst in Erik's hip, but his jaw was already clamped around Vernon's human neck, and he bit right through, decapitating the asshole.

Luna hit the brakes, and they skidded for several yards, spinning wildly until they crashed into a tree. Then silence.

"Erik," she cried out. "Erik?" She reached for him, grabbing his fur.

He turned and leaped back through the broken windshield to land on the hood and slide across it to the icy ground, where he could shift back to human form without hurting her. His bones protested with loud creaks as he shifted again so quickly.

"Erik," she screamed, opening the car door and running through the snow to reach him. "Are you okay? Oh, my God. Are you okay?" Her hands went to his bleeding hip and shredded flank.

"Yeah, I'm okay." He looked down. The bullet had gone right

through. He'd be poisoned by the silver for a couple of weeks, but he was still standing. He grabbed her and pulled her close, holding her tight. "Are *you* all right?" His heart rammed wildly against his rib cage.

She snuggled into his arms, her face warm against his chilled chest. "No, we have to get back. Francine and Allen were shot."

"They're okay. Konrad and Oakley are with them. We already removed the bullet from Francine's stomach," he said, smoothing her hair back. "I love you. You need to know that." Apparently, he should have said it long before now because who the hell knew what was going to happen in this life?

Tears streamed down her face. She looked up. "Are you sure you're okay?"

"I'm sure."

"I love you, too," she said, looking at the wild storm around them. "Thank you for coming to get me."

He kissed her then, hard, and then soft before leaning back. "I'll always come for you. Every damn time because you're everything in this world to me. Forever. I love you."

EPILOGUE

*L*una hummed happily at the main lodge of headquarters as she set out platters of food.

"Let me help," Francine said from her seated position near the buffet table.

"Don't even think it," Luna replied sternly. "You were shot a week ago and are still recuperating. Recovering from silver poisoning takes some time."

Francine was still pale but looked lovely in a pink sweater and jeans. "I'm better. I can help."

"Nope," Luna said.

"You've gotten bossy since you became the Alpha female around here." Francine rolled her eyes.

Luna chuckled. "Yeah, that's me. Bossy. How's Allen doing, anyway?"

Francine looked down at her hands. "He's better. It's going to take him longer to recuperate than me since he was shot three times in the heart. I did deliver some cookies to him earlier today. Don't worry, I didn't drive. One of the kids took me." A peach blush covered her cheekbones. "We were both fooled and betrayed by Vernon, and we're helping each other through the healing from that."

Luna paused. "Really? Am I sensing a romance?"

Francine lifted her shoulder. "I don't know. He's always been kind of a jerk, but I think that having his brother shoot him may have mellowed him out a little. He's reconsidering his life, and his actions, and I don't know, I think there's hope for the guy."

Luna unwrapped several platters of cold cuts, safely protected under the eaves of the porch. "I like that. He did try to save our lives, you know."

"Yeah," Francine said softly.

Luna looked out at the many people milling around, drinking mulled cider and hot chocolate as they celebrated the beginning of winter. The kids ran around throwing snowballs and chirping in excitement since they'd all go sledding later that day. It was nice to see the Frostland and Thunderhoof bands integrating so happily into the pack. They had strong numbers now, and she had truly enjoyed meeting all the new people. Everyone had taken their oaths, and they were all Copper Pack members now. It was a good thing.

"I see several romances blossoming," she said happily.

"Me, too." Francine said. "The Santerbury sisters are seriously matchmaking, and they're doing a pretty good job of it already."

Luna studied the crowd. "Speaking of, where are they?" She paused. "Did we make sure they had a ride here?"

"Oh, yeah," Francine said, a smug smile on her face. "They were baking some more pies, I believe, and then they'll be here."

"Oh, good."

A twittering sounded, and Luna looked up. Shock held her absolutely immobile for a moment.

Erik strode up the road and across the parking area, dressed in only dark gray boxers. Snow covered his feet and shoulders as he made his way to her, holding what looked like several pies and a big bucket.

"What is happening?" she asked.

Francine stood and walked to her side. "Oh, my! Has he lost his mind?" She chuckled and then returned to her seat, kicking her legs out to watch.

Luna hovered at the edge of the porch.

"Hi," Erik said, an odd expression on his face.

"Hi," Luna said slowly, looking over to see the Santerbury sisters arriving in a truck and jumping out, cute winter hats protecting their heads.

He handed over the stacked pies. "I was cooking with the sisters, and I made huckleberry, apple, and peach."

"Okay," she said slowly, accepting the pies and putting them on the table. What in the holy heck was happening right now?

"Here's the ice cream." He hefted over a big bucket. "It's vanilla. I made it myself, and I used Alpha strength." He spoke in curt sentences as if going down a list of necessary declarations.

She gulped and looked at the assembled crowd, who all watched curiously, especially the newer members. "Erik, why are you in your boxers?"

He threw up a hand. "I was told we didn't have to wear loin-cloths anymore, and believe me, I wouldn't even know how to make one."

What in the world was he talking about?

He set his stance and cleared his throat. "All right, so here it is." He cleared his throat again and started to sing.

Luna, you're the best thing that ever happened to me.

Before that, I was lost.

You're my Fortuna and I'd like to visit a Laguna, but if nothing else, we mated under the moon-a.

My sweet, sweet Luna.

Luna's jaw dropped open.

"Did he just say moon-a?" Francine whispered.

Luna looked wildly around to see Oakley doubled over in hysterics by the nearest tamarack tree and Konrad trying to hold back a laugh but failing miserably.

Francine gave up the fight and burst out laughing behind her.

Luna just looked at Erik. "Erik, I..." Had he lost his mind? Had the silver bullet somehow poisoned his brain? Did he need help?

He rolled his eyes and yanked a copper band out of the side of his boxers. "With this cuff, I vow to you my eternal love." He reached forward, took her left arm, and shoved the beautiful cuff onto her wrist. The bracelet was stunning with intricate copper tendrils intertwined with a strong line of silver.

"Erik," she gasped. "It is beautiful." So, he'd decided on a courtship. "Thank you. I love it."

"I also have a diamond ring when I propose, but I'm doing that privately," he said grumpily. "Was my song okay?"

She gulped. "Your song was...wonderful, but I don't understand."

He looked around. "I'm courting you."

"I know," she said.

He looked over at Yago, who was sitting with several of his buddies, all of them chuckling. "This is courting, right?"

"You bet it is," Yago snorted, holding his belly as he laughed.

Realization began to dawn across Erik's face, and he cut sharp looks at both of his Enforcers, who at this point were laughing so hard, tears streamed down their faces.

"Oakley," he said quietly.

Oakley pointed at Zelda. "Okay. The song might've been my idea. But the rest was hers."

Zelda was over near a bunch of the kids, packing snowballs and laughing wildly. "I'm sorry, boss."

"What the hell?" He looked over at Konrad.

Konrad wiped a tear off his face. "Don't ask me. I got here late and just joined in."

Oakley snorted and tried to speak several times before he could regain his breath. "We thought as a new Alpha, maybe a little hazing was in order. You know, to show everybody that you have a sense of humor."

Erik's chin ducked and he closed his eyes for a moment before opening them. "So, this isn't normal courting behavior?"

Luna's lips twitched and she tried to press them together and not laugh. Man, he was cute. Well, in a badass Alpha, hard-cut-muscle type of way. "No, just...just the copper band. That's the courting ritual."

"That's it. Not baking all day?" he muttered

The Santerbury sisters hustled up in their bedazzled snow gear.

"Yeah, but we had fun. We made great pies," Gladys said.

"We did have fun," Erik agreed, looking strong and tall, half-naked in the snow. "And the song?"

Luna shook her head, tears gathering in her eyes as she tried hard not to laugh. "No. The song, and the ice cream, and the nakedness are not part of our courting ritual. However, it was a lovely song. I've never heard the word moon-a used like that."

Erik looked at her and then threw back his head and chuckled. "Everybody should know that I believe very strongly in payback. So be prepared." Sighing, he walked up the stairs and kissed her.

His pack mates cheered.

He leaned back. "I love you."

"I love you, too," she said, wrapping her arms around his waist. "Please tell me you brought clothes."

* * *

IF YOU ENJOYED SHIFTER, take a look at One Cursed Rose! Here's a quick excerpt:

Alana

Panic stifles a scream in my throat. Somehow, this impossibly strong man has an arm around my legs as he runs through what appears to be a storage area and kicks open a door. Then we're running through abusive rain. I'm tossed into the back of an SUV and I roll over, my shoulders hitting the far side. The man jumps inside. "Go," he snaps.

The driver punches the gas, and we speed off down the alleyway. I scramble and sit up, trying to blink and focus my eyes in the darkened interior. "Who are you?"

The man turns toward me. Everything inside me goes quiet before exploding tumultuously alive. Even with a jagged scar that runs from his forehead, through his left eyebrow, and across the bridge of his nose to the other cheekbone, he is by far the most handsome man I've ever seen.

His mere presence is a warning as he takes up more than his fair share of the back seat. In comparison with the men in the bar I just left, he wears a rough black leather jacket, ripped and faded jeans, and battered but high end combat boots. Rain dots his thick black hair, making it curl slightly beneath his ears. The breath of his shoulders alone intimidate me, and that's before I notice the blood on his neck and the bruises on his knuckles.

So I turn, facing him, pulling one leg up on the seat in case I need to pivot on my knee and attack him. The difference in our sizes makes that idea stupid. But I know letting any kidnapper take you away from a public space is a death sentence.

"Who are you?" My voice trembles this time. His eyes are black with, I swear, flicks of silver. Not gold, not brown, not amber, but silver. I have never seen the color before, but I know those eyes. "You've been watching me." I flash back to the other night across the street.

"You're very watchable," he says, his voice deep and rich like a McMillan Sherry Oak 18 year old scotch. So he does not deny it.

I'm not sure if that should ease my mind or concern the hell out of me. I go with concern. "Listen, you don't know my father, but I can tell you he won't pay a ransom." It is the truth and a fact that has been drummed into me since I was a little girl.

My kidnapper's eyes twinkle for a second as if I've amused him.

"You're going to have to let me go," I say, reaching behind my back for a door handle.

"That door doesn't open," the driver says, sounding bored, even though he's driving so fast the buildings on either side of the rainy night meld together.

I look again at the man who carried me so easily away from danger and focus on the scruff covering his jaw—his very angled, cut, and masculine jaw.

All of a sudden, the driver yanks a phone to his ear and starts barking orders in Irish Gaelic. Something about three ports of entry and taking control of shipments.

My captor lifts his phone to his ear, his voice a low rumble that licks across my skin. What the heck is wrong with me? Did I hit my head? Am I suffering from some sort of nervous system malfunction from nearly being split in two by a bullet?

Snapping out a bloodcurdling series of clear orders dealing with movement, timing, and sanctioned bloodshed, the dark haired fantasy next to me ends his call and slaps his phone against his muscular thigh. His hard, nicely defined, badass of a thigh.

Yep. Short-circuited. "Listen," I say softly, scrambling again for a lever to open my door. Based on what I decipher from the calls, the mammoth man is orchestrating strategic hits against shipments of his rivals. There isn't a doubt in my mind that he's in the Irish mafia, which does not bode well for me. At all. The one good thing is that they have no idea I speak

Gaelic. "It's obvious you chaps are busy, so how about I take off now?"

He turns toward me, lifting his head slightly with his nostrils flaring, as if catching some kind of scent.

My ovaries roll over and jump up and down. Seriously. I'm losing my mind.

"Say something else," he orders. No man has ever looked at me like he's starving and I'm the perfect meal. Until now.

Air catches in my throat. I clear it. "Why?"

"Something sweet."

Okay. This is getting weirder.

"Damn it." The driver swerves, one hand still on the phone at his ear. "Thorn? We need to be at the port, damn it."

Thorn? As in Thorn Beathach? I gulp. "Um…"

"This is more important," Thorn growls. "The boys can handle the job."

My fear of the Irish mafia pales as reality slaps me upside the head. Hard. "You're Thorn Beathach?" I whisper, my heart clanging against my ribcage so fast my chest compresses. I hope I'm too young for a heart attack.

His lips slightly part. "Say my name again."

Oh, crap. There is a reason Beathach has stayed out of the public eye. He's nuts. Gorgeous…but crazy. "All righty, then." I can't find the door handle. "I seriously doubt your boys will succeed without you at the port, so how about you drop me off and go get your work done?" No doubt the job is illegal and I don't want to know anything more than what I just heard.

He breathes in as if he's breathing *me*.

His phone buzzes and he lifts it to his ear, instantly launching into a spate of Gaelic.

I have to get out of this situation before he wraps those humongous hands around my neck. If my door is locked, perhaps his is not. The guy is twice my size, if not more, and looks like solid head-to-toe muscle. But I know better than to let them take me to the woods or wherever they plan to kill me. So it's now or never. When he turns to look out the window at the darkened night and issues even more orders, I find my chance. Taking a deep breath, I launch my body across the seat, elbow him hard in the throat, and yank on his door handle. The door starts to open and my heart leaps into my throat at how fast the wet asphalt flies by. Doesn't matter. I have to jump.

Without seeming to move, Thorn manacles an arm across my waist, dumps me around to sit on his hard-assed lap, and slams the door shut.

I jerk and look up, meeting the driver's gaze in the rearview mirror. "Fuck," he says, the note almost admiring.

Sitting perfectly still, I try to calm my breathing. My skirt has ridden up to my thighs, and the material is trapped beneath my rear, so I can't pull it down. Not only are Thorn's thighs hard, his entire body is warm. Hot, even. The heat seeps toward me, circling me, tantalizing me in a way that negates any calming.

He finished his call and places his phone on the armrest. "Look at me, princess."

I push against him, trying to retake my seat. His abs are rock hard and ripple beneath the T-shirt. His arm doesn't tighten but I can't move. Is he the terminator or what? The arm is solid steel. So I turn, my breath catching at the raw heat in his eyes. "Let me go."

"No." His gaze drops to my lips, and they swell. Or at least, they feel like they swell with a shocking tingle. None of this makes sense. He continues in that devastatingly deep and now dominant tone. "I hadn't planned on establishing your rules until we arrive, but apparently I need to do so now."

Order One Cursed Rose today!

ABOUT THE AUTHOR

New York Times and *USA Today* bestselling author Rebecca Zanetti has published more than sixty romantic-suspense and dark paranormal novels, which have been translated into several languages, with millions of copies sold world-wide. Her books have received Publisher's Weekly starred reviews, won RT Reviewer Choice awards, have been featured in Entertainment Weekly, Woman's World and Women's Day Magazines, have been included in retailer's best books of the year, and have been favorably reviewed in both the Washington Post and the New York Times Book Reviews. Rebecca has ridden in a locked Chevy trunk, has asked the unfortunate delivery guy to release her from a set of handcuffs, and has discovered the best silver mine shafts in which to bury a body...all in the name of research. Honest. Find Rebecca at: www.RebeccaZanetti.com

Printed in the USA
CPSIA information can be obtained
at www.ICGtesting.com
LVHW091603140224
771863LV00007B/245